Advance Praise for *The Hyena Murders*

Ellen Frankel's wonderful novel, *The Hyena Murders*, sheds light on the exotic and compelling world of Ethiopian Jews. Intrepid intelligence agent, Maya Rimon, must face down the dark forces of revenge and witchcraft, exposing, in the process, the invisible faultlines in Israeli society. Racism, conflicting attitudes toward superstition and belief, the toxic consequences of partisan politics—Frankel reveals all with her incisive wisdom and wit. Most of all, it's fascinating and fun—an absolute page-turner.

—Jan Eliasberg, author of *Hannah's War*

Also by Ellen Frankel
The Deadly Scrolls, The Jerusalem Mysteries Book 1

THE
HYENA
MURDERS

The Jerusalem Mysteries, Book Two

ELLEN FRANKEL

WICKED SON

A WICKED SON BOOK
An Imprint of Post Hill Press
ISBN: 978-1-63758-360-9
ISBN (eBook): 978-1-63758-361-6

The Hyena Murders
© 2022 by Ellen Frankel
All Rights Reserved

Cover Design by Tiffani Shea

Post Hill Press
New York • Nashville
posthillpress.com

Published in the United States of America
1 2 3 4 5 6 7 8 9 10

To the members of the K'far Rishon Namutumba
Community in Eastern Uganda, who shared with
me their joy in being Jewish and African

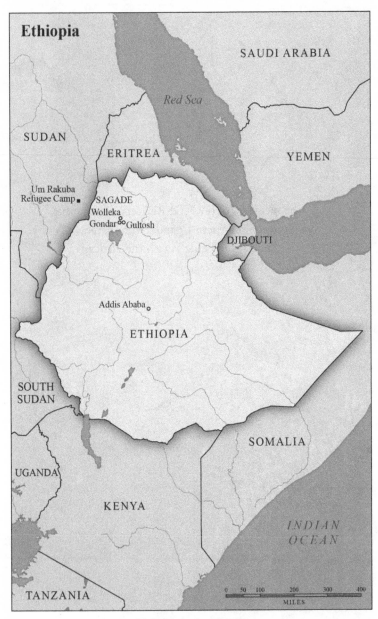

Credit: Mapping Specialists Ltd.

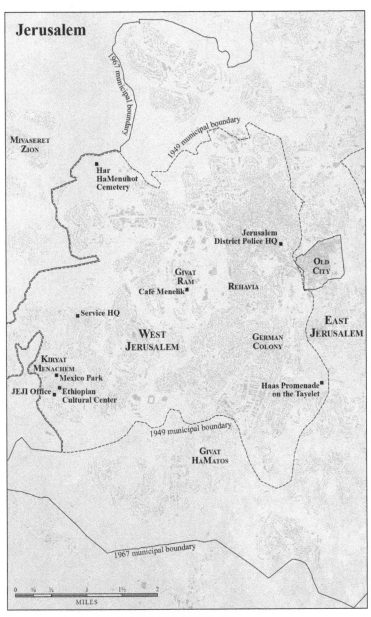

Jerusalem

MIVASERET
ZION

Har
HaMenuhot
Cemetery

1967 municipal boundary

1949 municipal boundary

Jerusalem
District Police HQ

OLD
CITY

GIVAT
RAM
Café Menelik

REHAVIA

Service HQ

WEST
JERUSALEM

GERMAN
COLONY

EAST
JERUSALEM

KIRYAT
MENACHEM
Mexico Park

JEJI Office   Ethiopian
Cultural Center

Haas Promenade
on the Tayelet

1949 municipal boundary

GIVAT
HAMATOS

1967 municipal boundary

0   ¼   ½   1   1½   2

MILES

Credit: Mapping Specialists Ltd.

Timeline

Pre-modern Times

3000 B.C.E.	Queen of Sheba Visits King Solomon; son Menelik I born in Ethiopia
4th century C.E.	Christianity comes to Ethiopia
7th century	Islam comes to Ethiopia
10th century	Jewish Queen Judit/Gudit conquers Axum and reigns for 40 years
15th–17th century	Jews in Ethiopia banned from owning land
1867	Joseph Halevy "discovers" the Beta Israel

Modern Times

1930–1974	Haile Selassie rules as emperor of Ethiopia
1934	First Ethiopian-Jewish immigrants successfully make aliyah together with Yemenite Jews from Italian Eritrea
1975	Civil War begins in Ethiopia
1984-5	Operation Moses: 8,000 Ethiopian Jews airlifted to Israel

March 22, 1985	Operation Joshua: 500 Ethiopian Jews rescued from Sudanese refugee camps and flown to Israel
May 24–25, 1991	Operation Solomon: 14,000 Ethiopian Jews flown to Israel in 36 hours
1996	First Ethiopian-born Jew elected to Israeli Knesset
2008	Sigd declared national holiday in Israel
2010–12	Operation Dove's Wings: 8,000 Falash-Mura Jews brought to Israel

DAY 1

Monday

1

By the time Chief Inspector Sarit Levine arrived at the Aklilus' imposing mansion, situated in the heart of Jerusalem's fashionable German Colony, the narrow street in front of their house was already clogged with police cars and a gaggle of reporters. The police had blocked off both sides of Cremieux Street and roped off the spacious front and side yards with red crime scene tape. Curious neighbors, mostly housewives and children with their nannies, jostled reporters to get a closer look. Moshe Aklilu was one of the more famous residents living on this street, a recently elected member of the Knesset and a frequent guest on television talk shows. He was often described as "the future hope of the Beta Israel" and "a role model for Ethiopian Jews." What could have brought the police to his house?

Sarit straightened her spine to stretch to her full five feet of height, squared her shoulders, and pushed through the crowd. As she strode past several uniformed police posted at the crime scene perimeter, she flashed her credentials. The men took a step back as if physically threatened by this petite embodiment of incontestable authority.

She marched up to the first crime scene officer she spotted, a dark, wiry man with a large mole on one cheek. He stood at the top of the mansion's front steps, eyeing the crowd nervously.

"Where's the body?"

He thrust his head backwards.

Sarit pushed past him and walked into the spacious front hall. Her dark brown eyes stared straight ahead, oblivious to the gleaming parquet floor under her feet, the plush Oriental carpets to her right and left, and the pendulous stalactite of glass crystals hanging overhead. Neither did she notice the small, dark housemaid, dressed in black from head to toe, sitting on the bottom step of the curving marble staircase, sobbing.

In seconds she was through the house and out the double glass doors leading to a magnificent backyard garden, which flamed with the pastel blooms of Israeli autumn. Dr. Avraham Selgundo, the Chief Medical Examiner of the Jerusalem District Police, looked up when the glass doors slammed shut, announcing Sarit's arrival.

"You haven't missed anything, Inspector. I'm just beginning my preliminary examination."

"And?"

"You know I can't say anything conclusive until I do the postmortem."

Sarit grunted.

Dr. Selgundo stood up from his crouch and brushed dirt off the knees of his crime scene whites with both hands.

Sarit pointed down at the slender body, lying face-up on the close-cropped grass. She put the woman's age at no more than twenty-five. Likely worked out compulsively at a gym, ate like a sparrow.

"His wife?"

Selgundo nodded.

"Her name's Titi," he said. "Age twenty-three. One of your forensic guys told me she was crowned Miss Beersheva a few years back."

Sarit peered down at Titi's slight body. So peaceful in death. Arms at her sides, relaxed. Eyes closed. She was dressed in a skimpy red halter top and shorts not much more ample than a thong. In the bright sun her ebony skin glistened as did the tight red coils of hair helmeting her head. Her face was meticulously made up: moist red lip gloss, heavy mascara, a flick of blush, and lashes too long to be natural.

Who gardened in such an outfit? And what was with all the makeup?

It looked like the young woman had been planting bulbs. A pile of them, not much bigger than shallots, lay in a mounded pile nearby. The woman's small hands were enveloped by bright red cotton gloves, their padded white palms flecked with red polka dots. A few tools lay beside the body. A small spade and a hand rake. The rake's tines and the spade's silver scoop, which gleamed in the brilliant morning sun, were unsullied by dirt. The family no doubt had a full staff of real gardeners to tend such a jungle.

"*Nu*, at least give me your first impressions, Avraham."

"The cause of death is almost certainly stabbing. But I won't know that definitively until I do the post."

Sarit ran her eyes over the beautiful corpse, from stiletto heels to henna curls.

"What sort of weapon?"

"You know I don't speculate about such things, Sarit."

Sarit's breathy grunt was meant as a rebuke, but the Medical Examiner showed no reaction. They had played out this scene dozens of times over the years. But Sarit would never give up bullying Selgundo at each new crime scene. So much valuable time was lost waiting for autopsy results! Killers profited from such scrupulous caution.

"So, what else can you tell me?"

Selgundo withdrew a large white handkerchief from the pocket of his Tyvek coveralls and wiped his brow. Although it was already November, Jerusalem was in the grip of an unusual heat wave. And the winter rains hadn't yet begun.

"She was stabbed in the back with considerable force."

Sarit waited for the medical examiner to turn over the body. But he didn't move. She bit her lower lip to curb her tongue.

"I haven't yet removed her gloves to look for defensive wounds, but I doubt I'll find any." Selgundo pointed one latex-gloved finger at the gardening tools lying on the clipped grass. "These were laid down carefully, not thrown. If she did see her attacker approach, she wasn't startled or frightened by him. So she probably knew him." He paused and looked down at the still form, breathtakingly lovely even in death. "Of course, if he snuck up behind her, she might not have had time to react. Or she could have put the tools down earlier." He turned to look at Sarit. "We'll know more when I open her up."

"You know this is top priority, Avraham. Moshe Aklilu is a prominent member of the Knesset. Extremely well-connected. He'll want to know the name of his wife's killer as soon as possible."

Selgundo nodded and sighed. Whenever Sarit Levine showed up at his crime scenes, the case was always top priority. Somehow, she was always the first to learn about high-profile murders—movie stars, politicians, military heroes, athletes, business moguls. Her ambition seemed to have endowed her with some kind of sixth sense. No doubt she would climb fast and far up the ladder.

"Oh, one more thing." Selgundo dug into a pocket of his overalls and fished out a small plastic baggie, filled halfway with white powder. "I found this in her shorts."

Sarit raised her sandy eyebrows, then bent forward for a closer look.

"Cocaine? You're kidding me! First thing in the morning? While she's gardening?"

Selgundo shrugged.

"I only dissect their bodies, not their minds." He chuckled, then immediately flattened his affect when he saw Sarit's taut frown. "Maybe she forgot she still had it on her."

"Give it to Golyat to enter into evidence. He's around here somewhere."

Selgundo looked around helplessly. He scanned the sprawling backyard. In-ground lap pool, fancy wet bar, chaise lounges. An elaborate playground set. A brand-new soccer ball nestled under a bush. The scene was crawling with uniformed police, crime scene officers, forensic photographers, and a suit from a government office. He raised his palms toward Sarit, imploring.

She ignored the gesture and thrust her pointed chin at him.

"Better get on it. As I said, top priority."

Not waiting for the medical examiner's protest, she spun on her heels and strode determinedly toward the glass doors of the back terrace. She shoved one side open, then slammed it shut behind her. Then she marched toward the living room, a path clearing before her.

Like the Israelites plowing through the Red Sea.

2

Moshe Aklilu entered his home office and sat down at the elegant mahogany desk.

Poor Titi!

He sighed. A heavy tear, unbidden but welcome, rolled down his dark stubbled cheek.

Picking up his new Montblanc Meisterstück Rollerball, a birthday present from the Prime Minister, he dangled it between two fleshy fingers. He was oblivious to the commotion roiling just outside the closed door of his home office. He stared at the pile of colorful "Get Well" cards sitting on the desk in front of him. Given that his young wife lay newly murdered in his backyard, no one at the Jewish Agency would fault him for reneging on his promise to the Director: to sign almost a hundred cards intended for Ethiopian children currently interned in Israeli hospitals. It was something he did every year since becoming the first Beta Israel MK elected to the Israeli parliament. Above his flamboyant signature, he would always add a personal note: "You're in my prayers, Hagit!" "Refu'ah shelemah, Baruch!" As he signed each card, he would remind himself that someday this child might be his constituent. It never hurt to start early.

If one didn't know that Moshe was once a poor immigrant from Ethiopia, his home office certainly wouldn't betray the fact. Two of the room's white walls were covered with several large paintings by avant-garde Ethiopian Israeli artist, Nirit Takele. No colorful folk art from the old country. No eye-catching weavings or pots.

Half the room was taken up by a seating area. One corner held a right angle of plush sectional couches marbled in earth tones. Facing the couches was a large round table. Its glass surface was covered with awards inscribed with Moshe's name—a deep cut-crystal bowl, a glass obelisk and globe, and a Lucite map of Ethiopia standing erect in a black plastic base.

The wall across from one of the sectionals was plastered with photographs: Moshe posing with Israeli and foreign leaders, businessmen, sports heroes, beauty contestants. The largest photo, positioned in the center of the wall in a gaudy gold frame, featured his second wife, Titi, wearing a gold mesh bikini. The cross-body sash read: "Miss Beersheva 2015." Next to her stood her proud husband, holding a gold tiara poised above her red curls. There were no photos of Moshe's daughter, his son and daughter-in-law, or his eighteen-month-old grandson.

A sharp rap on the door startled Moshe. He dropped the pen, which bounced and rolled toward the edge of the broad desk. He reached out to grab it before it tumbled onto the plush white carpet, but he was too late. He stood up, walked around the desk, and retrieved it, carefully placing it back into its dark teak tray.

Walking toward the door, he glanced down at his white shirt and decided to leave the top button undone. But perhaps he should shed the sandals and put on the stylish black shoes he always kept polished in the closet? No, dammit! He was at home. Why should they expect him to be formally dressed? His young wife lay dead in the garden!

He returned to the wooden desk and sat down. Then he folded his large hands together neatly on the blotter.

"Come in!"

The door opened, revealing Moshe's son Elvis, dressed even more casually than his father. Denim shorts, fraying at the edges. A white T-shirt. Barefoot. Such disrespect! Moshe hoped the damn media would cut him some slack on a day like this.

"What is it?"

"Hagar said you wanted to see me before we talk to the police."

Even making allowances for the shock of Titi's death, Moshe found his son's brusque manner offensive. Elvis's sharp chin jabbed at the ceiling, as if in defiance of some slight. His sandy hair, slicked down with too much gel, reached almost to his shoulders. And Moshe could smell his son's sweat from where he sat. The boy would forever be an embarrassment to him, despite all that his father had done for him.

"They told me they found drugs on your stepmother."

Elvis snorted as he did every time his father referred to Titi this way. Moshe's second wife was six years younger than her stepson. And her childlike innocence rubbed Elvis the wrong way. She seemed completely oblivious to her husband's many faults.

"What do you know about this?" Moshe demanded.

"Why should I know anything about it?"

"I assume you sold them to her."

Elvis shrugged and walked into the room, pushing the door closed behind him. He flopped down on one of the soft couches, placing his bare heels on the edge of the round glass table. Then he laced his hands together, placed them behind his head, and leaned back.

"And I suppose you think I killed her."

His pronouncement was not posed as a question. It was intended as a challenge—or a threat.

Elvis leaned forward and picked up the clear globe from its geometric glass base. He began tossing it from one hand to the other, the sweep of the globe's arc inching steadily higher. He stared at his father, grinning.

Moshe fought the urge to command him to stop. Or to rush over and snatch the fragile orb from his hands. Elvis was clearly trying to provoke him. He would not respond to the goad.

Both waited for the other to speak. The silence became oppressive, like clammy air before a storm.

Moshe couldn't breathe. A bony hand gripped his throat. His son's smile widened. Panicking, Moshe sucked in a mouthful of air and slowly exhaled. The skeletal fingers loosened their grasp.

"Didn't I tell you to cut ties with that shiftless gang of yours? You know they're all going to end up behind bars—or dead. What makes you think it won't happen to you?"

Elvis tossed the glass ball high into the air. It hit the stippled surface of the ceiling, shearing off flecks of white paint. The paint chips rained down upon the glass table, the couches, the carpeted floor, and Elvis's head. He giggled, then shook off a shower of white flakes.

"Why should I worry—when you can always get me off?"

Moshe slammed his large palms on the hard surface of his desk and rose from his seat. He felt blood burning his dark cheeks. His hands, slack at his sides, curled into fists.

"I'm so tired of this, Gidon!"

Elvis's head jerked back as if he'd been struck. His father never used his given name—unless he was really mad. Mad enough to throw him out of the house. Mad enough to turn him over to the cops.

"I swear I had nothing to do with this, Abba! Not the drugs. And definitely not Titi's murder."

"Don't lie to me! I know all about your dirty business with the Ukrainians. And the Maghrebis. The drugs. The extortion. The smuggling. I wasn't born yesterday."

He sank down into his chair and sighed.

"You just don't get it, do you? You and your friends are rank amateurs. They'll eat you alive, these monsters you're dealing with."

"Enough already! Stop treating me like some loser. You know nothing about me!"

Elvis sprang up from the couch, flung back his right arm, and hurled the glass globe. It hit the photograph of his father and Titi, shattering the framed glass into a haze of shards. Moshe ducked under his desk. Moments later he straightened up and stared across the polished wood surface at his son. Then he closed his eyes and slowly shook his head from side to side. When he opened them, his dark lashes glistened in the soft glow cast by the two recessed lights above his desk.

"I had such high hopes for you, you know. My only son. How I rejoiced when you were born!" Moshe's voice was muffled, as if strained through gauze. "And now look at you! A drug addict, a high school drop-out, a gangster. Why'd you have to drag her down with you?"

Elvis leaned back against the soft couch, threw his head back, and grunted. He wiggled one hand into the tight pocket of his jeans, fished out a cigarette and lighter, and lit up. He inhaled deeply and blew out a coiled weave of smoke, staring at it until it dissolved into threads, then dissipated. He leaned forward. Seeing no ashtray on the glass table, he flicked the ash onto the white carpet, muffling a giggle.

Then he stood up and retrieved the globe from the middle of the floor. Its glass surface was chipped and veined with hairline cracks. Grasping it with both hands, he walked back to the couch and flopped down. He gazed down at the globe, poring over its fissured skin as though it enciphered deep secrets. When he next spoke, he addressed the globe.

"And why'd you have to marry someone young enough to be your daughter? And throw out my poor mother like a piece of trash!"

Moshe was too tired to strike back. He spoke into the dark pockets of his hands.

"I'm begging you, Elvis. Take care of this before it's too late. I'll ask the police to provide better security for us. Maybe install a few more surveillance cameras outside."

Elvis leapt up from the couch and tossed the cracked globe to the carpeted floor. It rolled a few feet before coming to a stop.

The two men glared at each other across the broad, gleaming desk. Elvis broke free first, jerking his body away from his father like an iron bar freeing itself from a powerful magnet. He spun on his heels and strode out of the office. The wooden door whooshed closed behind him. Only a few of his receding footsteps could be heard before the room returned to its silence.

Moshe lifted his head and straightened his broad shoulders. He reached out his right hand and gently lifted the sleek silver and blue pen from its teak cradle, rolling it between his thumb and forefinger. He picked up the next "Get Well" card from the top of the tall stack and signed it. Then he added it to the others, not bothering to write a personal note to the sick child who would receive this card in the hospital.

What does it matter? he thought. *They don't know who I am, and I don't know who they are. They'll get well with or without my prayers. Or they won't. There's not much I can do about any of it.*

3

SARIT WAITED UNTIL TITI'S BODY was on its way to the Institute for Forensic Medicine in Abu Kabir before gathering the Aklilu family together for an interview. They convened in the Aklilus' spacious living room, furnished ostentatiously in leather, glass, and glazed ceramic. *Like the lobby of a celebrity law office*, she thought. *Impersonal and designed to dazzle.*

They were certainly a striking family: the patriarch, Moshe, broad-shouldered and barrel-chested, almost two meters tall, with jet-black hair and eyes, and a single gold upper tooth beaming like a searchlight. Moshe's daughter, Hagar, like her father, was tall and raven-skinned, with dark eyes and crinkly hair. Her thick black eyebrows formed a single line over the bridge of her sharp-edged nose.

Her brother, Elvis, on the other hand, seemed to have descended from a completely different bloodline. Perhaps he favored his mother. Esti, Moshe's first wife, was French. Elvis was slight and stoop-shouldered, with sandy hair and skin the color of a rusty nail. The only feature he shared with his father and sister were dark eyes, but his were set close together, making him appear to be always brooding.

The only other family member present in the room was Elvis's wife, Shulamit. Endowed with a high brow and cheekbones, dark arching eyebrows, and an aquiline nose, she evinced a regal beauty. *Like the Queen of Sheba*, thought Sarit, *legendary ancestor of the Ethiopian Jews*. Her hair was reddish brown, hinting of some European genes. But her most unusual feature were her eyes, honey-colored like amber. The young woman appeared passive, almost detached. As Sarit questioned the others, Shulamit glanced indifferently at her eighteen-month-old son, Bekeli, who was playing beside her on the carpeted floor, chortling to himself.

The interview did not begin well. It went downhill after that.

Before Sarit even had a chance to deliver the remarks she'd prepared on her way, Moshe Aklilu launched into a speech. Unlike the rest of his family and Sarit, he remained standing.

"I demand a full government investigation into my wife's death!" he thundered. Bekeli began to whimper. Shulamit made no effort to comfort him. "Her murder was indisputably a hate crime."

"I can assure you, MK Aklilu," said Sarit, "that our investigation is only preliminary. If we find *anything* pointing to a racist motive, I won't hesitate to kick it up the chain of command. The Minister of Security has made it abundantly clear to me that finding your wife's killer is our top priority. He's pledged to make all resources available to us."

Sarit's words seemed to appease Moshe, although she knew it wouldn't be long before he was posturing in front of the cameras outside, fulminating about this "travesty of justice." The man was a shameless publicity hound, always stirring up his constituents against the government. If she didn't crack this case within forty-eight hours, her commander would be breathing down her neck.

"Can you tell me where you were last night, MK Aklilu?"

Moshe harrumphed, then tossed back his head. His glutinous, tightly coiled hair did not stir.

"I was at home the entire time, watching the World Cup playoffs. I shut the TV off about midnight. When I got into bed, my wife was asleep. When I woke up this morning, at about eight, she was no longer in bed, but her side was still warm."

"Can anyone vouch for your whereabouts during this time?"

Moshe eyed her darkly.

"No one disturbed me while I was watching TV. And no one saw me go upstairs last night or come down this morning."

She ignored the large man's menacing tone and calmly wrote down his answers in her small black notepad.

"How about you, Gidon?"

She deliberately chose to call Moshe's son by his legal name, a name she knew the young man hated. He much preferred Elvis, which called attention to his retro pompadour. But Sarit had always found provocation an effective strategy when it came to hotheads like him.

Elvis glared at her, then smiled, twisting a renegade curl around his index finger.

"I was out clubbing in Tel Aviv, like I am most nights. Can't remember exactly where or with who or when. But if you insist, I can probably come up with some names."

Sarit thought about asking him why he was out clubbing without his wife but decided not to push it. No sense alienating him too much this early in her investigation.

When she turned to question his wife, Shulamit, Elvis didn't give her a chance to speak for herself. And the woman showed no signs of resenting her husband's presumption.

"My wife was home asleep at the time of the murder. Our two maids can vouch for her."

Shulamit sat still as a stone, neither affirming nor denying her husband's claim. Not even blinking her eyes.

"How about you, Hagar?"

Hagar looked up, startled. Her eyes opened wide, like an animal's caught in high beams.

"I was at a three-day conference for primary school teachers in Haifa until early this morning. As soon as I heard the news, I headed back to Jerusalem. I got here just after the police cordoned off our house."

As she spoke, Hagar twisted the hem of her patterned skirt tightly between her hands. The muscle under one of her eyes began twitching involuntarily. Sarit crossed her off her list of suspects. The young woman was obviously too skittish to commit murder.

That left only the two live-in Ethiopian maids, a mother and daughter. Neither spoke much Hebrew. They seemed terrified at the thought of talking to the police. Sarit suspected that the mother had entered Israel illegally, perhaps wasn't even Jewish. As for her daughter, she was a pathetic little thing, small as a dwarf, lame in one leg, her face pocked by disease or by some intractable skin condition. Sarit first questioned the mother, with Hagar translating, but got nowhere. The daughter wouldn't even make eye contact. Her coal-black eyes darted all over, rudderless. Sarit was relieved when the interview was over. The two small, dark women gave her the creeps.

Sarit knew it was pointless to try to break any of their alibis. The Aklilus had powerful friends in the Ethiopian Jewish community and well beyond. The police had long suspected that someone in the family had ties to organized crime but had never been able to prove it. If she was going to nail any of them for Titi's murder, she'd need incontrovertible proof.

She stood up, put her cap back on, and turned to leave.

"I'll get back to you if I have more questions. Please don't leave Jerusalem for the next few days."

None of them called goodbye to her when she opened the door and left.

4

Shulamit's Diary

Monday, November 2

They finally carted her body away! She looked surprisingly composed in death.

But the red crime tape's still there, circling our house like a big, fat target. No way the two cops posted outside can keep away the paparazzi or the nosy neighbors. You'd think they'd have the decency to leave us alone. But murder is so exciting! I bet that photos of Titi's lovely corpse are already trending online.

I'm sure they didn't want me to find this out, but I saw what that doctor showed the police inspector. Titi had drugs on her when she died! Must have gotten them from Elvis. I warned her to stay away from that stuff—and from him. But she told me to mind my own business.

Given Elvis's criminal record, they're gonna try to pin this on him. But I'm sure they'll question all of us. What should I say if the cops ask me about him? Maybe I should ask the MK what to say. He's an old pro at dealing with the authorities.

Way-ya! If only Emayay was still alive. She'd know what to do!

5

BY THE TIME SARIT LEVINE checked into headquarters in Kiryat Menachem Begin, it was already early afternoon. She felt drained. She sat down at her gray, steel desk and stared wearily at the stack of pink slips impaled on the brass spike. Frustrated that their boss ignored so many of their emails, her officers and staff had recently resorted to bombarding Sarit with paper messages. Not that she paid much attention to those, either.

She slipped the Glock out of her waist holster and shoved it into the bottom drawer of her desk. Then she removed her rimmed cap. With a sweaty hand, she brushed back the few sandy curls that had escaped her ponytail. The November heat wave was testing her patience. What she most liked about living in Jerusalem was its cool autumns and winters. But some were now saying that such pleasant weather was going the way of the dodo. Global warming. One more reason to pressure the minister to upgrade their unreliable air-conditioning system. Although the attractive white stone building that now housed the Israel National Police was new, the government had skimped on the HVAC system. Another consequence of perennial budget cuts.

Sarit pressed "esc" and woke her desktop out of sleep mode. Dozens of new emails popped up, most encumbered with attachments. There were also a few blinking alerts reminding her about upcoming meetings. On the departmental listserv, the debate about new sentencing guidelines handed down by Israel's Supreme Court raged on. All of it would have to wait. The Aklilu murder case came first.

She reached for the manila file at the top of her overflowing inbox. When she lifted the cover, she found inside only two pieces of paper: A copy of Titi Aklilu's birth certificate and a speeding ticket the young woman had received seven months ago. No postmortem report yet from Dr. Selgundo. Nothing from Toxicology. Nothing from Forensics. She slammed the folder shut and exhaled an exasperated blast of air.

"Golyat!"

Moments later, a large, burly police officer, his prominent belly straining against the two bottom buttons of his blue short-sleeved shirt, sallied into Sarit's office. His giant jaw mashed gum like a steam press. He approached Sarit's desk and stopped just short of its edge, planting his large frame in front of her, arms akimbo.

"Yeah, boss? Whadya want?"

Sarit resisted the urge to make him turn around and come back in again, this time with his shirt tucked neatly into his pants, the gum gone, his flaming red hair combed and slicked down, and his black shoes shined. Why bother? The man was born rumpled and impertinent. But he was invaluable to her team. He had a nose for no-goodniks. And where brains were lacking, Golyat's prodigious muscle and unusual height took their place. Few criminals slipped out of Golyat's clutches. He had earned his nickname more than once. Goliath.

"Bring me Gidon Aklilu's file."

"Who?"

"Gidon Aklilu. The MK's son."

"Oh, you mean Elvis. No one calls him Gidon."

"Whatever. Bring me his file."

As soon as Golyat left, Sarit turned back to her screen and brought up the online chess game she'd abandoned earlier to attend to the Aklilu crime scene. She wasn't surprised to learn that her opponent, a young man from Crimea whom she'd never beaten, had demanded a win by forfeit from the judges. She didn't much care. She disliked these arrogant young Russians, who cared more about winning than about strategy. She much preferred the Americans, especially the young mavericks who earned their chops in New York's public parks, some of them so poor they lived on the street. She admired their *hutzpah*. Their strategies tended to be unexpected, bold. And they didn't mind losing—if they could learn something from their defeat to use against their next opponent.

She scanned the list of players looking for a game. Her dark brown eyes lit up when she saw Slapdog XXX's name on the roster. Although the boy was only ten, Sarit was certain that he was destined to become a world master. Too bad he hadn't chosen a more self-affirming moniker. "Slapdog" was so demeaning. Maybe he would reclaim his real name once he achieved a measure of public recognition.

Sarit typed in her name, informing Slapdog that she was ready to play. But before either could make a move, Golyat barged in, grasping a manila file folder in one meaty hand.

"Not much here. Considering."

Sarit took the folder from his hand and placed it down on the desk in front of her. Golyat leaned forward, looking down. She glared at him. He grinned but did not retreat. She shrugged her shoulders and opened the folder.

Despite his youth, Elvis Aklilu had already racked up quite a sheet. Two arrests for possessing more than one ounce of marijuana. Two arrests for grand larceny, stealing a Mercedes and a BMW. One arrest for breaking and entering. One arrest for possession of cocaine with intent to sell.

"It seems that Mister Aklilu has been our guest a number of times," she said.

She glanced again at the file. Then she saw the pattern; she'd missed it the first time. Within hours of each arrest, Elvis had been released "on his own cognizance." The charges had been quickly dismissed. The kid hadn't served a single day in jail.

Sarit scoured the sheet for an explanation. And there it was: "Remanded to his father's custody." At each arraignment, Moshe Aklilu had assured the judge that his son had learned his lesson from his brush with the law. He swore that he would personally monitor his son's behavior. Sarit wondered how much *baksheesh* had exchanged hands behind the scenes. Or maybe there had been a quid pro quo between Moshe and the judge. A fixed traffic ticket, a dismissed fine, a deleted file. In her fifteen-year career, Sarit had seen plenty of *protekzia* greasing the wheels of the criminal justice system, but this instance was among the most flagrant.

"Looks like your friend Elvis has a guardian angel."

"He's no friend of mine!"

She was surprised by the vehemence of Golyat's reaction. She hadn't meant anything by her remark. It was just a figure of speech.

Golyat seemed embarrassed by his outburst. He looked down at his feet, then out the window of Sarit's office. He reached into the pocket of his pants and ferreted out a few fresh sticks of gum, unwrapped them, mushed them together, and popped the soft lump into his mouth. He began to chew, his jaw muscles sawing back and forth, then up and down. He gulped down a wad of saliva and licked his lips.

"Look, boss, if you're liking Elvis for this murder, forget it. It's his father who's the real criminal in the family."

"I'm not liking anyone yet. Just gathering information. But say more. What do you know about Moshe Aklilu?"

"He started with nothing and built an empire of foreign domestic service workers. He has branches in six cities now. And he's since 'diversified,' if you know what I mean. I hear he's connected with a couple of big mob families, some here, some in New York. Maybe in Central Europe too. In pretty deep with some real bad guys. Smuggling, human trafficking, extortion, drugs. I mean, compared to him, Elvis's crimes are penny ante. If you're looking for a killer, that's where I'd look first. And if he didn't do her, he hired someone."

"But what's his motive? Okay, so he had the means and opportunity. And no good alibi. But why would he kill his young wife? They've been married less than two years."

The large policeman turned his broad palms toward the ceiling and grinned.

"Who knows why men kill their wives? Maybe she wouldn't put out. Or maybe she was too dumb. Or maybe he met someone even younger. You'd have to ask him."

Golyat paused, swallowed another gob of spittle, then spit out his gum into the small trash can next to Sarit's desk. The wad clanged when it hit the metal bottom.

"Forget about Elvis," said Golyat. "Killing's not his thing."

It was true, thought Sarit. *None of his previous crimes had involved violence.*

"Okay, bring me the father's file."

Even as she pronounced these words, Sarit knew there would be no such file. Of course, she would make note of that in her report, hoping that her boss would see the absence of a file as evidence of Moshe's corrupt influence in the police department. But she knew that a missing file would be taken as a sign of the man's innocence. Or of *protekzia* too powerful to challenge.

As soon as Golyat was gone, Sarit stood up from her chair and walked into the room next to her office, known as the "Incident Room." The new name was yet one more sign of America's encroaching influence on Israeli culture.

She pulled the heavy blackboard away from the wall and placed it at the front of the room, facing three rows of empty plastic chairs. She noted that there were four broken pieces of yellow chalk in the tray, but no eraser. Pretty different from what they showed on American crime shows with their smartboards, see-through Lucite panels, and holographic projections of autopsied bodies. The Israeli police were lucky if they got whiteboards. Despite all the high-tech inventions and gizmos emerging from tiny Israel—Google and Intel both had major operations here—their own law enforcement system was still in the Dark Ages. Still dependent upon their wits and old-fashioned police work. Maybe that was just as well. Sarit knew she was smarter than most in her business. She didn't need fancy equipment to solve crimes.

Golyat returned and showed Sarit his empty hands. She smiled at him and winked. The big policeman laughed, causing one of his shirt buttons to pop off and land on her desk. She carefully picked up the white plastic button and examined it, as if it held the key to their case. Then she handed it back to Golyat and waved him away. He shoved the button into his pants pocket and drew out another few sticks of gum. Then he turned around and lumbered back to his cubicle.

When he was out of sight, she turned her attention back to her desktop screen. To her surprise, Slapdog was still there waiting for her. He probably played several games at once.

She typed: "Ready for combat?"

The boy's response came back immediately: "Prepare to meet your doom!"

She smiled. A little distraction wouldn't hurt. Sometimes even helped her solve a case.

She typed: "King's pawn to e4."

Slapdog's reply was instantaneous: "You're toast, Levine! Might as well resign now!"

Sarit laughed out loud. This was so much more fun than chasing killers.

6

NONE OF MAYA'S COLLEAGUES LOOKED up when she rushed into headquarters just after 3 p.m. The mercurial young agent was notorious for her odd hours. She often showed up in the late afternoon and worked into the early morning hours. No matter how many times her boss, Roni Qattawi, reprimanded her, she persisted in her eccentric habits. The joke in the office was that the Messiah would show up the day that Maya Rimon followed agency rules.

Maya's office at the Service, the special branch of Israeli Intelligence that focused on international crime and criminal networks, was located in a three-story apartment house in the middle of a posh residential section of West Jerusalem. Like many buildings in this area, the building was a hybrid of European and Ottoman styles: imposing iron gates, a capacious first floor vestibule, front balconies framed in wrought-iron filigree, painted wooden shutters, and a domed copper roof. Behind the massive structure was a fenced-in back garden. Like other buildings on the street, this one was in a state of perpetual disrepair. And it would remain so. The Service specialized in avoiding notice.

Sitting in his office at the far end of the first floor, Roni watched Maya push through the massive front doors and enter her office. Her small room was flanked on both sides by similar glassed-in offices that were reserved for senior agents, who'd earned the enviable perk of having doors and blinds they could close. Unlike the Service's large support staff and most of its junior agents, who worked in cubicles massed together in the central open section of the floor. Roni had often considered evicting Maya from her private office to punish her for her unrelenting noncompliance with agency protocol. But he worried about the bad influence she'd have on the junior agents if she worked out in the open. Better to contain the damage.

When he was sure that Maya's door was closed, its glass window shielded by white mini-blinds, Roni called out to his new assistant, Tasha, whose desk was situated just outside his office.

"*Nu*, so where's my Turkish coffee?"

There was no response.

"Dammit, Tasha! I asked for that coffee twenty minutes ago!"

Still no reply from the coquettish young Russian, whose unreliable work ethic was beginning to eclipse her physical charm.

Roni stood up, pushing back the metal chair. He stuck his head out of his office door. Tasha's chair was empty. The screen of her desktop was pulsing with tantalizing images of lacy lingerie on sale. Her in-basket overflowed with files and unopened mail.

He charged down the stairs into the basement and stormed into the canteen room, which was located at the end of a long, dim corridor. There he found his new assistant, deep in conversation with Agent Masha Petrovna. The small room was filled with the pungent aroma of bitter coffee, mint, and cinnamon. Masha, a stocky blonde with pointed breasts like old Russian Scuds, was seated at a Formica table, facing the door. Tasha was bent over her colleague, her back to Roni, her plump bottom straining against her tight skirt. For a moment, Roni forgot his irritation. Then his pique resurfaced. He stamped loudly on the floor.

"What do you think I pay you for, Natasha? To hang out and drink coffee with the other *rooskis* here? Get back to work! And bring me my mud, *chik-chak*!"

Without waiting for her to turn around, Roni wheeled around and disappeared into the dark corridor. Back in his office, he flopped down into his chair with an exasperated *whoosh*. From his back pocket, he fished out a cigarette and a tiny box of matches. He flicked a match with his thumbnail, lit the cigarette, then took a deep drag and held it. Seconds later he blew out two perfect smoke rings, which drifted slowly toward the ceiling and dissipated.

Damn that Arik Ophir, dumping Titi Aklilu's murder into his lap! Probably responding to pressure from the husband, that pompous black prick. What did the murder of an Ethiopian beauty queen have to do with the Service? Not a goddam thing! Their resources were already spread too thin. Roni couldn't spare his highly trained agents to chase down some lowlife thugs killing one of their own. Most likely had something to do with drugs. He definitely needed to push back on this one. Politics!

His mouth felt dry. He rammed his half-smoked cigarette into the can of Coke sitting on one corner of his desk, then licked his parched lips. Where was his coffee?

"Tasha! If you're not here with my mud in thirty seconds, you can clear your desk!"

A moment later, the young woman dashed in, clutching in her hands a steaming hot-cup filled with dark, viscous liquid. As she neared Roni's broad desk, she tripped over a computer cable taped to the floor. She let out a piercing yowl and flung the cardboard cup in front of her. The hot liquid splashed onto the gray metal surface of the desk, spraying the front of Roni's white shirt. He jerked backwards in his chair, slammed against the wall, then shot forward, landing face-down on his desk.

Tasha stood before him in tears, staring down at the floor.

For the next few moments, Roni remained face-down on the desk, motionless. Slowly he raised his head. A thin stream of blood trickled down his left temple. His dark eyes glared at his assistant, who was carefully examining her long, neon-pink nails. Tasha looked up at him.

"Roni, you all right?"

Because he was Egyptian, Roni's complexion was too dark to reveal the hot bloom of blood that flushed his cheeks. But with the sudden infusion of blood, the large diamond-shaped port-wine stain on his left cheek vanished. His stare speared his young assistant's wide blue eyes, drilling into her like hot lead.

"If things weren't so crazed around here," Roni said, "I'd fire you right now. But I need you to do some things for me. Lucky for you, you've got useful skills. No brains, but skills."

Tasha ran out of the room and returned seconds later with a stack of damp paper towels. With quick, efficient movements, she wiped off Roni's desk, his desktop monitor, the manila folder sitting in front of him, the photograph of his two children, and lastly, his soggy shirt-front, which had turned a fecal brown from the coffee. She balled up the damp towels and dropped them into the metal trashcan next to the desk.

"Anyt'ing, Roni! What I can do for you?"

"Tell Maya to come to my office. Now."

Tasha spun on her heels—hot pink four-inch stilettos with thin straps around her ankles—and shimmied toward the door.

"And Tasha..."

She halted in her tracks but did not turn around.

"Fetch me another mud. And please do your lingerie shopping during your off-hours."

7

MAYA TOOK HER TIME RESPONDING to her boss's summons, even though—no, precisely *because*—he had ordered her to report to him immediately. She knew it was unprofessional, but she didn't like the way he ordered them around like house servants. He was such an officious bureaucrat! Forever currying favor with the Big Boss, Arik Ophir, whose only qualification to serve as Israel's Minister of Security, as far as she could tell, was his illustrious Zionist lineage. Ophir was the grandson of two pioneers from the First Aliyah. Maya suspected that Roni aspired to inherit Ophir's job someday. But he was dreaming. As a Mizrachi Jew whose parents had been ordinary merchants back in Alexandria, Roni Qattawi would never be anointed by any major party. She suspected that was the reason he was so mean-spirited toward his staff. No matter how hard he tried, he would never be anything but a big fish in a tiny puddle.

She walked quickly to the back of the floor, striding down the wide left aisle that separated the mid-floor cluster of particle-board cubicles from the outer perimeter of glassed-in offices. As she passed Masha's cubicle, she noted that her partner was still not back from her coffee break. Maya was eager to talk to Masha about the new neighbors who'd just moved in next door. A young Ethiopian couple with a new baby. Maya had heard troubling stories about the newest immigrants from Ethiopia. Some said that they brought with them a few pretty primitive superstitions and bizarre folk practices. Witchcraft and black magic. But these were probably just racist smears against Israel's black Jews. As their numbers grew, so did the popular animus against them. She promised herself to keep an open mind.

As soon as Maya stepped into Roni's office, her nose wrinkled up. What was that stink? It smelled like a mixture of cleaning fluids and stale smoke. She took a step closer, coming right up to the edge of Roni's broad desk. The odor was on his breath, but she couldn't quite identify it. Definitely too strong for wine.

Although Maya knew that Roni liked to drink, she was surprised to find him doing it so openly on the job. Whenever he caught any of his agents with liquor or drugs, he threatened all sorts of dire consequences, which he never carried out. But she wouldn't call him on it. Not yet. It might be a chit she could redeem later.

"What do you want, Roni? Your new Barbie doll said it was urgent."

Roni trained his dark, close-set eyes on her, his glance barreling down both sides of his sharp-ridged nose.

"Jealous, Maya?"

"Oh, give me a break! Save the boyish charm for the newbies."

Unconsciously, the small, wiry director flexed his ropy biceps, making the short sleeves of his white shirt ripple. His thin lips curved up into a grin.

Roni reached for a small cardboard box near the edge of his desk, shook out a cigarette, then lit a match with a flick of his clipped thumbnail. He lit the cigarette just before the match's flame burned his fingertip. He tossed the dead match into the small metal wastebasket alongside his desk.

Maya drew in the smoky air through her nostrils. She eyed the sloppy heap of butts in the metal can. One day they'd have to dig him out from under his own debris.

"We just got a new assignment," he said. "Seems like someone's murdered the wife of an MK. Moshe Aklilu. They found her body in the backyard this morning. Knifed in the back. Ophir wants us to take the case."

"Why isn't this being handled by the Jerusalem District Police? Ophir knows we don't do local homicides."

"Except under special circumstances."

Roni sucked in a lungful of dark smoke and blew out a few smoke rings. Maya watched them rise until they hit the speckled ceiling and dissolved.

"Such as?"

"When the victim's husband is a Knesset member. Aklilu told Ophir that the knife was really meant for him. They killed his wife by mistake. Claims he's received several death threats."

Maya raised her auburn eyebrows, then chuckled.

"Who would want to murder Moshe Aklilu? Everyone knows he has no power in the present government. They only tolerate him because he brings their party the votes they need to prop up their razor-thin majority."

Roni grinned. He took another drag on his cigarette and spit out the smoke in a breathy exhalation. With his thumb and index finger, he plucked a few shreds of tobacco from his tongue.

"You and I both know that, but Ophir is nothing if not political. Always working the angles. Some say he's going to challenge the PM in the next election. He probably figures it can't hurt to curry Aklilu's favor. The MK will be in his debt."

"So, we're going to take the case? Even though you don't believe Aklilu's story?"

Roni examined the smoking ember of his cigarette. His grin widened.

"I'm guessing Missus Aklilu was murdered over some drug deal. Yet another casualty of an Ethiopian gang war. So no, *we're* not going to take the case. *You* are."

Maya, who had been standing all this time, not having been invited to sit down in the hard wooden chair opposite her boss, angrily stamped one sandaled foot on the concrete floor. Then she tossed back her loose skein of auburn curls.

"C'mon, Roni, you can't be serious! You know this is a matter for the local police. You can't just sideline me like this. It's not fair!"

Which was precisely why, Maya now realized, he was doing this. He was getting back at her for making him look bad during their last big case. It was only because of her own tenacity and investigative instincts that they'd managed to foil that plot to blow up the Temple Mount, recovering a lost Dead Sea Scroll in the process. Roni had tried to upstage her but had ended up pinning a medal on her chest.

"It's not your call, Maya. I already told Ophir the Service will take the case. With you as lead investigator. If you don't want to remain sidelined, then solve this murder quickly. Here's the case file."

He picked up the thin manila folder that lay on the desk in front of him and handed it to Maya. She grabbed it from him with both hands. Roni flapped his hands as if they'd been torched. Then he blew on his fingertips. Maya noticed that the pads of his thumb and index finger were grimy with soot.

"Have fun," he said. "And don't bother reporting back 'til you've nailed the killer. Ophir was quite clear that he only wants to hear from us when it's done."

"Who's my liaison at the Jerusalem Police?"

Roni smiled. A chuckle came from deep within his throat.

"Your old nemesis, Chief Inspector Sarit Levine. I know how much you two enjoy working together."

Roni let out a hearty guffaw. He dismissed Maya with a curt nod. She spun on her heels and stomped out of the office, slamming the door behind her.

In the unsteady light of the overhead fluorescent rods, he bent down, yanked open a bottom drawer, and straightened back up in his chair. In his right hand he held an almost full bottle of amber liquid. The label read: Lagavulin 16. He reached down into the drawer to retrieve a short glass, streaked with water stains. He poured himself two fingers of the sharp, smoky liquor. The black beads of his eyes sparkled in the flickering light.

He raised his glass and addressed Maya's retreating back.

"L'chaim!"

8

DANI SOLOMON SAT QUIETLY AT his desk, his right hand resting on the mottled wooden surface. His soft palm felt the nubby grain of the wood, splintered and gouged from decades of use. He placed his left hand down next to his other, thumbs touching. His scarred palm felt only smooth, uneven contours. He smiled. His two hands were a metaphor of his character. One sensitive to every nuance in human interactions; the other, calloused.

Today was his second day as the new Director of JEJI, an acronym for Justice for Ethiopian Jews in Israel, the national legal aid society for the Beta Israel. Yesterday he had met for the first time with his small staff of four: two other lawyers, a social worker, and an admin assistant. He was not surprised to discover that all were Ethiopian Jews. Smart optics. But he wondered whether they were up to the daunting task facing their agency: obtaining justice for the Beta Israel community. He was especially dubious about the social worker, Esther Azezew. She struck him as overbearing, as if her seniority at the agency gave her the right to criticize her superiors.

But perhaps it was only his own insecurity that made him feel that way about her. He was coming to this job with no experience outside his law degree from the University of Haifa. What did he know about the troubles afflicting the majority of Ethiopian Jews in Israel? True, he'd grown up on the wrong side of the tracks in Ashdod, getting into trouble as a teenager. But he'd caught a lucky break at the end of high school. A rich British donor had plucked him out of his Ethiopian ghetto and sent him to Oxford on full scholarship. Now that he was back among his own people, he'd have to reacquaint himself with his roots.

He stood up and walked out into the small room that served as a reception area for clients and visitors. Two men sat in orange plastic chairs which lined two of the yellow-brown walls. One was an old man missing most of his teeth. His back was bent, his skinny legs bowed. The other man was young, probably in his twenties. He sat ramrod straight like a cedar. His bright teeth flashed in the sunlight streaming into the room from a row of high windows. Both had the same furtive look in their dark eyes. They stared at the floor, occasionally looking up at the white ceiling tiles, then back down at the floor, shuffling their sandaled feet over the worn speckled linoleum. Behind him, Dani heard the clicking sounds of Esther's keyboard, the gurgle of boiling water, and the occasional ringing of a phone.

Moments later, when he passed Esther's desk on his way to the morning staff meeting, she looked up from her screen and raised her severe eyebrows. He noticed that her ebony skin was pocked with small, shallow craters.

"The Adanech file. Kidist and her daughter." Her voice was high-pitched, urgent. "Are you going to follow up on it?"

Dani stared at her. Her eyes, shining dark pearls floating in cream, seemed about to pop out of their bony sockets. It was obviously a congenital condition, but he felt assaulted by her gaping stare. He looked away.

"The Adanech file," she repeated.

"Excuse me?"

"The case was never resolved. Left pending. The mother's diary was found in a Sudanese refugee camp in 2015. The UN forwarded the diary to the Jewish Agency, and they sent it on to us. When it came here, I logged whatever information I could ferret out of it into our database. What your predecessor, Mister Senbatu, liked to call 'the demographic particulars.' On my own initiative I found out that the mother died in the camp. Cholera. No word on the daughter.

Mister Senbatu told me not to bother looking for her. I'm hoping you'll be more interested in this case than your predecessor was."

What *hutzpah* this woman had! His second day on the job, and already she was making demands. Still, her heart was in the right place. This was why JEJI existed. To make sure that Ethiopian Jews got a fair shake.

"Write me a short memo about the case, Esther. I'll make it a priority."

Then he noticed she was grasping a small notebook in her hand. She thrust it at him. The book's worn leather cover was seamed with spidery lines like veined marble.

"Kidist Adanech's diary." She hesitated, gulped, then took a deep breath. "As soon as I heard you were hired, I took the liberty of re-reading it. You'll see why I feel so strongly about this case."

Dani took the small notebook from Esther's hand, then transferred it into his right hand so he could feel the weathered grain of the cover. He feathered the pages, the stiff, cheap paper.

He looked at Esther and smiled sympathetically.

"As I said, I'll make it a priority."

She continued to stare brazenly at him. He wasn't sure she even blinked. Then, without a word, she nodded curtly and returned to her typing.

He waited until after his meeting to turn his attention to the diary. Seated back at his desk, he laid down the notebook and bent back the leather cover. On the reverse side, the writer had written her name in black ink. *Kidist Adanech*. The writing was in a beautiful hand, written by someone who'd probably been trained as a scribe or maybe a professional letter-writer.

He began reading the first entry.

> *Why should it be so hard to leave this place? How often have I cursed my life here!*

Have we Jews ever been truly welcome? Hyena people, they call us. Sorcerers. Buda. Constantly accusing us of cursing them with the evil eye. And even when they leave us in peace, what else have we known here but famine and disease? Why should we want to call this wretched place home?

And yet. How my heart breaks to leave this village! My garden, my kiln, even that stubborn goat!

Qes Yeshak has divined that we will soon go up to the Promised Land. Three thousand years we have waited! How blessed are we, the generation privileged to witness a miracle!

But the qes has told us almost nothing about how we will make our way there. I know it's a long, arduous trek across the desert and mountains to reach the Sudanese border. No doubt we'll encounter many perils along the way—wild animals and snakes, the lack of water, and ruthless bandits. Not all of us will survive. Do I dare risk my children's lives for the sake of a dream?

As we wait for the qes, I watch my littlest one perform the bunna coffee ceremony for her doll. How well-crafted is the little clay jebena she has made with her own hands! How skillfully she pours water out of its delicate spout. Already she follows in my footsteps as a potter! Of course, she is too young to understand why we are leaving Gultosh. This is the only world she has ever known—a mud hut, her father's forge and her mother's kiln, the garden where we grow our food, the small side yard where we keep the goat and chickens. Why are we uprooting her from her peaceful, happy world? Are the dangers she faces here any worse than those she will face in the days ahead?

My mother tells me that my fear betrays my lack of faith. Ever since we decided to leave, she's had several visions. They have convinced her that we have been destined to make this journey. She has sworn to leave even if the rest of us lose our nerve.

Makari has promised to go with her. He wants our children to grow up as free Jews in the Holy Land. He fears for their future in Gultosh. He swears that he will protect us on our journey. He fully trusts in the providence of his name. "Makari. *He who is wise.*" *He urges me to trust in mine.* Kidist. "*She who is blessed.*"

Dani lifted up his head and sucked in a deep breath.

The writer's Amharic was simple but eloquent in its directness. What Ethiopian village woman knew how to write like this?

He exhaled with a loud huff and returned to his reading.

Why then do my limbs tremble when I think about fleeing from here in the dead of night?

Hawi assures me that Negasi will lead us safely to the refugee camp in Sudan. She swears that this tall, young man is fearless, possessed of immense strength, carrying himself with the bearing of a warrior. I know full well that she has other reasons for singing his praises. She is already twelve. Almost ready to be a wife and mother.

Perhaps my husband is right in upbraiding me for my lack of faith. If God wills that we return to the land of our fathers, who am I to doubt Him? He promised that He would carry us there on the wings of eagles!

Dani put down the notebook and rubbed the bridge of his nose. Deciphering such ornate handwriting strained his eyes. The woman's story was not unusual. Like a thousand other Ethiopian Jews who had fled the remote villages of Gondar Province, this woman and her family had risked everything to come to Israel. They had left behind all their worldly goods and faced overwhelming odds to make it to refugee camps or to Addis from which they would eventually be air-lifted to Israel. So why was Esther Azezew so obsessed with this par-ticular case? Who knew if this woman's daughter had made it out of Sudan? So many succumbed to the deadly diseases so common at these overcrowded camps—cholera, dysentery, pneumonia, or deadly malnutrition.

Shaking his head, he opened his top desk drawer and slid the worn, leather-covered volume in among the jumble of envelopes, post-its, stationery, and other office supplies. Like so much else on his "Urgent" to-do list, it would have to wait.

He pushed the drawer shut and lifted up the black receiver on his desk.

"Esther, please call the AG's office and arrange a lunch date with him as soon as possible. Tell his secretary it'll be my treat. You choose the restaurant. But remember we're a non-profit. Dairy and salads."

After he hung up, he thought about retrieving the diary and read-ing a few more entries. Maybe the woman's story wasn't as common-place as it seemed. Maybe.... But then he looked at his inbox, spilling over with memos, files, requisition requests, and pink telephone slips.

Maybe when he had some free time.

9

It was late afternoon when Maya arrived at the Abu Kabir Institute for Forensic Medicine, part of Tel Aviv University. The mud-brown stucco building, located in a former middle-class neighborhood, stood alone on the street, surrounded by a stone wall. It was the only facility in the country that handled autopsies of unnatural deaths.

When Maya had called to arrange the visit, Dr. Selgundo told her that she was too late to attend the autopsy of Titi Aklilu, which had taken place several hours earlier. She told him she was on her way to Tel Aviv to view the body and get his take on what he'd found. What she neglected to tell him was that she wasn't authorized to do either. Sarit Levine had made it quite clear that Maya was to stay out of her way. Fortunately for Maya, the Medical Examiner didn't ask any questions.

A little more than an hour later, Maya walked through the unlocked front door of the facility and headed toward the frosted glass door marked "Laboratory" at the end of the foyer. A set of concrete stairs took her down to the basement, a vast area that extended well beyond the perimeter of the two-story building that sat above it. The rough concrete walls and tiled floor muffled her footsteps. The air was cool. Like the bodies that inhabited this underground realm.

She walked past a number of gurneys lining both sides of the long corridor, noting that some bore bodies covered by white sheets. When she reached Avraham Selgundo's office, she found him seated at his desk, dressed in street clothes. The surface of the desk overflowed with papers.

"I want to see her," said Maya.

The Medical Examiner didn't argue. He soundlessly rose, exited the small room, and led Maya to Room 1B, a large room dimly lit with an array of fluorescent lights, one of which sputtered sporadically. Lining the white concrete walls were large wooden cabinets faced with glass. Inside the middle cabinet was a torture chamber of medical instruments: handsaws, forceps, drills, hammers, power saws, and various bowls and trays.

Selgundo walked over to one of the cabinets and removed two blue disposable autopsy gowns. He handed one to Maya. He slipped his on over his short-sleeved shirt and fastened the ties. From a cardboard box sitting on a shelf near a stainless-steel sink, he plucked two sets of magenta latex gloves. He gave one pair to Maya. Then, pulling on his own, he headed for the large rectangular steel table, which occupied the center of the room.

A body lay on the table, covered by a green rubber tarp. Maya noticed a drainage pipe running from under the table into a metal bucket. Suspended over a nearby sink hung a large showerhead connected to the faucet. Water dripped slowly from the showerhead into the deep sink.

The room reeked of chemicals, body fluids, disemboweled organs, blood, feces, and undigested stomach contents. The pungent perfume of death.

Selgundo carefully pulled off the tarp, revealing the body underneath. Titi's beautiful corpse lay, face-up, on the stainless-steel surface. A bright halogen light on a swivel arm hung over her. The Medical Examiner switched on the light and aimed its beam at Titi's chest. Her small breasts lay almost flat, the dark nipples sunken.

"We have to turn her over."

Maya stepped close to the steel table and looked down at the body, which had begun to stiffen as rigor mortis set in. The center of her chest was disfigured by a Y-shaped-incision, now sewn shut with large basting stitches. Her eyes were closed, as if in sleep.

The preliminary report had stated that the young woman had been gardening in the backyard when she was killed. Maya noticed that none of her manicured fingernails had dirt under them. Her makeup was still perfect. *She couldn't even garden without putting on lipstick and mascara!* The tight red coils of her hair glistened in the harsh light. Her skin, the color of antique bronze, was unmarked. Unlike many of the Ethiopian girls in Israel, Titi's flesh displayed no tattoos on her face, neck, chest, or arms. Lying naked like this, she seemed much younger than her twenty-three years. Innocent. Why had she been murdered?

Standing flush against the metal table, Selgundo reached over Titi's body and grasped her left shoulder with both gloved hands. He thrust his chin toward her legs. Maya reached over and grabbed Titi's left hip and thigh. Together they tugged gently until the body rolled over, her arm and leg slightly overhanging the table. Selgundo nudged the body back into the center.

They both stared down at the corpse. Blood had pooled under the skin of her buttocks, shoulders, and heels, leaving purple bruises. The back of her hair was matted. Maya's green eyes quickly zeroed in on the primary focus of her inquiry: the large vertical gash in the center of Titi's back, a long, raw cut running from her delicate shoulder blades down to her thin waist. Despite a thorough washing prior to the post-mortem, the wound remained crusted with dark blood, distinguishable from the woman's brown skin by its viscous sheen.

"It's one of the longest stab wounds I've ever seen," said Selgundo. "Almost forty centimeters! But that's not the only thing that's unusual about the wound. The weapon that killed her appears to have been double-bladed." He pointed with one gloved finger at the ragged edges of the wound. "And when we opened her up, I noticed that the blade didn't go straight down but curved upward so that it entered the heart from below. Never seen anything like it. And believe me, I've seen plenty of stab wounds. Knives, axes, screwdrivers, ice picks, even a mezuzah once. But I can't identify the weapon this killer used."

Maya bent down to examine the bloody cut. The opening was wider than many of the knife wounds she'd seen. The cut was straight and precise as though drawn by an architectural draftsman. No hesitation shown by this hand. The bleeding must have been profuse. She had probably died almost instantly.

Judging by the depth of the wound, Maya suspected that the attack was personal. Was the killer close to the victim? A crime of passion? Did the viciousness of the wound indicate rage or jealousy? Maya doubted that it was either. The stabbing had been too methodical and controlled. Definitely not done by mistake, as Aklilu had claimed. So, what had motivated the killer? Was Roni right, that it was a drug deal gone wrong, a gang killing? But then how to explain the unusual weapon? Gangs tended to use weapons easily obtained, easily concealed, easily disposed of. Handguns or small blades. Maybe it was some kind of ritual killing. She knew so little about the culture of the Beta Israel. Filling in those blanks had to be her first order of business.

"Are we done here?" Selgundo asked.

Maya stared at him blankly.

He began stripping off his rubber gloves, turning them inside out and tossing them into a blue metal can. He then untied his gown and tossed it into an open plastic bin on top of several others.

Maya hurriedly removed her own autopsy gown and gloves. The smell had begun to get to her. She had forgotten to bring Vicks to smear under her nostrils.

"Sorry I can't be more helpful about the knife," Selgundo said. "I assume the Service has a pretty extensive database of weapons. I'm guessing you'll find your double-bladed curved weapon there."

Maya said a hasty goodbye then slammed through the double steel doors of the examining room. She just managed to keep her gorge down until she reached the women's bathroom.

10

SHORTLY BEFORE DARK, ELVIS DROVE to Kiryat Menachem. He walked two blocks to the small community garden where he'd arranged to meet his contact. None of the people he passed paid any attention to him—a skinny young black man wearing torn jeans, a Bruce Springsteen T-shirt, scuffed sandals, and a dark baseball cap.

His contact showed up twenty minutes later, dressed in civilian clothes similar to what Elvis was wearing. But the other man's white skin and flaming red hair attracted stares from some of the dark-skinned couples strolling through the park. He met their stares straight on, gazing down at them through icy blue eyes from a height of two meters. Heads down, they hurried past.

The two men sat down side-by-side on an iron bench. Each lit a cigarette and took a few drags, peering in opposite directions, not speaking.

Finally, Elvis brushed aside a limp hank of sand-colored hair from his forehead and turned to face his companion.

"*Nu*, what was so important that we had to meet in person? It's risky for us to be seen together."

"I thought you'd wanna know that Levine's looking at you for Titi's murder."

Elvis spit the smoke out of his lungs and threw his cigarette onto the gravel path. He stamped out the embers with the heel of his sandal.

"Go on."

"She had me bring her your file. She's asking questions."

"Standard police procedure. They always suspect family members. She must have seen from my file that I've had no convictions. No time served."

The burly cop thrust his large hand into his pants pocket and dug out a slim pack of gum. Deftly he unwrapped all five pieces, then wadded them together and stuck the gob into his mouth, chomping down with his back teeth. Slowly his massive jaw relaxed into rhythmic mastication. *Chews like a camel*, thought Elvis. *About as smart as one too.*

A grin soon appeared on the large man's face, stirring the sea of freckles covering his pale cheeks.

"Don't underestimate her, Elvis. She's pretty sharp."

"Yeah, well, so am I."

He reached into his pocket, fished out a slim box of cigarettes, and thrust one between his lips. He lit it and blew out a thin stream of smoke. A jogger running by, beads of gleaming sweat pouring down his black face, glanced at him with undisguised censure. Elvis thrust his middle finger at the man, then spit out a globule of spit. The big cop laughed and gave Elvis a high five. Elvis had to raise himself off the bench with one arm to clap the giant's palm.

"I hope you gave her someone else to focus on."

The cop smiled broadly and nodded.

"Your Abba. Plenty of bad behavior there."

Elvis laughed. He inhaled a lungful of smoke, tossed his head back, and pursed his lips, sending several perfect smoke rings up into the cool night air.

"Good man! That should keep her busy." He laughed again. But he stopped abruptly when he saw that his companion's pale blue eyes had taken on a grave expression.

"What?"

"She's not the only one looking into this murder."

"You're kidding me!"

"Your father's also leaned on the Minister of Security. Arik Ophir. Demanded that the Service launch a full investigation. Claims someone's trying to kill him."

Elvis sprang up from the bench and began pacing back and forth. His sandals scraped the gravel. Like a shovel digging. He muttered under his breath, punctuating indecipherable words with gusts of smoke.

"*Dikkalla*! Thinks he's so goddam important he needs spies working for him! Hey, you gotta help me out here!"

The giant cop leaned forward and spit his gray gobbet of chewing gum onto the ground. It landed close to the blob of spittle Elvis had launched moments earlier.

"No fucking way! It's one thing for me to stick my nose into a police investigation, but if you think—"

Elvis cut him off.

"You forgetting how much money you lost at that Jericho casino, *havivi*? If I hadn't paid your debt..."

Elvis flicked his half-smoked cigarette toward a row of flowering bushes on the other side of the gravel path. In the dusky light, the red spark glowed brightly for a moment, then winked out.

The tall cop looked down at his feet, then scuffed at the gravel with one shoe.

"Never mind," Elvis said. "I'll handle the Service myself."

Then he bent over to hiss into his companion's ear.

"We've stayed here long enough. Do what you can to keep your boss off my tail." He leaned in closer, his lips tickling the fine hairs sprouting from the cop's puckered ear. "And next time, call me on your burner, not your police mobile."

Elvis sprang up from the bench, spun on his heels, and began walking back rapidly to Dominican Republic Street. He hoped that none of the neighborhood kids had keyed his new car or stolen his tires in the fifteen minutes he'd been gone.

11

Shulamit's Diary

Same day, evening.

Now that his sexy young wife is dead, he's hornier than ever.

He came looking for me when I was nursing the baby. My back was to him, but I could feel those greedy eyes boring through my skin. He grew impatient pretty quick and cleared his throat, letting me know he was close. I refused to turn around. So, he walked into the middle of the living room and stood right in front of me, ogling my swollen breasts while Bekeli suckled. His mouth was open, his tongue hanging out, panting like a bitch in heat. I stared at his gold tooth, glittering in the sunlight flashing through the front windows. He couldn't take his eyes off my tits. I thought about pulling Bekeli off my tit and buttoning up my shirt, but I didn't want him to think he could intimidate me so easily. Instead, I plucked the baby off my nipple and waved my dripping breast at him, the milk spattering all over my dark blue tunic. His panting increased. He took a few steps toward me. When he was almost on top of me, I shoved my breast back into my shirt and twisted to one side, quickly buttoning myself up. He growled at me—growled!—like a wild beast cheated out of a sure kill. I laughed in his face. He drew back his hand, those big, fat fingers splayed like a palm leaf, ready to hit me, but then he stopped. Maybe he was afraid I'd tell the cops. How would it look as they're investigating Titi's murder? Her husband a domestic abuser! Under his breath he muttered something I couldn't make out, his voice rumbling with anger. Then he stormed out of the room. His footsteps were so loud he scared the baby, who began to cry. I picked him up, pulled out my other breast, and gently placed his little pink mouth on my nipple. He began to suck and was soon asleep.

I've never liked being in this big house when other people aren't around. Moshe prowls around like a hyena, sniffing for twat. I wish he'd go satisfy his needs with the baryas. I can understand why he's not attracted to the younger one, with her crooked leg and ruined face. Not that he cares much about what a woman looks like on the outside. They have no choice but to submit to him. They're baryas. But he should show more respect for me, his daughter-in-law!

Well, we'll see what happens to Mr. High-and-Mighty once the cops dig into his past and poke around his business. I hope he gets what's coming to him!

12

MASHA PETROVNA WALKED INTO MAYA'S office a few minutes before 5:00 p.m. Most of the staff and other agents were already gone for the day. By now, she was used to her friend's odd hours and idiosyncratic MO. She'd given up trying to persuade Maya to try to conform to the normal rhythms of the agency. Even if Maya had agreed, she couldn't have followed through. She was just wired differently. Maybe it was her OCD, though neither she nor Maya had ever given Maya's eccentric behavior a psychiatric label. Maya preferred to describe her conduct as "focused" or "single-minded." Masha never corrected her. Whatever fueled Maya's engine, Masha was convinced it made her the best agent in the Service. Too bad it also constantly got her into trouble. Roni liked to joke that she had never learned to color inside the lines.

This new case struck Masha as an odd one for the Service to take on. Why not leave it to the Jerusalem Police? That was the first question Masha meant to put to her friend.

When she walked into Maya's office, Masha found her fellow agent absorbed in one of her byzantine puzzles. This one was an interlaced cubical matrix of wooden rods, which Maya was methodically pushing and pulling to unlock. She didn't look up when Masha walked up to the large gray steel desk and hopped up on one corner. She sat silent and motionless while Maya finished working out the puzzle. Only when the last few rods broke apart and clattered to the desk's metal surface did Maya look up and see her friend gazing at her, a broad smile on her flat-featured face. Masha's warm brown eyes twinkled in amusement.

"How long have you been sitting here, watching me?"

"Would you believe me if I said two hours?"

They both laughed. Not because Maya was incapable of remaining oblivious for such a long period, but because no puzzle yet invented would take her that long to crack. Keeping her gold-flecked green eyes fixed on Masha, Maya began putting the wooden puzzle back together, her small hands connecting the pieces without hesitation.

"Since when do we investigate Jerusalem homicides?" asked Masha.

"The victim's the wife of an MK, Moshe Aklilu. Aklilu leaned on Ophir, who leaned on Roni..."

"Who leaned on you."

Maya nodded, slipping the final puzzle piece into place and carefully setting the wooden cube down among the motley array of puzzles, fidget toys, and mechanical gadgets lined up in the middle of her broad desk. She stared at the collection, then nudged the wooden cube with her index finger so that it aligned precisely with the two wooden puzzles flanking it. She looked up and smiled sheepishly at Masha. Then she straightened her shoulders. The smile evaporated into a hard line.

"Okay, so here's what we know so far."

Maya reached for a manila file folder sitting to her right, slid it in front of her, and opened it.

"Moshe Aklilu is an Ethiopian immigrant, first generation. Serving his first term in the Knesset. Apparently an up-and-comer. Came here in '95, started a domestic employment agency in Beersheva. A few years later he expanded into other cities around the country. At first, he mostly placed Ethiopians, but they now recruit temporary workers from all over. Seems to have done quite well for himself. Married, divorced, and remarried. Two grown children from the first marriage. His son is now married with a baby. Daughter still single. Aklilu was elected to the Knesset in 2012. Moved to Jerusalem, built a fancy new villa in the German Colony. Married his second wife in 2018. Titi Akilu, aged twenty-three. Miss Beersheva 2015. Our murder victim."

"A meteoric rise, as the tabloids would say."

"Which usually warrants looking into," said Maya. "The whole family lives together in their McMansion. The parents, the unmarried sister, the married son with his wife and baby. And two female servants."

"Anything pop out at you?"

"Plenty. For one thing, there's no Service file on Moshe Aklilu. Not a single note. I find that odd, given his prominent position. He's claiming that the knife that killed his wife was meant for him. Her killing was a mistake. I want to find out why he thinks someone wants him dead."

Masha looked down at her fingernails, which she'd recently had done. Two nails chipped already. She'd need an emergency manicure as soon as possible. Then she glanced down at her bare toes, peeking out of her new Christian Louboutin open-toed pumps. The pedicure was still unspoiled, thank God. She couldn't afford to do both this month.

"Something else doesn't add up," continued Maya. "I haven't been able to find anything on Aklilu before he came to Israel. Maybe he changed his name. Maybe he left something behind in Ethiopia that he doesn't want found."

"What about our vic, Titi?"

"Nothing that raises any red flags. Daughter of Ethiopian immigrants. Attended school in Beersheva. Active in the local Scouts. Finished high school, served two years in the IDF. Secretarial Support. Went to modeling academy. Won a beauty contest. As routine as it gets."

"So, what's next?"

"I want to look into all the members of the family. For now, they're our only suspects. I'm counting on them to point us to more leads."

Masha looked down at her watch, a slender lady's model with diamond chips in place of numbers.

"It's late. Past six. Maybe we should pick this up tomorrow?"

Maya bent her chin down and eyed her friend under auburn eyebrows.

"Have a hot date tonight?"

Masha blushed.

"You know I don't! But there's a sale at Nahmani's. I thought I'd go—just to look."

Maya laughed and waved one hand toward her office door.

"Go! Spend your retirement savings on more shoes! You only go 'round once."

Masha bounced off the desk and wobbled toward the door on her stiletto heels. The door closed softly behind her.

Maya ran her eyes over the puzzles lined up across her desk. She'd been saving the newest one—a modern variation on the Kongming lock—for her next day off, but she couldn't wait that long.

With an itching palm, she scooped up the wooden puzzle, which was a bewildering wooden knot of a dozen pieces. She set it down in front of her. Gently she began poking at each piece until one yielded slightly to her touch. Within moments she was lost in the matrix of intersecting rods, trying to envision their secret turnings in her mind's eye. She didn't hear the heavy double doors of HQ's front entrance clang shut when Masha left for the night.

13

It was just before seven that Dani Solomon stepped into his apartment in Mevaseret Zion, a northwest suburb of Jerusalem. He carried his wrinkled sports jacket draped over one arm. The back of his white short-sleeved shirt was drenched with perspiration. Even at this late hour, the 183 bus had been so crowded that he'd had to stand during the entire fifteen-minute ride.

He was ravenously hungry. Flinging his jacket onto the yellow vinyl couch on his way to the kitchen area, he noted with a sigh that the piles of laundry still awaited sorting. So did yesterday's mail. He yanked open the small red refrigerator, finding inside only a container of hummus, a few cucumbers, some olives, and two hard-boiled eggs. A glass jar of home-made tej. From a paper bag on the counter, he shook out the last pita, tore it in half, and stuffed the contents of the fridge into each oval pocket, which he wolfed down in a few bites. This would have to do for his dinner. He was too tired to venture out to a restaurant or to the little grocery store around the corner.

After a quick shower, he changed into a T-shirt and shorts. Then he retrieved his briefcase from the spot where he'd dropped it on his way in and brought it over to the couch. Pushing aside the pile of wrinkled clothes, he flopped down on the middle cushion. For a while he just rested there, watching night darken the apartment house across the street. Then he leaned forward and bent down. From the worn briefcase, he withdrew a small leather notebook, which he placed gently on the low wooden coffee table in front of him.

Two damp fingerprints darkened the dusty cover. He should have dried his hands more thoroughly after he'd eaten! It was bad enough that he'd taken the diary home with him—a flagrant violation of agency rules—but he was also damaging it. What kind of example was he setting for his staff?

Wiping his damp hands on his shorts, he leaned forward and gingerly opened the diary to the writer's second entry. He had left her on the brink of fleeing her village. How had their small party managed the long, difficult trek? How had the diarist found the strength to write it all down? How many had survived?

He squinted in the pallid lamplight and began to read:

We have only been on our journey for two days, but already our old life seems like a vanished dream.

I am glad that we chose to leave Gultosh after Sigd. It is good that we were able to have one last celebration at home before starting our new lives in the Holy Land. The older children will certainly remember this day! The whole village traipsing up the mountain wearing fresh white shammas, the qesoch toting colorful umbrellas for shade. How splendid Qes Yeshak looked, carrying the Orit despite his advanced age. How steady his voice rang out when he chanted the Ten Commandments!

I was so proud of Noham for joining Hawi, Kabede, Makari, and me in fasting this year. Only six years old! Of course, the baby was hardly aware of what was going on. I thank God that he still possesses such innocence. As for his beautiful little sister, I doubt she'll remember the last Sigd here, being only four. Her first memories will be celebrating the festival in the Holy City of Jerusalem! How I envy her!

It is good that Ebo and his family have decided to come with us. It is a shame that his parents had to leave most of their beautiful handiwork behind—his father's elegant metalwork, his mother's graceful pottery—but our hands and backs are too weighed down with necessities to carry any more.

I am so pleased that Ebo and Negasi are once again on friendly terms after so many years of estrangement. I remember when Negasi was expelled from the Jewish school in Ambobar shortly before he became bar mitzvah. Hawi insists that Ebo was just as guilty as Negasi for starting that fight with the younger boys. But because of his great wealth and influence, Ebo's father was able to arrange it so that only Negasi carried the blame. And it is only Negasi who still bears a scar on his neck from that fight. Perhaps Negasi's offer to guide Ebo's family as well as his own family and ours to freedom is his way of showing that all is now forgiven. Ebo does seem to look up to Negasi as our leader.

We will all need to support each other on this dangerous journey. Negasi has warned us to stay vigilant. He is especially worried about attacks by bandits or government soldiers along the way. That is why he has decided that two of us are to stand guard each night. But with only a billawa and some smaller knives as weapons, how can we possibly defend ourselves if we're attacked?

Yet despite the dangers, I am grateful that we are finally on our way! I refuse to believe the stories I've heard about what our people have encountered when arriving in Israel. That other Jews look down on us because of the color of our skin. That their rabbis challenge our understanding of Torah and Jewish law. Some in our village—government informers, no doubt—even claim that the Israelis are more hostile to the Beta Israel than Christians and Muslims here in Ethiopia. All lies meant to discourage us from leaving! Like Pharaoh in Egypt, the Ethiopians now regret letting our people go!

Dani leaned forward and gently set the slim leather volume back down on the coffee table. He was relieved to see that his dark prints had become almost invisible. He removed his glasses and rubbed his eyes. As much as he wanted to keep reading this woman's story, he was too tired. He'd spent his day listening to an endless litany of grievances. Clients complaining about unfair housing practices. Discrimination in employment. Institutional racism. Crime and vandalism in their neighborhoods. He had tried to listen sympathetically, to help solve their problems. But as soon as he resolved one issue, three more seemed to pop up. The community's complaints were like a hydra on steroids!

He carefully tucked the diary back into his briefcase and snapped the clasp. Then he padded into his bedroom and lay down on his single bed without putting on any lights. But sleep eluded him. The whining voices kept nattering in his head like buzzing gnats.

Clicking on the bedside light, Dani saw the familiar photograph of his family on his night-table. It brought a tired smile to his lips. But that feeling, too, soon slipped away.

He closed his eyes and tried to picture his grandmother, Ayati Abaynesh. Despite her advanced age and small stature, she was a powerful voice in their village. Her words were few but always ripe with wisdom. Even years after her death, her folktales and proverbs frequently floated up into Dani's mind.

Ayati, he whispered to himself as he finally drifted off to sleep, *give me strength. Help me heal this broken people.*

14

Driving on automatic pilot, Maya turned off Hebron Road and guided her silver Toyota Corolla down the exit ramp into Givat HaMatos. Past the ramp, the bright sodium lamps disappeared, replaced by much dimmer lights, spaced far apart, many flickering or burnt out. When she drew near her building, she saw that the streetlamp across from the four-story apartment building was now dark. It would be weeks before the municipal authorities got around to replacing it. Fortunately, the yellow bulb lighting the building's entryway still cast its pallid glow.

She parked on the street, clicked the fob, and headed toward the side door of the building. She preferred not to use the front entrance this late at night. The recessed entryway, extending back beyond the tight cone of yellow light, was dark as pitch. Not so the steel-reinforced side door, which stood flush with the exterior concrete wall. Nothing could hide from its bright yellow bulb.

A row of black plastic trash cans and blue recycling buckets lined the concrete path leading to the side door. Maya had forgotten that tomorrow was trash day. But she was too tired to walk up and down four flights of stairs to bring out her garbage. That made two weeks in a row she'd missed the pick-up. Fortunately, she and Vered didn't accumulate much trash. It had been her ex-husband, Rafi, with his glossy magazines, take-out boxes, and foam peanuts and Bubble Wrap from online purchases, who'd accounted for most of their domestic refuse.

Just before she was about to insert her key into the heavy steel door, Maya noticed a large black plastic bag lying next to the trash can positioned closest to the outside wall. The bag had been stuffed so full that it had split open, spilling its contents onto the macadam walk. In the bright yellow light, she could make out baby clothes—onesies, bibs, footie pajamas, tiny dresses and skirts, a few blouses, a matching jacket and cap—as well as an assortment of nursery items—rattles, rubber bath toys, board books, a stuffed lion, bunny, and fox, pacifiers, a Minky baby blanket, and a musical mobile with nursery rhyme characters dangling on strings. Some of the clothes still had labels attached to them. A few of the other items remained in their original packaging.

Maya was puzzled by such extravagant wastefulness, especially here where so many of the residents were new immigrants. Had these new parents received so many baby gifts that they had no qualms about tossing the duplicates out? Why hadn't they passed them on? Plenty of the families here could use them. She debated carrying some of the things over to the donation bins a few streets over. But that would mean climbing up four flights to her apartment, grabbing a large garbage bag, walking down all those stairs, filling the bag with all this stuff, and then shlepping the heavy bag over to the bins. She was just too damn tired.

Suddenly the heavy steel door swung open towards her. Out walked Nigist Fredo-Wasa, a short, bespectacled Ethiopian woman who lived on her building's second floor. The woman's two plump arms embraced a green plastic trash basket, which was almost as tall as she was. Maya leapt out of the way as the woman hoofed breathlessly to the end of the line of black plastic barrels and emptied her trash into the last one with a grunt.

Nigist wiped her forehead with the back of one hand. Then she noticed she was not alone. She squinted her dark eyes to identify the stranger. The thick lenses of her glasses distorted her eyes, so they looked like black yolks swimming in milk.

"Ah, Maya! What you doin' out here this time of night?" She looked around anxiously. "Not safe for young woman like you."

Despite having lived in Israel for more than three decades, Nigist still spoke with a heavy Ethiopian accent. Her Hebrew was full of grammatical mistakes. But that had never stopped her from speaking her mind.

"Just getting home from work," said Maya.

Nigist waggled a chubby black finger at her.

"You work too hard, *fikire*. Too young for t'at. Should have fun! As we say in Ethiopia: 'Even in monastery comes time to sing and be merry.'"

Maya laughed. So did the other woman, her loose flowered house-dress jiggling like a full-bellied sail.

Then Nigist noticed the split-open garbage bag lying near Maya's feet, the clothes and baby things tumbled onto the dark walk.

She shook her head, then ran her fingers through her close-cropped hair.

"Bad business, t'at." She spit three times onto the desiccated grass and mumbled something under her breath. "Poor Fewesi! Her baby girl die last night. All of sudden. No mark on her. Some say killed by evil eye. Bad business."

She muttered a few more syllables, then abruptly swiveled on her pink slippers, jerked the metal door open, and disappeared inside the dark building.

Maya had not yet met the new immigrant couple from Ethiopia. They'd moved next door only two weeks ago with their newborn daughter. She'd often heard the baby crying at night. It had reminded her of those first few months with Vered, getting up every two or three hours to nurse. She'd been planning to drop by their apartment, bring them a bowl of fresh fruit, maybe a toy for the baby, but she hadn't gotten around to it. And now it was too late. She owed them a condolence call. She knew nothing about shiva customs among the Beta Israel. She'd have to query Reb Google.

As she thrust her key into the lock of the steel door, she heard a rustle behind her. She froze and listened. Nothing but the muffled swish of traffic on the Hebron Road. Then she heard it again. The scuff of a paw on pebbles. Or a shoe. She whipped around and caught a glimpse of something glinting in the chalky light. The gleam of an eye or a shiny earring. She could just make out a shadowy form. Medium height, topped by a tumulus of dark hair. Then only mute darkness.

She stood for a few more moments, ears cocked, straining to hear the rustle again. But whoever it was had departed.

Inside the dark hallway of the first floor, she groped around near the door until she found the button controlling the stairwell lighting. When she pushed it in, lights flickered on, illuminating the four floors of stairs. She hurried up the stairs, trying to reach the top before the lights died.

She almost made it. As she reached the top steps of the metal stairwell, everything went dark. Stepping warily, she made her way to the square electric plate situated in the middle of the fourth-floor hallway and depressed the button. She felt ashamed of her fear. Forcing herself to slow her breath until she was breathing normally, she slid her key into her front door and pushed inside. She was glad her six-year-old daughter was sleeping over at her parents' again tonight. She didn't like Vered to see her like this, agitated and afraid.

Before she could snap on the overhead light in her living room, she heard noises from across the hall. The apartment of the newly bereft parents. She could make out the voices of a man, loud and angry. She couldn't tell whether he was speaking Hebrew or Amharic. Suddenly there was a crash, the jangle of broken glass. Then came a woman's high-pitched scream, followed by a roar of male rage. Maya stood in the dark, her ear pressed to the inside of her front door, debating whether to intervene or leave them to it.

Before she had time to decide, the door to the neighbors' apartment burst open and crashed against the unpainted cement wall of the landing. Maya cracked open her door and peered out. A large black man stood in the hall. His broad back, covered only with a thin white undershirt, faced Maya. The pencil-thin ray of light streaming from his apartment daubed only the back of one of his heels. He held a flimsy suitcase in one hand, a bulging burlap sack in the other. He was shouting at his wife. Maya caught the Hebrew words, "witch," "baby," and "murder." The man's wife shouted back at him in Amharic and then began to wail at the top of her lungs. Flinging one last curse at her in his native tongue, the man pounded down the dark stairs, his sandals slapping the metal treads like a jackhammer. The sounds grew fainter, then ceased altogether.

Maya gently eased her door shut and walked over to the sagging orange loveseat in her living room. She sank down into the soft cushion. The silver light of a quarter moon streamed through the window.

That poor woman, thought Maya. A new immigrant. A dead baby. And now deserted by her husband; although, she might be better off without him. She certainly needed a friend now. Tomorrow morning before she went to work, she would bring Fewesi some dinner.

Then the thought struck her. Why not ask Fewesi to babysit Vered occasionally? The woman could probably use the money. And maybe Vered's presence would partially fill the hole that had just been ripped open in the young woman's heart. She would definitely discuss it with her new neighbor tomorrow.

15

Shulamit's Diary

Midnight.

Can't seem to get any sleep tonight. As usual, I'm by myself. The bastard's out carousing with his home-boys. At least the baby's asleep. For now, at least.

I've been thinking a lot about poor Titi. I can't believe that I once envied her. I thought she had it all—a beauty crown, a promising career as a model, marriage to an important man. A grand villa in Jerusalem and lots of money. It's what I once dreamed of for myself. As a kid, I used to imagine that I'd become a model someday, or maybe a famous TV or movie star.

What a fool I was!

I have come to accept that I was simply born on the wrong side of fate. What does it matter that my beauty outshines hers? So what if I inherited my mother's topaz eyes and her silky hair, the color of a blood rose? Or that I have a royal nose like the Queen of Sheba? What good is beauty if you're doomed to a cursed life! The day I was born, the die was cast. From the moment I drew breath I was destined to be betrayed, orphaned, raped, and abused. So much for the name my parents gave me at birth: "omen of good things." Everything I've touched has rotted on the vine.

But I will not lose hope. I will yet change my fortune!

I look around at all the fancy things in this pretentious house—the expensive furniture and carpets, the modern art on the walls, the designer clothes, the fancy cars—and spit on such useless vanity. As the Orit says: A man of faith will reap abundant blessings, but he who hastens to be rich will not go unpunished. I now realize that I was better off in our poor village than this family will ever be! Our thatched tukul *was full of treasures—my father's beautiful metalwork and his skillfully honed knives, my mother's exquisite bowls and calligraphed scrolls. All of it was left behind when we fled. But at least* Emayay *let me take with me my precious Gudit. How I loved her yellow corn silk hair and carved bone buttons. When she gave me Gudit, Ayati Lebna told me that she blessed this doll with her own special magic.*

But even that he took from me. He stole everything, God curse him!

DAY 2

Tuesday

16

GOLYAT DROVE THE BLACK-AND-WHITE KIA Cadenza into the Aklilus' broad driveway and turned off the ignition. The engine clicked twice, then died. He felt a twinge of longing for the old Corolla patrol car he used to drive. That engine had purred, never clicked and twanged like these Korean jobs. But word was that the department had gotten a sweet deal to replace the old fleet of Toyotas with Kias. No doubt there was *baksheesh* involved.

Golyat's boss, Chief Inspector Sarit Levine, sat stock-still in the passenger seat. Her dark brown eyes stared into the open two-car garage, where a black Mercedes sat, tail out. She reached back and grabbed her ponytail with both hands, yanking it apart so that the navy-blue scrunchie tightened the sandy hair blanketing her head. Then she let her arms drop to her sides. She reached her right hand into the brown leather shoulder bag perched on her lap and withdrew a small black pad with a pen attached in an elastic loop at one edge. Still not saying a word, she tossed her head toward the dark garage and exited the patrol car. Golyat unbuckled his seatbelt and followed.

As always, he kept a few paces behind. He wasn't sure why she'd brought him with her, except to show the paparazzi that she had an underling to chauffeur her to crime scenes. And to keep the rubber-neckers at a distance.

Sarit strode briskly to the back of the garage. She flicked on the overhead light, then whirled around and walked to the driver's side of the sleek car. Shielding her eyes with her hand she peered through the clouded glass. Golyat stepped up behind her, looking over her shoulder.

The dead woman sat in the driver's seat, tilted back as though asleep. She was dressed casually in a light-colored pants suit. Her black hair was neatly cropped close to her scalp. Just above her sunglasses, her thick black eyebrows met above the bridge of her straight-edged nose. She wore glossy lipstick that shimmered through the milky glass. From her small ears dangled shiny silver spirals.

Golyat gasped when he recognized the earrings. Although Sarit had told him the victim's name back at the station, he hadn't really let it sink in. But seeing her like this, so peaceful—and so dead—and wearing the earrings he'd given her for her birthday last June, he had no choice but to believe his eyes. Hagar Aklilu wasn't the prettiest girl he'd ever dated nor the sexiest, but there had been something about her, a gentleness, an earnestness, that he'd never encountered in another woman. She was so devoted to her third graders, believing that the months she spent teaching them would make a real difference when they grew up. The few times they'd been together, she'd delighted in telling him about her latest classroom triumph. Teaching the slowest boy in the class to read his first words in Hebrew. Getting a bully to apologize to his victims. Relishing the wonder in her students' eyes as they watched an Israeli space-lander reach the moon. For some reason Golyat had never tired of listening to her. Her enthusiasm, shining in the dark pools of her eyes, had mesmerized him.

"Gloves!"

Sarit's commanding voice broke through his reverie. He dug out a pair of white latex gloves from his pants pocket and forced his large fingers into them, pulling the gloves tight with a final snap.

"Don't touch anything!" she barked at him. "Selgundo gets first crack. I just want a quick look-see."

When Sarit tried the door handle, she wasn't surprised to find it unlocked. She stamped her foot impatiently on the cement floor and snorted. She'd specifically ordered the cops at the crime scene not to touch anything. The maid who'd found the body wouldn't have dared. But of course, they hadn't listened. How likely was it that the dead woman had been found reclining so peacefully in the soft leather seat, her designer sunglasses perfectly poised on her sharp-prowed nose? Sarit bent down and peered into the young woman's dark lenses. Her ebony lids were closed, the long lashes curled neatly upward toward the car's plush ceiling.

The body had obviously been moved!

As Sarit straightened up, a shaft of bright light from the car's overhead lamp flashed on the dead woman's forehead. The light revealed a bloody glyph carved into the victim's dark skin. Sarit recognized the loops and whorls of Amharic writing.

"Hey, Golyat, come take a look! Can you read this cockeyed language?"

Golyat peered into the car and shuddered at the sight of Hagar's mutilated brow. He quickly stepped back, then shook his head when Sarit turned around to look up at him. Hagar had tried to teach Golyat the Amharic alphabet as well as a few common expressions, but he hadn't been interested. Foreign languages had never been his strong suit. Hebrew was hard enough.

"Go get someone from the family down here. Now!"

Golyat walked to the steel door at the back of the garage and knocked. A moment later, a small dark woman with a horribly disfigured face opened the door. As soon as he said a few words to her in Hebrew, she shook her head peevishly and threw up her hands. But when she heard the name, "Aklilu," she abruptly turned around and limped up a short flight of stairs into the house. Golyat followed her.

When he entered the spacious living room, he found the surviving members of the family, seated far apart from each other on a long white sectional sofa. All of them stared down mutely at the plush white carpet under their feet. Off to one side, a small boy sat on the floor and babbled as he played with an assortment of colorful plastic shapes.

Moshe Aklilu looked up when Golyat entered the room. The whites of the MK's eyes were bloodshot. The black pips at their centers glistened in the harsh morning light.

Today Moshe was dressed in a crisp dark suit with hairline stripes, a collared white shirt, and shiny black shoes. On his head he wore a large white kippah embroidered with gold tracery. His face was drawn, making him look much older than his forty-three years. His face bore an expression midway between consternation and grief.

"We haven't even set up the mourning tent for Titi, and now Hagar is dead too!"

Moshe's large, closely shorn head dropped heavily into his cupped hands.

Elvis looked up at the giant cop, then quickly looked away.

"We can't bury either of them until after the autopsies," Golyat said.

He couldn't tell from the younger Aklilu's expression or tone of voice whether Elvis was offended or depressed by this fact. Elvis remained slumped back against the soft, white cushions, his hands thrust deep in his pockets. His eyes were hidden behind his shaggy forelock.

"Sorry for your loss," muttered Golyat.

Although he tried to sound sincere, he knew that no bereaved family was ever fooled by cops' messages of condolence. He cleared his throat and looked at the ground.

"I need one of you to come to the garage, to translate something in Amharic."

Elvis looked over at Golyat. Then he flung his head off to one side, uncovering his dark eyes. They brimmed with tears. *What an actor*, thought Golyat. Or were the tears real? His wily friend always played his cards close to the vest.

Nodding curtly to Golyat, Elvis now stood up. He walked briskly past the giant policeman, trotted down the stairs, and entered the garage through the metal door. He let it swing shut behind him.

17

ELVIS STOOD FOR A MOMENT at the metal door, waiting for Sarit Levine to acknowledge his presence. When she finally swiveled her head toward him, he walked over to the driver's side of the car. Standing beside her, he drew himself up to his full height, which even at a modest five foot six dwarfed the diminutive police inspector.

Sarit pointed her index finger at the bloody lines carved into his sister's forehead.

"What's it say?"

Involuntarily Elvis shuddered. His dark eyes glistened in the dim light. He waited a few moments to regain control of himself.

"*Jib*. It means 'hyena' in Amharic."

Sarit's dark brown eyes yawned wide.

"What?"

"You know, the animal. A hyena. They're common in Africa. I hear there are even some left in the southern Negev."

"I know what hyenas are!"

Sarit's hands flew back to her ponytail, which she yanked fiercely. The skin at the corners of her eyes tightened, making her eyes narrow into a suspicious squint.

"Any idea what it means?"

Elvis snorted and tossed back his shank of sandy curls.

"It's what they used to call us back in Ethiopia. *Jiboch*. Hyenas. Our good Christian and Muslim neighbors thought that we Jews could turn ourselves into hyenas at night in order to prey on them."

"So, the killer's a member of the Beta Israel."

"Or wants us to think he is."

Neither of them noticed when Golyat slipped through the door and stood in the shadows at the back of the garage. With growing alarm, he watched his boss and Elvis spar with each other. He had warned Elvis that Levine was shrewd. The more she probed, the closer she would get to the truth. She needed to be thrown off the scent. And quickly.

He took a few steps forward, letting the bare bulb overhead reveal his presence.

"The Beta Israel were often scapegoats back in Ethiopia," said Golyat. "People thought Jews were witches 'cause they were metal smiths. They knew how to control fire."

Sarit pivoted to face him.

"And how do you know so much about them?"

Was that surprise or suspicion in those laser-beam eyes?

"When I first started out as a beat cop, my turf was southwest Jerusalem. Kiryat Menachem, Ir Ganim, Giv'at Massu'a. Lots of Ethiopian immigrants in those neighborhoods. Some of them told me about the hyena thing."

Sarit peered up at the giant cop, her sandy brows angled like a guillotine.

"Okay. So why do you think this poor girl's face was branded like this?"

Elvis cleared his throat. Sarit swung around to face him.

"Your officer might be onto something, Inspector. Wouldn't be the first time someone tried to frame a *kushi*."

Golyat gave a thumbs-up to Elvis behind his boss's back. A smart move, playing the race card. The son had clearly learned a thing of two from his canny father.

Sarit grunted and turned back to the corpse. For the first time she noticed splotches of blood staining the driver's bucket seat and the right side of Hagar's pants.

"We need to look at her back!"

"I thought you wanted to wait for the ME," said Golyat. "You know how mad Selgundo gets if you touch a body..."

"We're not going to flip her. Just bend her forward. We'll put her back exactly the way she was."

Golyat sucked in an exasperated breath and walked to the other side of the car. He opened the passenger door and leaned in. While Sarit grabbed hold of Hagar's left shoulder with both hands, he grasped her right. Together they gently nudged the body toward the steering wheel. But the absorbent cloth of Hagar's suit jacket, sodden with blood, stuck to the leather seat. With slightly more force, they tugged at her shoulders. The leather released her body with a sucking sound, like strips of Velcro tearing apart. Where the body had pressed against it, the leather was smeared with blood, glutinous like wet paint.

Golyat stared at the back of Hagar's bloody jacket. The cream-colored material was slashed vertically with a long, serrated cut. Ragged along all edges. The sort of cut that could only have been made by a double-edged blade.

Then his eye was caught by a triangle of clear plastic sticking out of Hagar's pants pocket. While his boss was busy scrutinizing the wound at close range, he grasped the plastic between two gloved fingers and jerked it out of the pocket. It was a small Ziploc bag, half-filled with white powder. He quickly stuffed the bag into his pocket.

Sarit gazed at the bloody slash for a few more moments. Then she looked back at Elvis, who was clearly sickened at the sight. Golyat tried to hide his own horror. He recalled his last encounter with Hagar. She'd walked out on him before they'd even finished dinner at the fancy restaurant he'd saved up to take her to. She'd called him a cheat, a sham cop. Just because he'd given her a bottle of expensive perfume that Elvis had illegally smuggled in from France. Why'd he have to tell her where he got it? And what was the big fucking deal, anyway?

And now she was dead.

Sarit pointed at the stab wound exposed under the torn jacket.

"Can't be a coincidence. Same MO."

Golyat opened his mouth, then clamped it shut.

If you cross her, she'll get suspicious. Tread carefully. Let Elvis take it from here.

But Elvis was silent. A single tear trickled down his sandy cheek. He made no move to wipe it away.

Suddenly he spun around and walked rapidly toward the door leading into the main house. He paused, his hand on the steel knob.

"Let us know as soon as you have a suspect, Inspector. They won't get away with this!"

He twisted the knob and disappeared into the house. The door swung shut with a soft click.

"Gotta be a gang killing," Sarit muttered under her breath. "Golyat!"

Still leaning into the car, the tall policeman lifted his head and banged it against the Mercedes's soft ceiling. His eyes fell upon Hagar's bloody back. He gasped out loud.

"Help me ease her back into the seat," said Sarit. "Selgundo'll be here any minute."

When the corpse was once again in a reclining position, Golyat slowly backed his huge body out of the passenger side and stiffly straightened up. He began walking back toward the driveway.

"Where do you think you're going?" said Sarit. "We stay until Selgundo's done here."

She bent over to take another look at the pretty young corpse.

"This is definitely payback. We just have to figure out for what."

18

As soon as Maya stepped out of her apartment, she smelled the coffee. The rich, pungent fragrance of Ethiopian beans. Mixed with the slightly acrid odor of incense. She walked up to her neighbor's door and gently knocked.

"Who there?"

The woman's voice was halting, wary.

"It's Maya Rimon. I live across the hall. Just wanted to introduce myself."

Maya heard the slide of a chain bolt, the click of a lock.

The door opened slightly to reveal a small woman with skin the color of ironwood. She was dressed in a thin, pink nightgown buttoned up to her chin. Maya noticed that the floor-length hem was frayed. Two white buttons were missing from the bodice. Peering out at Maya, the young woman blinked several times, then squinted.

"Wait! I get glasses. And I must to change my clothes."

The door gently closed. Maya heard light footfalls, the opening and closing of a door, the splashing of water, the clanging of heavy pots. Five minutes later the door swung open.

Fewesi was now dressed in a floor-length white cotton robe. Wrapped around her hair and neck was a gauzy white scarf edged with fringes. *Like a tallit*, thought Maya. Against the dark lustrous skin of Fewesi's oval face, her bright white teeth shone like mother-of-pearl. Her ink-black eyes, now magnified behind thick lenses, sparkled in the amber light of the table lamps scattered on low brass tables around the living room.

"How kind for you to visit," said Fewesi. "I know such few people here."

She smiled shyly at Maya. She was so young that the smile summoned no crows' feet to the corners of her eyes.

"One of our neighbors, Nigist Fredo-Wasa on the second floor, told me about your baby."

Maya was tempted to say more, but what could she offer except the usual platitudes? *Sorry for your loss. I can't imagine how you feel. May God console you among all those who mourn in Zion.* So, she said nothing. Comforting the bereaved, she had learned from her mother, required, above all, silence.

With both hands, Maya held out a covered glass bowl. It was filled to the brim with *harira*, a thick, spicy Moroccan soup made with tomatoes, beans, lentils, and chickpeas.

"I don't know much about your customs, but I know that food is always welcome in a house of mourning."

In silence the two women sat across from each other in high-backed armchairs. Fewesi's eyes glistened in the soft light. When Maya proffered a hand of sympathy, the other woman gently deflected it, then ran into the bedroom, closing the door softly behind her. When she returned moments later, Maya noticed that the whites of Fewesi's eyes were spidered with tiny red veins, her eyelids pink and wet.

Maya quickly looked away, then fussed with a loose thread on her shirt sleeve.

"I brew coffee." Fewesi waved her hand toward the stove. "Ready in one minute."

Maya sank back against a plump cushion. Glancing around at Fewesi's vibrant decor, she felt ashamed of her own drab second-hand furniture. Everything here was daubed in bright primary colors: blue, red, yellow, green, purple, white. The couch and two armchairs were covered with a flannel-like material, patterned in a riot of greens. On the walls hung weavings displaying scenes of Ethiopian village life. Women drawing water at a well. Boys herding goats. Men praying in a simple thatched hut. A procession of villagers climbing a mountain, some carrying colorful umbrellas. The throw pillows were similarly embroidered with village scenes.

Fewesi bustled around the small kitchen area, constantly eyeing a small cast iron frying pan heating up on one of the gas rings. Suddenly she whirled around and snatched the frying pan from the stove. Dark smoke spiraled toward the ceiling and into the living room, mingling its spicy fragrance with the sweet incense smoldering on the coffee table. The smells made Maya feel light-headed.

Fewesi padded into the living room, carrying the still-smoking pan filled with lightly charred coffee beans. With her free hand she fanned the smoke toward Maya, who breathed in the aromatic smoke and held it in her lungs. Fewesi poured the roasted beans into a large wooden mortar on the floor and crushed them into powder with a heavy pestle. She scooped out the grounds and poured them into a *jebena*, a tall clay vessel with a delicately curved neck and spout. Into this she poured boiling water, swirling the mixture a few times. Finally, she poured a little of the coffee into a small cup, tasted it, wrinkled up her small nose, and poured the brew back into the pot.

From a lidded basket woven out of colorful coils of dried grasses, she scooped out some sugar and ladled it into two cups. Crouching down on her haunches, she lifted the *jebena* high above the cups and poured out streams of rich, black liquid, not spilling a single drop. She lifted one of the steaming cups and offered it to her guest, who accepted the cup with both hands. Maya purred as the sweet coffee pleasured her tongue.

"This ceremony we call *bunna*," said Fewesi, sipping from her own cup. "Special time for us. We invite guests to drink coffee, bring news, share stories. Get to know each other better. Pleasing to Zar also. So different from coffee in West. You gulp down too fast! For us, the longer *bunna*, the better."

"It's wonderful!" said Maya. "Not bitter at all. And the aroma is intoxicating!"

They sat across from each other without speaking, sipping their coffee. When Fewesi thrust her chin toward the *jebena*, Maya nodded. As she drank her second cup, she sampled one of the cakes Fewesi had set out on a brass platter. Her tongue identified cinnamon, cardamom, honey, and something similar to oregano. The silence grew. Maya waited, aware that the wrong words could spoil their nascent friendship.

Finally, Fewesi set down her empty cup and lay back against a cushion.

"I had hope my daughter know better life than me."

Maya leapt through this small chink in Fewesi's reticence.

"Tell me about her. Your daughter."

"What to tell? She born healthy. One morning she not wake up. Dead. No mark on her."

Fewesi stared, unseeing. Her eyes were dark hollows.

"Such death not sent from God. Is punishment."

Maya didn't like where this conversation was headed. She preferred not to look for reasons for life's miseries. And she had no patience for those who insisted on vindicating God.

With a bright smile pasted back on her face, Fewesi lifted up her empty cup.

"*Bunna* not complete until three cups."

Maya could tell that Fewesi's cheerfulness was feigned, the requisite stance of a proper host. Like most women from traditional cultures, she'd had lots of practice repressing her feelings.

Sipping the hot, sweet beverage, Maya took another look around the large room. For the first time she noticed a curved dagger hanging on the back wall.

Fewesi followed Maya's gaze and chuckled.

"Wedding gift from my father. Billawa. My father was very good smith in Ethiopia. He make billawas as wedding gifts for Christian neighbors."

Maya stood up and walked over to the dagger. It looked to be about a foot long. The knife's hilt and the curved wooden sheath hanging beneath the dagger were painted red and gold, decorated with circles and triangles connected by swirly lines. She brought her eyes closer to the knife's blade. Both of its edges were honed to razor sharpness. She took a step back as if fearing she might be sliced open simply by gazing too closely.

Fewesi came over to her. "Once in while my father make billawa like this, sharp on *two* sides. He say someone who own this type of dagger is danger to himself and to his enemy."

"Why would your father give *you* such a knife for a wedding present?"

Fewesi sighed, then shrugged her thin shoulders.

"He not want me marry this man. He say he not good enough for me. He not want my husband to have good luck."

Both women laughed. Fewesi's toothy smile returned to her face, loosening the taut skin of her cheeks and brow. Maya felt something shift between them. The shared burden of an unhappy marriage.

"My father die soon after my wedding. He fortunate not to see death of first grandchild."

Fewesi's smile disappeared, immediately replaced by a dark mask of grief.

Maya glanced down at her watch. It was almost ten! The day was getting away from her.

"I have to go, Fewesi. Thanks so much for the coffee."

She walked over to the door, grasped the knob, then looked back over her shoulder.

"I was wondering..."

Maya hesitated. *Was it too soon? Would Fewesi resent taking care of Maya's healthy child when her own child lay so newly dead?*

Fewesi stared at Maya, her dark eyebrows raised.

"Would you be interested in babysitting my six-year-old daughter Vered once in a while? I work late some nights. Occasionally I have to go out of town for work."

Fewesi said nothing. She looked down at the floor and shuffled her bare feet.

"Of course, if you don't want to..."

"No, I love children!"

Maya detected no bitterness in Fewesi's voice. Only a yearning that filled Maya with both sorrow and relief.

"I'll bring her over soon to meet you. I'm so glad we're neighbors, Fewesi!"

Without waiting for a response, Maya jerked the door open and walked out into the dark hallway.

19

MAYA PARKED HER COROLLA IN her usual spot around the corner from headquarters. On her way, she popped into the hole-in-the-wall falafel restaurant to pick up a quick bite. By the time she rushed through the double front doors and sat down at her desk, she had completely devoured the spicy pita sandwich and washed it down with Rahamim's hot, bitter coffee.

She didn't even have a chance to check her email when the desk phone rang. It was her brother-in-law, Avi. Her knuckles whitened as she gripped the black receiver. Her blood began to boil whenever she heard his smarmy voice. And her sympathetic nervous system snapped into high alert.

"Just wanted to let you know that Rafi has formally asked for sole custody as soon as he's released. I filed the papers this morning."

Though Maya had been expecting this news, she was nonetheless shocked. She sucked in a sharp breath and slammed her free hand down on the gray steel desktop.

"*Mamzer!* On what grounds?"

"I shouldn't have to go over this again, Maya. My brother has ample grounds to prove you unfit as a parent."

Look who's talking! She loosened her grip on the black plastic handset, switched it to her other hand, and rubbed her sweaty right palm on the seat cushion of her desk chair. *Don't let him steamroll you!*

"So says the parent speaking from his prison cell!"

Avi's husky breath rattled in her ear. She waited patiently.

"If the court were to side with him," continued Avi, his voice like brushed wool, "which I'm predicting they will, then I guess Vered will have to go into public care until he's released."

"You wouldn't dare! He wouldn't dare! His own daughter!"

Maya screamed into the phone, so loudly that her voice penetrated through the glass panel of her office door. Masha looked up from her computer screen, her brown eyes gaping wide in alarm, and began to rise out of her seat. Maya waved her back down, attempting a smile. Masha hesitated, then sat back down in her cubicle. But she kept her eyes fixed on Maya through the glass.

"I'm sure we can work something out that will satisfy both of you." Avi's silky voice purred into her ear. "Maybe increase Rafi's visits with Vered to every other week. Including some private time for father and daughter, supervised by prison personnel, of course."

Maya bit down on her tongue, then swallowed hard. Even from a jail cell, Rafi was still tormenting her.

"Say I agree. What do I get in return?"

The laugh at the other end toggled between a cackle and a bray.

"The satisfaction of knowing that your child is able to console her lonely father."

Now it was Maya's turn to laugh. But her throttled rage twisted her amusement into bitterness.

"Still no child support?"

"I'm afraid Rafi's finances continue to be tied up in litigation. His assets have been frozen until the forensic accountants finish their investigation."

"Fine. You win—for now! But I'll see that bastard burn in hell before I agree to sharing custody once he gets out. Tell that to your lonely client!"

She slammed down the receiver with such force that many of the delicately balanced puzzles on her desk toppled over. She would put them back into the proper order later. When she calmed down.

But her hands had a mind of their own. Moments later her fingers were stretching toward the center of her desk, carefully aligning each puzzle, setting them up like a grandmaster preparing his side of the board for a championship match. When they were all back in place, she felt much calmer. Centered. In control again.

She reached for her aluminum water bottle and took a long swallow. Then she stared at her office door for several minutes. Her breathing slowly returned to its normal steady rhythm.

She turned her attention to the two manila folders sitting in front of her on the large steel desk. She picked up the olive-green one first and opened it. Quickly she riffled through the thin sheaf of paperwork inside. The Service had very little on the most recent murder victim, Hagar Aklilu. No arrests, not even a caution. Just multiple parking tickets, all of them paid. It looked like the young woman had been a model citizen. A white sheep in a very black herd. Paid her taxes, did her army service, volunteered at a local hospital. Nothing to indicate why she'd been targeted for murder.

Maya shut the folder and set it aside. Then she picked up the second folder. Inside were copies of the interviews that Sarit Levine had conducted at the Aklilu home and at Hagar's workplace. Maya had been surprised by how quickly the Police Inspector had sent her the files. It was not Sarit's usual MO when the two agencies worked together on the same case. She should remember to thank her the next time they spoke. Maybe throw her a bone from her own investigation. She still owed Sarit big-time for quickly shutting down cell service under the Temple Mount when Maya was pursuing Mashiak through the tunnels. Her decision to trust Maya on that call had prevented a catastrophe.

It appeared that Hagar Aklilu had been a popular teacher at the secular elementary school where she taught third grade, beloved by students and staff. Most of her colleagues said she kept pretty much to herself after work. But another third-grade teacher had shared in confidence that she thought Hagar had been involved with someone.

When pressed by Sarit, the teacher had mentioned a "giant police-man." *I don't even think she came up to his pupik*, she said about the man. The woman didn't know his name. But when Sarit had questioned Hagar about him, she'd brushed her off. *Just a casual acquaintance. There was never anything there.*

Maya closed the red folder. She furrowed her brow. Then she shook her head, tousling her mane of auburn curls. What was she missing? What connected Hagar to Titi, Moshe's young trophy wife? Why had they both been murdered? Had it been the work of the same killer? If so, what was his motive? What did these two young women have in common?

Maya returned to the olive-green folder and took out the color photograph of Hagar. She stared at the image. It had been taken at some glitzy political function a few years ago. Aklilu's daughter was certainly pretty, with close-cropped black hair, dark eyes, and high cheek bones. One might even call her features regal. Her thick black eyebrows, which met over the bridge of her straight-edged nose, made her look like an African Frida Kahlo. Her dark skin gleamed under the chandelier like polished obsidian.

Titi's beauty was of an altogether different sort. Her complexion was like antique bronze. The tight ringlets helmeting her egg-shaped head were dyed red, and her face was painted like a courtesan.

But they were both striking young women. Was beauty their common bond? Should she be looking for a serial killer who targeted pretty young Ethiopian women? Were these murders the work of an obsessed psychopath who killed the same woman over and over again? Or were they gang-related, as Sarit thought? But why would a gang want to kill innocent girls? A punishment for betrayal? Something to do with drugs or prostitution?

She needed to dig deeper into the Aklilu family. Both father and son smelled rotten. Could they be in this together? She needed to figure out the killer's motive. She would find her murderer when she figured out who benefited from these killings.

But at least she now had a lead on the murder weapon. It was most likely an Ethiopian billawa, the kind of double-edged knife she'd seen in Fewesi's apartment. At Titi's autopsy Dr. Selgundo had speculated that the lethal blade was sharpened on both sides. Although the ME hadn't yet performed a post-mortem on Hagar, his preliminary findings at the crime scene had suggested a weapon similar to the one that had killed Titi.

It wasn't much to go on. Fewesi had told Maya that billawas were generally not sharpened on both edges. But for certain occasions they were sharpened on both sides of the blade. Who might possess this kind of special billawa? Clearly the smiths who made them. And the Ethiopians who received them as gifts. And maybe certain high-ranking officials who received them as bribes or in exchange for favors. Could the list include the first Ethiopian member of the Knesset?

She needed to know more. She turned to her keyboard and typed "billawa" into her browser. Nothing came up. She tried several different spellings. Still nothing. The phrase, "billawa knife," likewise yielded no hits. She smacked the metal desk with her open palm. *I thought Google knew everything!*

She tried a different tack. Swiveling toward the keyboard, she began typing furiously. Her gold-flecked green eyes bored into the screen.

Within seconds her screen filled up with a list of Ethiopian cultural resources in Israel: government departments, restaurants and food suppliers, tour companies, Amharic language schools, nonprofit organizations. With 130,000 Ethiopian Jews now living in Israel, it wasn't surprising that such resources had proliferated since the Beta Israel first began arriving in 1984. Even though they now made up only 2 percent of the Israeli population, their impact on Jewish life and culture was much more sizable.

Maya printed out screenshots of the first two pages of her search. Then she stood up and opened her office door. Masha was hunched over her desktop, typing at breakneck speed. When Maya touched her shoulder, she jumped.

"You know I don't like it when you sneak up on me like that!"

"I need a cultural informant on Ethiopian customs. For background."

"This for the Aklilu case?"

Maya nodded. She told Masha about her visit that morning with Fewesi. And about the accursed dagger hanging on the young immigrant's wall. Then she handed Masha the print-out.

"I need to know more about how this particular type of knife is used, what types of people own them, and what they mean in Ethiopian culture. Do you know anybody at any of these places?"

Masha held up a finger, freshly manicured, the shapely nail painted pearly white. With her other hand she brushed back her honey-blond hair.

Masha skimmed over the list, then pointed a glossy fingernail at one of the non-profits listed near the middle of the screen.

"JEJI. Justice for Ethiopian Jews in Israel. I've consulted with their new director once or twice. Dani Solomon. A smart cookie. And *so* handsome. Educated in England. You know how I *love* the accent!"

Maya chuckled. Masha was often like this, bubbling like uncorked champagne. Except when she was going after bad guys. Then she scalded like bathtub hooch.

20

THE JEJI OFFICE WAS LOCATED in Kiryat Menachem, an immigrant neighborhood in southwest Jerusalem. Maya decided to leave her car behind at HQ. At this time of day, she'd be better off taking public transportation.

Once the bus dropped her off, it took her almost half an hour to find the JEJI office. Tucked away in an alley off Dominican Republic Street, not far from Mexico Park, the two-story stone building was shoehorned between a shawarma shop and a coin laundry. *Why are all the streets in this neighborhood named after Latin American countries instead of rabbinic sages or Zionist icons like most Jerusalem streets?* She made a mental note to look that up in her spare time. But she knew she'd never get to it.

At the end of the alley, a construction crew was bulldozing an old Ottoman-era apartment building into rubble. Jackhammers pounded the cobbled sidewalk that fronted the half-wrecked structure. Dust plumed high into the air, mixing with the tangy smoke from shawarma roasting on vertical spits in the glassless windows of the restaurant. The idle construction workers sat on broken stone blocks, smoking, guzzling from water bottles, and shouting to each other over the noise. The open storefront of the laundromat displayed facing rows of washers and dryers, chugging and tumbling in percussive dialogue. Hot, soapy steam billowed out into the street. Inside, a number of women sat on folding chairs, holding babies and yelling into cellphones. Some stood at long tables folding clothes. Several stood outside, smoking and chatting with each other.

Maya walked briskly to the front of the JEJI building. She noticed a hand-lettered sign leaning against the cement wall, drawn with a thick black Sharpie: "National Headquarters of Justice for Ethiopian Jews in Israel." A giant black index finger pointed down several stone steps to a wooden basement door. A cardboard sign was tacked on the door, but without an overhead light, it was hard to read the writing. She bent down and could just make out the letters: JEJI.

She carefully descended the cracked steps, twisted the iron knob, and walked inside.

Maya found herself in a large room. The cinderblock walls were painted the green of underripe bananas. Lining three of the walls were plastic folding chairs of various colors. In one corner, a pile of glossy brochures in Hebrew, English, and Amharic and some dog-eared magazines lay on a scratched wooden table. Two half-window casements were located up near the unpainted plaster ceiling, giving those inside a glimpse of the feet, pants, and bare legs of passersby.

Two closed wooden doors interrupted the cinderblock walls. Next to one of them sat a young Ethiopian woman dressed in a plain dark-blue shift, typing on an antiquated PC. She looked up to see who had entered. Catching her gaze, Maya was startled by the gleaming whites of her eyes, which seemed about to pop out of her head. The young woman's skin, black like charred wood, was badly pitted, as were her arms and neck.

"Can I help you?"

The young woman's voice was as unnerving as her eyes. High-pitched and loud. Maya recognized in her speech the halting rhythm of newly acquired Hebrew. Maya flashed her a simple grin of encouragement. The woman's dark lips immediately broke into a radiant smile, exposing perfect white teeth and a dimple in her right cheek. Maya felt ashamed of her harsh snap judgment. It was a personality trait she was constantly working on—with very little to show for the effort.

"I called earlier," said Maya. "I spoke to your director. Is he available?"

The young woman picked up a cellphone lying on her small desk, whose wooden veneer was as pockmarked as her own. She hit a button. Maya noticed for the first time that there was no standard-issue office phone on her desk.

"Dani!"

Her voice was so loud that the occupant of the adjacent room must have been able to hear her without needing to pick up his own mobile.

"A lady here to see you!"

Moments later the door opened. Dani Solomon emerged from his office. He strode briskly toward Maya, his right hand extended.

As she'd been taught in her training classes, Maya drew a quick mental picture of the JEJI Director. Nothing about him struck her as particularly remarkable. He was of slight build, maybe five foot eight, with black kinky hair cropped short, military-style. His hair was beginning to gray around the temples. His eyes were dark black, the skin around their outer corners deeply wrinkled. From laughter or stress. Under his high forehead and thick eyebrows, a prominent nose fanned out like a river delta. His skin was a rusty brown, smooth and almost hairless.

But when she glanced down at the hand extended toward her, she identified the man's trademark feature. The palm of his right hand was almost completely encased in pink scar tissue. He saw her staring and quickly folded her small hand in his.

"Agent Rimon, right? So glad I was able to accommodate your request to meet."

Unlike his assistant's heavily accented Hebrew, the director's was elegant and crisp. She detected the vestige of a British accent.

With his unblemished hand, he motioned her into his small office, then into a slat-backed wooden chair facing his desk. He closed the door. Then he walked over to his desk and sat down in an identical chair facing her. Like the lobby, this room was framed by green cinderblock walls and an unpainted ceiling. Besides the desk and two chairs, there was only a brown couch made of some synthetic material and a small bookcase, crammed with paperbacks and some textbooks. On the desk sat an antiquated desktop computer and a small table lamp. There was no desk phone, in-box, or tray for office supplies. A tall stack of manila folders teetered in one corner.

Maya's eyes wandered away from the desk to the light-green walls. Behind and above Dani, secured by yellowing tape, was a map of Ethiopia with an inset of the Gondar region in the northwest. Next to it a few framed academic degrees. The wall to her left displayed a map of Israel with pins flagging the major areas where Ethiopian Jews now lived. Next to it, covering about a quarter of the wall's surface, was a photo array of smiling black faces, many of the photographs signed. Present and former clients, Maya guessed. Cases they'd won.

She swiveled her head to look at the opposite wall. Hanging on the wall were handicrafts native to Ethiopia: woven reed baskets, textiles depicting colorful village scenes like those she'd seen in Fewesi's apartment, and framed pieces of parchment covered with calligraphed verses in an alphabet Maya didn't recognize. And above all of these hung a billawa! The curved dagger with its ornamented sheath aimed its sharp, pointed tip toward the bare plaster ceiling.

Maya gasped. She turned toward Dani, pointing a trembling finger at the dagger suspended from the ceiling molding by a thin steel cable.

Dani smiled, his straight white teeth offering a sharp contrast to the rich red-brown hues of his skin. The corners of his eyes crinkled as though pulled taut by invisible wires.

"It's called a billawa."

"I know. I saw one just like it at my neighbor's. She told me that Jews in Ethiopia often give these knives as wedding presents to Christian or Muslim friends. On rare occasions, they make them with double-edged blades."

She craned her neck toward the dagger on the wall.

"Looks like this one's double-bladed."

Dani pushed back in his chair, tilting it up against the wall. He grunted, his smile extinguished. When he spoke again, his tone was bitter.

"You're more knowledgeable than most."

A grin briefly creased his mouth but soon fled.

"What our non-Jewish neighbors back home never figured out," he continued, "was that the symbolism of this knife is as double-edged as its blade. For centuries, we explained to them that the double-bladed billawa represents the relationship of Jews and non-Jews in our country. One side of the blade symbolizes our gentile overlords; the other, the Jews subordinate to them. But what we never revealed to them was that this symbolism cuts both ways. As sole masters of fire and forge, we Jews have long intimidated our gentile masters. We've chosen to keep this joke to ourselves."

Maya sat staring at Dani in stunned silence. Did any of this shed new light on her case? Did it perhaps provide a clue to the killer's motive?

Dani leaned forward. Maya noted his strong chin, the determined set of his jaw.

"Why are you so interested in the billawa?"

"I'm working on a double murder investigation for the Service."

Maya fished her credentials out of her shoulder bag and flipped them open to show him.

"That's why I wanted to see you," she said. "We're pretty sure that the killer is Ethiopian. Both victims were stabbed with a weapon sharpened on both sides of the blade."

Dani nodded.

"I'm no expert about such things," he said, "but I know that quite a number of Ethiopian Jewish immigrants worked as metal smiths back home."

He began rubbing his scarred palm with the fingers of his right hand, then swept that hand up to his head, threading it through his thin nap of bristly hair.

"Most people don't realize that in many respects Ethiopia remains a primitive country," he continued, "still filled with ancient superstitions and primitive rites. Especially in the provinces where most of the Beta Israel come from."

"Hyena people."

Dani stared at her. She thought she read hostility in his dark eyes, but it quickly gave way to resignation.

"Yes, that's what they called us back home. *Jiboch*. Hyenas. Not that different from werewolves. They believed we could turn ourselves into hyenas at night to bewitch them."

As soon as Dani uttered the Amharic word, a memory flashed into Maya's mind. Fewesi's husband had hurled this word at his wife when he'd walked out on her. *Jib*. Hyena. Were the Beta Israel now turning on each other, accusing fellow Jews of perpetrating the same evil that they were once accused of?

"This word—*Jiboch*—was carved into the forehead of our second murder victim."

Now it was Dani's turn to gasp.

"How horrible!"

The conversation stalled. Maya didn't feel comfortable disclosing more details about the case to someone she'd just met. And Dani was clearly too upset to probe further. Both of them stared down at the floor. The cracked concrete surface was covered with dust and dead insects. Into this silence intruded sounds from the street—jackhammers, shouting workers, whirring laundry machines.

The awkward silence dragged on. Maya realized with a jolt that she was strangely drawn to this man. It was not that he was particularly handsome. But she found his toothy smile and disarming candor comforting, like a lost melody recovered from childhood. In his dark eyes she saw deep compassion; in his sinewy hands, hidden strength.

She was intrigued by that disfigured palm. What had happened to him? How had it shaped who he had become?

She stood up to leave. She was due at her parents' place in an hour. "Wait!"

Dani leapt to his feet, scraping the back of his chair against the wall.

"I have a suggestion," he said. He leaned forward on the desk, pinioning her gaze. "We're holding a fundraiser tomorrow night at the Ethiopian Cultural Center. Why don't you come? There'll be dancing and music, home-cooked dishes, and drinks. You can do further research for your case." He smiled. Maya felt a stream of molten metal pulsing just under her skin. "Eight o'clock. Plan on a late night. I'll meet you there." He paused, then winked at her. "No hyenas on the guest list."

They both laughed. Maya nodded and left. She didn't stop to say goodbye to Esther Azazew, Dani's assistant, who had just scooted her chair back to her desk after eavesdropping—unsuccessfully—at Dani's door.

21

MAYA'S BUS DROPPED HER OFF near her parents' apartment just after 7 p.m.

The Rimons' apartment was located in Rehavia, a fashionable district in West Jerusalem. Modeled on the "Garden Cities Movement" of the early twentieth century, the neighborhood was well-tailored with gracious apartment houses hewn from white Jerusalem stone, leafy trees, lush gardens, and manicured pocket parks. The residential area was interlaced with narrow streets and alleyways to limit traffic. Commercial activity was restricted to a few streets. In addition to private homes, the area was home to a number of schools and research institutes.

Many of the neighborhood's residents were professors, intellectuals, and well-to-do Ashkenazi Jews. When Moti Rimon had been promoted to a senior agent at the Service, his wife, Camille, had immediately insisted that they move here.

In her recently remodeled kitchen, Camille stood glaring at her daughter, who had moments before rushed into the apartment and flopped into a kitchen chair, breathing hard. Maya apologized for her lateness, promising to arrive earlier next time.

"It's always 'next time,' Maya!" Camille snorted through her prodigious nose. "As my mother used to say, 'Evening promises are like butter. Morning comes, and it's all melted.'"

Maya sank lower into the kitchen chair and sighed. There was just no winning with her mother. Ever since Maya had decided to become an intelligence agent like her father, Camille had been relentless in expressing her disapproval, especially after Vered was born.

What kind of job is that for the mother of a young child? You want her to go to bed every night wondering whether you'll be there in the morning? You want her to grow up an orphan?

"I'm hungry, Ima." Maya made no effort to disguise her irritation. "I haven't eaten since breakfast."

"And whose fault is that? If you had been here on time, you could have had fava bean soup and lamb tagine. I made it just the way Vered likes it, with dates and apricots."

Maya could not believe how much her six-year-old daughter liked Moroccan food. When she'd been Vered's age, she'd balked at her mother's spicy cooking, preferring the bland, brown cuisine of her father's Eastern European ancestors.

"Can you please warm up some of the leftovers for me?"

Sniffing through her august nose, Camille shuffled over to the double-door refrigerator, slid out a glass bowl, and shoved it into the microwave. As the machine hummed, she poured some freshly squeezed mango juice into a tall glass and placed it in front of her daughter, who greedily gulped it down. The microwave dinged. Camille scooped out a generous portion of the steaming lamb stew, ladled it into a bowl, and placed it in front of Maya. She sat down across from Maya and watched her eat. Through the table's clear surface, Maya saw her mother's right foot, swathed in pink satin slippers, tapping impatiently on the gold tile.

"I truly am sorry to be so late. I'm working on a complicated case at the moment."

Her mother opened her mouth to respond, but Maya held up her hand, palm out, to silence her.

"And no, they're *not* all this complicated. I've got a double murder to solve, carried out with a bizarre weapon. With no clue yet about motive. That's why I'm late. I was meeting with an informant."

Maya looked across the table at her mother's hands. She noticed a new ring on Camille's left index finger. A giant onyx encircled by pearls. It dwarfed the other two rings on that hand.

Camille sighed loudly. "Ah, *ya binti*! You're married to that job! You're thirty-six years old. When was the last time you went out on a date? I still don't understand why you let that nice American professor get away, run back to the States. At this point you'll be lucky to land a divorced man or a widower with children."

As always, her mother's reproach stung Maya. But though she still felt raw from her recent divorce and her thwarted relationship with Hillel Stone, she realized that she had begun to move on. She pictured the laugh wrinkles at the corners of Dani's dark eyes. The strong chin and jaw. His scarred palm. All of a sudden, her skin tingled, and she shivered.

Before she could stop herself, she blurted out: "I may have met someone."

"What do you mean, 'may have met'? Did you meet him or not? Who is he? What do you know about him?"

"His name's Dani. He's a lawyer who defends Ethiopian Jews in the courts. He's helping me with my new case."

"Is he a...*kushi*? You know they all carry HIV in their blood. Bad genes."

Maya felt her blood begin to boil. She hated that word. *Kushi*. Black man. When it was accented on the first syllable—as Camille had pronounced it—the Hebrew word stung like the word, *nigger*, in English. Her mother carried so much baggage—prejudices against Arabs or anyone with darker skin—but she also carried a grudge against Ashkenazi Jews for their snootiness. What had possessed Maya to bring up Dani? She'd only met him this morning.

"So what if he *is* Black, Ima? He's highly educated. Went to college in England! And he's doing good work for his community. We conferred about my case. I liked him. End of story."

Camille thrust her great nose into the air. With her right hand she plumped her steeple of frosty blond hair.

"I certainly hope so for your sake! It's bad enough you married that *jnoun* Rafi, may he rot in prison! No sense making another mistake. Getting involved with one of *them*."

"I happen to live next door to one of *them*, Ima. A new Ethiopian immigrant. Her name's Fewesi. A sweet young woman. Her baby died two days ago. Then her husband walked out on her."

Camille held up a plump index finger as if to say: *You see? What did I tell you!*

Maya swallowed hard and took a deep breath.

"I've asked her to babysit Vered. You won't be burdened with her care anymore."

Why had she told her mother this? *What was the matter with her? First opening up about Dani and now Fewesi.*

Camille clapped both hands over her heavily lipsticked mouth and wailed.

"*Wili wili wili*! You will not leave my granddaughter in the care of a *kushit*! Certainly not one who'll be jealous that you have a healthy daughter when hers just died? Don't you know that their women practice witchcraft? She'll curse Vered with an evil eye!"

Camille pressed the back of her hand to her brow as though about to faint. Maya called these her mother's "Sarah Bernhardt moments." The phrase always made her father laugh.

"I'm not asking your permission, Ima. Tomorrow night I'm going to a fundraiser at the Ethiopian Cultural Center. With Dani. It'll help me with my investigation. You told me you weren't free tomorrow. So, I asked Fewesi to babysit."

"We'll change our plans! I never wanted to go to that boring play anyway." Camille's pink satin slipper tapped faster. The tiled floor tolled like a ticking clock. "And what's this nonsense about Vered being a burden? We're always glad to have her."

"That's news to me," said Maya. She slapped the table with her palms and rose from her chair.

As Maya walked toward the living room, she could hear her father and daughter on the couch, glued to the giant flatscreen TV, giggling together. She walked up behind Vered and planted a firm kiss on her mop of auburn curls.

"C'mon, Sweetie, time to say goodnight to Jeddah and Saba. It's a school night."

Vered jumped up and ran over to Camille, who sat at the kitchen table, drowning her sorrows in lamb tagine. Camille kissed her absentmindedly and returned to her sulking. Vered then ran back to Moti and quickly pecked him the cheek. Then she skipped over to Maya and held out her hand.

Together they walked to the door and out into the night.

22

Maya and Vered emerged from the Rimons' apartment building onto Gaza Street to find themselves in the dark. The streetlamp that usually illuminated the sidewalk wasn't working. Maya had been in such a rush on her way in that she hadn't noticed the broken light. She grabbed hold of Vered's hand. They carefully made their way along the narrow walk, bordered on one side by a white stone knee-wall, on the other by the street. Occasionally they had to walk off the curb into the street to get around cars parked on the sidewalk up against the stone wall.

The November air was cold, a stiff breeze making it feel even colder. Vered shivered in her thin T-shirt. Maya took off her blazer and draped it around her daughter's bony shoulders. A few stray cats scampered out of their way. At this time of night, Gaza Street was usually filled with people—walking their dogs, strolling, heading to a café or a friend's house. But tonight, the streets were empty.

They approached a stone staircase that led down to a snaking wooded path. The path would take them through a grove of trees and past several backyards to Benjamin of Tudela Street, which ran parallel to Gaza. There they could catch a late bus to Givat HaMatos.

Maya had been on this path countless times. When they had first moved here when she was three, she would spend hours in the dense grove, sometimes alone and sometimes with friends. She and her friends would pretend that the wooded stretch between Gaza and Benjamin of Tudela Streets was a secret kingdom hidden from grown-up eyes. They'd bring their dolls here for picnics or chase terrorists away with wooden knives and blood-curdling cries.

But she had never been on this path at night. In the whispering dark, the tall trees loomed overhead like menacing giants. The leaves rattling in the wind sounded like restless bones. A cat in heat yowled nearby. Vered squeezed Maya's hand and began to whimper.

"Shhh," Maya said. She wrapped her arm around Vered's shoulder and drew her closer. "There's nothing to be afraid of."

Then Maya heard the tap-tap-tap of footsteps. They came from behind them, drawing closer.

She forced herself to stay calm, to walk deliberately in measured tread. *Rehavia is one of the safest neighborhoods in Jerusalem,* she told herself. *Many people who live here use this path as a short-cut, even at night.*

The steps continued to come closer. Whoever it was now stood directly behind them.

Maya stopped walking. She gently pushed Vered in front of her.

"Just do as I say," said a man's voice. "And nobody will get hurt."

The speaker was young, confident. His words weren't muffled. So he wasn't wearing a mask. He didn't care if they saw his face. Judging by his light tread, Maya guessed he was of average height and weight. Was he a harmless beggar? A thief? Or someone more dangerous?

"What do you want?" She kept her voice steady, neither defensive nor hostile. "You can have all the money in my wallet. It's not much. I have no jewelry. No credit cards."

She didn't mention her grandfather's Poljot watch on her wrist. It had little street value but was precious to her.

"I'm not interested in robbing you."

"So, what do you want?"

Vered began to cry. Maya placed both her palms on her daughter's shoulders. The gesture only made the little girl sob louder. She sucked in a gob of mucous, then began to howl.

"Shut up, kid!"

Vered instinctively picked up the menace in the man's voice. She clamped her lips shut, stifling protest. But her shoulders continued to tremble under Maya's firm hands.

"You're Maya Rimon, right?"

Maya nodded.

He knows my name. Do what you want with me, but please don't hurt my baby!

"You're investigating the murder of my step-mother."

It was Elvis, Aklilu's prodigal son! What did he want from her? Why had she exposed Vered to such danger!

"As if that witless ninny could ever pass herself off as anyone's mother!" The young man snorted in feigned amusement. Then he sucked in a deep breath and spit it out. "And you're looking for the killer of my sister, Hagar."

Maya heard the catch in Elvis's voice when he said his dead sister's name. Immediately he hawked up a gob of phlegm and spit it at the ground.

"What do you want?"

"You gotta stop investigating me!"

He waited for a response. Maya kept silent.

"My father's setting me up. I didn't kill either of 'em. I swear!"

"What kind of a father would do this to his own son?"

She was goading him, hoping he'd disclose more. She knew it was reckless. Could make him do something rash.

"I'll tell you what kind of father! Someone who's willing to kick my mother to the curb like a piece of trash so he can screw some young piece of ass. Someone who only loves himself. Who uses people to gratify his own needs. Ladies and gentlemen, I give you the illustrious, the esteemed, the one and only Moshe Aklilu!"

She heard both rancor and heartache beneath the young man's sarcasm. And enough rage to ripen into murder.

"But why would your father want to kill your stepmo—" Maya stopped abruptly, deftly backpedaling. "Why would he kill his wife and daughter?"

"How should I know? Maybe the two of them got wise to his criminal schemes and threatened to expose him. Or maybe he's a psychopath. It's your job to figure it out. But I'm not taking the rap for his crimes. I'm no *freier*! So, I'm warning you: you come after me, you'll pay for it."

Maya knew she'd gain more control over the situation if she could look Elvis square in the eye. With her back to him, it would be too easy for him to kill them and run away.

"I'm going to turn around now. But first I'm going to put my hands up in the air. My daughter, Vered, will stay behind me."

Vered began to shake. Her auburn curls flailed like leaves in the wind. Maya leaned over and whispered in her ear.

"Nothing bad's going to happen to you or me, Vered. I promise. Just stand behind me and don't move. Everything's going to be all right."

Slowly Maya raised her hands into the air and swiveled around on her heels. She slowly lowered her arms and let them hang by her sides. She kept her palms toward the man so he could see she was unarmed.

Then she saw the switchblade in his right hand. The slim silver knife glinted in the soft light coming from the streetlamps on Benjamin of Tudela Street. When the wind feathered the branches overhead, the metallic gleam flickered like a sputtering flame.

Her first thought was to lunge for the knife, but she felt Vered's skinny arms squeezing her thighs, holding on for dear life. What if she wasn't fast enough? What if…. She peered into Elvis's face. In the uncertain light, she thought the young man's face looked desperate. Like a wounded animal. She suddenly became aware she was holding her own breath. She let it out slowly, then smiled coyly at Elvis.

Dani sat down on the couch in his small living room and laid back against the stiff vinyl cushion. He could feel the sweat beading on his broad brow, even though the autumn air had turned cool by now. He knew it wasn't heat that was causing him to sweat. It was thinking about Maya Rimon. He'd been dazzled by her eyes. The flecks of gold floating in the sea-green irises. He'd never seen eyes that color. And her hair was not the henna-dyed red so popular among Ethiopian women but was coppery like lightly roasted arabica beans. Her soft curls bounced and fluttered like dazzled moths. So unlike the stiff, crinkly hair of North African women. He could tell she had a razor wit, which could probably slice off a guy's manhood without his feeling any pain. But he was certain that her keen intelligence could just as skillfully deliver great delight.

As Dani pictured Maya sitting across from him, warmth began seeping into his lower body. The sensation made him uncomfortable. He stood up and walked to the tiny bathroom. The hot water scalding his body quickly neutralized the distressing sensations. He let out a deep sigh, stepped out of the shower, and padded into his room, where he changed into jeans and a short-sleeved shirt.

Why had he invited this woman to the JEJI fundraiser tomorrow night? He needed to be on his toes at that event, buttering up donors, charming board members, networking with his counterparts in other agencies. Being seen with Maya, a beautiful white woman, would throw him off his game. He might even start stuttering as he sometimes did around pretty women. And she might embarrass him by saying the wrong thing or laughing inappropriately. It wasn't too late to un-invite her. *The venue is too small. Practically claustrophobic. Too loud for conversation. I'll be too busy playing host to introduce....*

No, she would see right through him, probably take offense, call him a coward.

What was he really afraid of?

A scene from his Oxford days flashed into his mind.

He and Jemma were punting on the Cherwell. She was dressed rather provocatively in a low-cut summer dress. Her long, blond hair was hidden inside a broad-brimmed white hat. She stared up at him, smiling, popping ruby-red grapes between her moist lips. He stood at one end of the narrow boat, pushing on the long pole, trying to smile but nervous about losing his balance and falling in. This was his first time punting, but he hadn't told her that, fearing her derision. He'd tried so hard to get her to notice him in philosophy class. Then to join him for coffee. And finally, to go boating on the river. He didn't want to blow it now! But of course he had, not by toppling into the water but by recoiling when she'd suddenly thrust her hand down his pants as they sat picnicking. And then he'd made things worse by overplaying his hand, ripping open her bodice. She'd slapped him and called him a "savage monkey." Then she'd jumped into the punt, pushed off, and left him stranded on the island. He'd waited until dark to swim ashore near Magdalene College and sneak into his chambers.

No way he was going to make the same mistake with Maya. He'd keep their relationship professional—unless she gave him clear signals that she wanted more. And then he would proceed with caution. Better yet, he wouldn't even start up with her. He'd spend a few hours with her at the fundraiser, then cut things off. What did he know about murder anyway?

He walked barefoot into the living room and sat back down on the couch. He reached into his worn briefcase and extracted Kidist's diary, which he'd not yet returned to the office. He knew it wouldn't be missed. He was the only one looking into this old case.

He took a sip of ice-cold water. Suddenly, he realized he was famished. He was too tired to get up and prepare something for himself in the kitchen. Maybe after he rested for a while.

He flopped back against the stiff yellow cushion. He opened the diary and paged to the middle, eager to find out how Kidist's family had fared further along on their perilous trek.

When we began this journey, we all knew the risks. Wolves and jackals, mountain vipers, bandits, hunger, and thirst. But Negasi promised to protect us.

"I've spoken to many others who've traveled safely to the border," he told us. "On my life, I will do the same for you."

We all believed him, especially after Hawi stood up for him. O, my sweet daughter! Such a fool for love!

Who would have imagined he would betray us like this!

At first, I refused to believe him capable of such evil. When we ran low on food and water, I trusted Negasi to ration fairly what remained. But then I noticed he was the only one among us not growing weaker. A few days later, my poor old mother lay down by the side of the path, demanding that we go on without her. Why did he accept her sacrifice so readily?

From the beginning, he had been planning to abandon us!

Two days later, when everyone awoke, he was gone. With all our food and water. And with our scant valuables, which we had turned over to him to bribe the Sudanese border guards. Including the beautiful hair clasp Makari fashioned for me. Even Sisayu's precious doll.

It didn't take us long after that to begin to die. The baby was first. My milk had dried up. I wasn't drinking enough water. I wrapped poor little Tenanye in a scarf. We buried her in a shallow grave under the shade of a giant kosso tree. We prayed for her soul.

The next day both Noham and Kabede died. Ebo's family lost two of their children that day as well. The four members of the other family all succumbed the following day. We only had the strength to cover them with stones. Hawi held on for one more day. I think she died of a broken heart. Ebo's parents died the same day in each other's arms. Ebo tried to dig a grave for them, but he quickly collapsed. He was gone by nightfall.

Dani lay the small volume down on the rough wooden table in front of him. He hadn't seen this coming. To walk all that way—only to be stabbed in the back by one of their own! They'd all died, except for Kidist and her young daughter. Esther Azazew had later discovered that Kidist had died in the Sudanese camp. But what about her young daughter? Had she perished there too?

Dani thumbed back through the last few passages in the diary. With a shock, he realized that Kidist had never revealed her surviving daughter's name.

DAY 3

Wednesday

24

Shulamit's Diary

Icy rain today. The beginning of winter. I'm chilled to the bone.

That bull-headed lady agent just won't quit! She's like a honey badger with her teeth sunk into a juicy carcass. She has no idea what she's dealing with!

Well, let's see how she does when she comes up against the full power of the Zar!

As a child, when I used to get those terrible headaches, Ayati Ga'wa would always explain to me that they were a blessing in disguise, a sign that I'd been singled out by the Zar for a special destiny.

"Never forget that you are one of the elect!"

What a great awakiy balazar *she was!*

Even though I was only ten years old when they placed me with that foster family, I could already sense that she was different. Much more powerful than my mother and grandmother. Those two women knew only good magic, the kind used to heal and bless. But old Ayati Ga'wa was trained in the dark arts, magic so powerful and deadly that only another shaman could oppose her.

How glad I am that she took me under her wing. Passed her potent secrets on to me. Out of that whole sorry lot, she was the only one who loved me. And I loved her. Nobody else in that cursed foster family recognized her for what she was. Or understood what I had become under her tutelage.

Okay, Miss Agent Honey Badger. Let's see how you stand up against my Zar!

25

MAYA STOOD ON THE CRACKED sidewalk in front of the Beta Israel Cultural Center, craning her neck. The Center, located in Ir Ganim, an Ethiopian enclave in southwest Jerusalem, wasn't much to look at. It occupied the bottom level of a four-story concrete building overdue for demolition. The three floors above the Center were rental apartments, housing recent immigrants. Laundry fluttered from a number of balconies. The mud-brown cement walls of the building were weathered and stained and marbled with serpentine cracks.

Maya glanced down at the scratched crystal face of the Poljot, her grandfather's old watch dating back to the Stalin era. It was almost 8:30. The neighborhood around the Center was cloaked in darkness. The few streetlamps in front of the entrance cast haloes of watery yellow light on the pavement like yolks puddled on burnt toast. In the nondescript blocky building, Maya recognized the brutalist style of public housing that had been hastily erected in the 1950s, when Holocaust survivors and Jewish refugees from the Arab world had flooded the fledgling state.

She found herself reluctant to go inside. Why had Dani Solomon invited her to this event? They had only just met. What did he want from her? She recalled her mother's disquieting words: *They all carry HIV. Bad genes.* Maya had seen the Service's files on some of the bad actors who'd snuck into Israel during the rushed airlifts from Ethiopia in the '80s and '90s—smugglers, pimps, thieves, wife-beaters, pedophiles. Had she been taken in by Dani's British accent and natural charm?

Unconsciously, her right hand floated up toward her chin, rubbing the rough skin, looking for bristly hairs. Suddenly aware of what she was doing, she dropped her hand to her side and brushed the patch of skin she'd just touched with a daub of ivory concealer. She'd spent too much time making her face pretty for tonight to ruin it now.

Her mind ricocheted back to her apartment, where Fewesi was babysitting Vered. Her mother's ominous words again tolled in her ears: *Their women practice witchcraft! The evil eye!* Was she endangering her daughter by entrusting her to this stranger? What did she really know about Fewesi? About how her baby had died? Had Fewesi had something to do with...?

Stop it, Maya! You're acting paranoid. You're still upset about your run-in with Elvis last night. Maybe it's time to make an appointment with Isabel. Talk through what you're feeling. You're not made of flint!

She sucked in a deep breath. Then she threaded her fingers through her russet hair, brushing a few rebellious sprigs to one side of her high forehead. She ran her open hands down the front of her cowl-necked burgundy blouse, pressing out a few last wrinkles. Brushed some invisible dirt off her beige chinos. Then, taking a second deep breath, she pushed her way through the dark-gray steel door into the Cultural Center.

The party was already in full swing. The large social hall had been dressed up to look like a banquet hall, but the colorful bunting and balloons couldn't hide the room's shabbiness. Brown paint peeled from the walls in several places. The cheap linoleum was worn, its geometric pattern faded. The drop paneled ceiling no doubt concealed a multitude of sins. The fluorescent lights bathed the room in a ghastly pallor.

On the walls hung familiar scenes of traditional Jewish life in Gondar, vividly depicted in colorful photographs, large-scale textiles, and paintings in vibrant acrylics. Israeli flags hung limply on brass poles in two corners of the room. At the back of the hall, a troupe of young black dancers whirled and capered on a low stage. Behind them a small ensemble of drummers thumped out an Ethiopian beat. The men wore multi-colored capes over long, white robes; the women, white shawls fringed in colored stripes draped over floor-length white caftans.

Clustered around tall cocktail tables throughout the room, couples and small groups sipped wine from clear plastic cups and nibbled on Ethiopian hors d'oeuvres. Maya realized that she was ludicrously underdressed for the occasion. All the other guests wore formal attire—long gowns, cocktail dresses, stiletto heels, black tie and tails. The Center's staff wore traditional Ethiopian garb: white cotton *shammas* and pants, head coverings, fringed netelas and scarves. Maya noted that all the staff members and servers were black. The guests, on the other hand, were a mix of races. Mostly they kept to their own kind. From where she stood, the room looked like a giant chessboard—blacks and whites consigned to separate squares.

Then she saw Dani striding toward her. Like his colleagues, he'd gone native. In place of the dark pants, white shirt, and sports jacket he'd worn in his office, he now wore a long white robe adorned with a striped woolen scarf draped over one shoulder. His white pants peeked out just below the robe's hem. His head was uncovered.

When he saw her looking at him, he grinned sheepishly. Embarrassed by his theme park costume perhaps? Or embarrassed by her own sartorial blunder?

"I thought maybe you decided to skip tonight," he said.

"No, I'm always late. A bad habit I can't seem to break."

"Well, you haven't missed anything yet. It takes a long time to warm up a Beta Israel party. But once the fire's hot, the flames burn all night."

He reached out and grabbed one of her hands and pulled her over to the makeshift bar. Without asking her what she wanted, he ordered two identical drinks. When they were ready, Dani handed her a tall glass filled with a thick tangerine-colored liquid.

"*Tej*. Honey wine. Made with gesho leaves. A bush that grows wild in Ethiopia."

She took a sip. It was sweet but left a bitter aftertaste, like the sour tang of hops. She couldn't gauge its potency. She continued to take small sips until the glass was empty. She decided it was too sweet to pack much of a punch.

The music changed tempo, then became slower, more sensual. A space cleared in the center of the room. A sparkling disco ball began to spray the room with a fusillade of colored light. Dani took hold of Maya's hand and pulled her onto the dance floor. Despite his long robe, he moved sinuously to the drums' rhythm, swaying his lean hips, raising Maya's arms as though they were kites on a string. She began to match his movements, feeling her head lift off her neck and float up to the acoustic tiles. So tej wasn't so harmless after all! Together they moved like a giant paper dragon in a Chinese New Year's parade, diving and rising as though buoyed on the music's undulating currents.

Maya felt all her senses awaken. Blood rushed from her toes up to her head, then surged back down through her torso, a stream of incandescent light that set her body on fire. Where her fingers joined with Dani's, her skin tingled and pulsed. She looked at his face. His eyes were closed. He was lost in the dance. But the two of them remained connected by tensile wires of mutual attraction. Time flew and dragged and circled back. She paid no attention. She could go on like this forever.

Then the music stopped. She and Dani stood alone in the middle of the room. She quickly glanced around and noticed that everyone's eyes were fixed on them. Was she imagining it or were their stares filled with judgment? Or condemnation? She heard them whispering.

She broke free of Dani's hold and walked quickly toward the food table. Dani pursued her, calling her name. When he reached her, she kept her back to him.

"What's the matter, Maya? Is something wrong?"

He touched her shoulder. She threw him off. She realized she was trembling. Biting down on her lower lip, she forced herself to become still.

"Why were they looking at us like that?"

"Like what?"

"Like criminals. Or perverts!"

Dani shrugged his shoulders.

"Back in Ethiopia," he said, "we were taught that Israel was a great, big melting pot. Jews came from all over the world and magically became one people." He tried to laugh, but it came out as a snort. "It was only when we moved here that I learned it was all bullshit!"

A few people standing nearby moved away from them. Dani lowered his voice.

"It's such a lie. For many Israelis I'll never be anything but a dirty *kushi*. Just as Jews from Arab countries will always be considered primitive and uneducated by many European Jews. I won't even mention what most Israelis think about the Palestinians. Israel has a caste system every bit as entrenched as India's."

Like a scythe, his arm swept over the room. Over the past hour, more people had arrived. There was now standing room only.

"The white donors have come here tonight to assuage their guilt over the demeaning way Ethiopian Jews have been treated in this country. Or they've come to slum, to ogle at our quaint customs and dress. Do you know how long it took the government to fund and set up this cultural center? Fifteen years! And look at it! It's pathetic."

Maya's head was spinning from the tej. She couldn't deal right now with Dani's bitter social critique. She couldn't deal with any of this. She needed to regain control. No, she needed to get away.

"Look, Dani, the main reason I came here was to gather background for my case. I see now that it was a stupid idea. Neither the time nor the place. Thanks anyway."

Not waiting for Dani's response, she vanished into the dark.

DAY 4

Thursday

26

SARIT PARKED HER CAR BEHIND Golyat's Cadenza and clicked the fob. She and the sergeant were the first to arrive at the scene. The red crime tape was still strung around the Aklilus' house, cordoning off the street in front.

At least it's not another murder, she thought. *Just ordinary vandalism.*

From the street she was able to read the messy scrawl of black graffiti spray-painted on the front wall of the house.

Your A Traitor To Your Own Peple!
YOUR A TRAITOR TO YOUR OWN PEPLE!

Black Jewish Lives Matter!

Justice for Solomon Teka!

Were Watching You! WERE WATCHING YOU!

Your Next! YOUR NEXT!

The pranksters had also spray-painted the two-car garage door. The white surface displayed a cartoon image of a hyena, with brown-spotted fur, a dark muzzle, and large ears. The creature's face was an unmistakable caricature of Moshe Aklilu.

Normally Sarit wouldn't get personally involved in this kind of petty vandalism. She'd let her officers handle it. But given the two recent murders in this family and Moshe's press conference yesterday denouncing the "ineptitude and indifference" of the Jerusalem police, she needed to make an appearance here. She expected cameras and reporters to show up any minute.

Moshe and Elvis Aklilu stood on the manicured lawn in front of the white-stone mansion, their faces contorted with rage. Sarit drew in a deep breath, straightened the lapels of her navy-blue blazer, and strode starchily toward them.

"I would think that after two murders, the police would protect my family better!" Moshe's voice was loud and belligerent. "Look what these animals have done! It's disgraceful!"

The imposing MK, dressed in a crisp white shirt and sharply creased dark trousers, directed his comments to the empty air above Sarit's petite frame. *Rehearsing his lines.* Sarit nodded, trying to disguise her annoyance at his predictable grandstanding. She recognized the haughty outrage of privilege. And she reminded herself that it was often those who yelled the loudest who had the most to hide.

"Any idea who might have done this, MK Aklilu?" she asked. "Can you think of anyone who might wish to embarrass you?"

"Who doesn't want to embarrass me! They're all jealous. I work my ass off to get them better housing, defend their rights, secure more funding for their schools, and this is the thanks I get! I'm only one man. This is obviously the work of Benny Tzagai and his gang. That *ars* has been after my Knesset seat for years."

Sarit hesitated before asking more questions. Government affairs lay far outside her comfort zone. But if she wanted to work her way into the upper echelon of Lahav 433, the elite unit investigating government corruption, Israel's equivalent of America's FBI, she would have to get over her repugnance of politics and dive in head-first. Although she'd never admit to anyone, she dreamed of becoming the first woman to head Lahav.

"Do you have any proof that Tzagai's behind this?"

"Who else could it be? Lately he's been stirring up the extremists just to humiliate me. It wouldn't surprise me if my own son is mixed up in this."

Elvis stared at his father. His sleek eyebrows arched up and disappeared into his sweeping mane of black hair, which he fretfully tossed aside. His eyes narrowed over the bridge of his sharp nose.

Sarit saw her chance to drive a wedge between the two. Make them careless.

"How about you, Elvis? Any idea who might be behind this attack?"

Elvis sneered at his father, hawked up some spittle, and launched it into the grass.

"Just some street punks getting their jollies." He twisted sideways and pointed toward the garage. "That's a pretty good likeness of you, Abba, don't you think?"

The elder Aklilu eyed his son with blatant contempt.

"Any 'punks' in particular?" asked Sarit. "Friends of yours perhaps?"

Elvis glared at Sarit. His eyebrows creased into a tight V above his nose. She hated to admit to herself how much she was enjoying the men's smoldering feud. Then she remembered the commander's warning: "Don't let 'this Aklilu affair' suck up too much of your time or budget."

"I've left all that behind, Inspector," Elvis said. "I no longer have anything to do with gangs. My current business interests are all legitimate. If I were you, I'd consider this vandalism a hate crime. You know how much most Israelis despise us."

Moshe Aklilu grunted. His body language telegraphed his irritation with his son. He turned away, his shoulders hunched up, his square chin thrust into the air.

Just then, a small, dark woman, dressed all in black, scurried out the front door. Sarit recognized the younger of the family's two Ethiopian housemaids. The woman's face was grotesque, etched with pockmarks, indigo tattoos on her neck and forehead, and scarring on her cheeks and chin.

Carrying a small bucket of soapy water, she limped rapidly toward the garage. When she was in front of the wide door, she set down the bucket, reached her arm into the water to grab hold of a wooden brush with stiff bristles, and attacked the cartoon image of the hyena. Sarit heard her mumbling in Amharic under her breath.

After a few moments of vigorous scrubbing, she stepped back. The paint was not yielding to her efforts. She resumed her scouring, throwing her whole tiny body into it, occasionally pummeling the painted animal with the brush and kicking the door.

"Hamor!"

Moshe Aklilu shouted at her, then clapped his hands together. But the maid didn't slacken her brisk scrubbing.

"You stupid donkey! Stop! You're accomplishing nothing!"

Still the small black-clad woman persisted. She dropped the brush back into the bucket and began clawing at the cartoon hyena with her splintered nails. Sarit could finally parse her words, although she didn't know what they meant.

"*Jib! Buda!*"

Sarit looked at Elvis and Moshe, bewildered. Elvis threw up his hands and grinned. Moshe looked away. Sarit raised her eyebrows, inviting either man to enlighten her. But they said nothing.

Suddenly Moshe turned and shouted at the tiny maid: "Go inside!"

Moshe's tone made her freeze. She bent down and lifted up her bucket. Then she hurriedly limped inside the house, letting the heavy door close behind her.

"I'm sending my officer back to headquarters," said Sarit.

She waved her hand to summon Golyat, who was standing in the driveway. He had watched the interaction between the male Aklilus and his boss with undisguised amusement.

Why did that man always look like a cat who'd just made off with the cream? He always had a stupid grin on his face. What did he know that she didn't?

"He'll write up a report and open a new case file. As soon as we learn anything about this incident, we'll let you know."

Golyat nodded to Sarit, then trotted toward his car, his large arms swinging at his sides.

Sarit tilted her chin up toward one corner of the house, where a security camera beamed its cold eye at them.

"Glad to see you took my advice and installed surveillance cameras around the perimeter. Maybe we'll get lucky."

"Luck seems to have lost my address." Moshe laughed mirthlessly. "I checked the video as soon as I was told about the graffiti. The cameras caught nothing. It's as if they knew exactly where to stand to be out of camera range."

Sarit shrugged her shoulders. She checked her watch. Where were the paparazzi?

"I'm going to stick around 'til the press gets here," she said. She smiled coyly at the elder Aklilu, who appeared not to notice. "Let's see if we can keep a lid on things, Okay? You know how eager these reporters are to blow things out of proportion."

Moshe grunted and marched up the front staircase into the house, slamming the door behind him. Elvis winked at Sarit, then tossed his thick hank of dark hair to one side and followed his father.

Sarit walked over to the front stone staircase and sat down on the top step. She was no closer than before to solving the murders. But at least she hadn't made things worse.

27

Shulamit's Diary

November 4

Today's the 25th anniversary of my mother's death. Twenty-five years! Hard to believe.

Even though I was just a child when Emayay died, that day is forever engraved in my memory. Like a scar.

I could tell that Emayay was very weak when we reached the Sudanese border. You could see her bony cheekbones through her papery skin. Her eyes were dark hollows. But she refused to give up. I think it was her love for me that kept her going. We snuck across in the dead of night, cutting ourselves as we crawled under sharp brambles. Emayay tied my mouth shut with her netela so I wouldn't cry out.

When we reached the gates of Um Raquba, it was just before nightfall. As soon as she read the name of the U.N. camp on the wooden sign, Emayay stumbled and collapsed. I remember being lifted up by strong white arms. Eating injera and beans on a dented tin plate. Drinking rusty water from a tap. Being jabbed with a sharp needle.

She was so weak. Gone before the sun came up.

Emayay was only twenty-three when she died. Six years younger than I am now.

May you rest in peace, my beloved mother.

As she lay dying on the hard ground, she made me promise to seek justice for our family. Not that I understood at the time what she was asking of me. I was only four years old!

"You must live for all of us, yene fikir! *Be strong!"*

She made me repeat the words after her: I swear by Igziabeher *to live for all of you. I swear by* Igziabeher *to seek justice for your death.*

An hour after she died, they took her body away. I don't know what they did with it. I was moved into a tent with several other orphans. I remained in that camp for six long, terrible years.

Every year on this day I renew my vow. I am the only witness. It's my duty to remember. And to see justice done.

28

MAYA SPENT MOST OF THE next day cooped up in her office, tracking down leads in the Aklilu case. Though it was already November, the first floor of Headquarters still felt like August. Her white shirt stuck to her skin like wet leaves on pavement. Her auburn curls lay limp on her scalp. But Roni, claiming budget concerns, refused to turn on the air conditioning.

By the end of the day the muscles in her upper back felt especially tight. She stood up and flexed her shoulders. But it didn't help much. She sank back into her chair and laid her head down on the cool metal surface of her desk.

She thought about leaving early. No one here would bat an eye if she did. She'd clocked more than her share of long shifts. She was eager to get home. To find out how things had gone with Fewesi and Vered. Today was their first full day together. She had tried to keep busy to distract herself. But it hadn't worked. All day long her mother's grim admonitions had whacked against the bony walls of her skull: *Their women practice witchcraft! The curse of an evil eye!*

Of course, her Moroccan mother was always blaming the evil eye for the world's ills. Maya had long ago outgrown Camille's superstitions. For the most part.

In this case, it was just Camille's racism talking. She looked down on Ethiopian Jews almost as much as she looked down on Arabs. Why should Maya pay attention to her mother's deep-rooted xenophobia?

But Camille's words had eaten at her all day.

On second thought, she wouldn't leave early. If she did, Roni would no doubt needle her about it. No, better to keep working on her case. Do a deep dive into Ethiopian culture, fill in the many gaps in her knowledge. How ridiculous she'd been to think she could pick up valuable intelligence at a fundraising party!

She began with the Service's extensive digital archives.

She did a little more digging into the likely murder weapon. The Ethiopian billawa. Some of these knives featured handles and sheaths even more elaborately decorated than Fewesi's. And many of them had blades sharpened on both sides, looking deadly even in pixelated two dimensions.

Then she turned to jib, the Amharic word for "hyena." She needed to know why Hagar's killer had carved this particular word on her forehead. She needed to understand why non-Jews in Ethiopia call the Beta Israel, "hyena people"? Was it meant as an insult, or were they claiming that Jews needed to be feared? Was the killer then a non-Jew from Ethiopia? Or was he a Jew disguising his true identity?

As she dug deeper, her uneasiness increased. Scrolling through half a dozen scholarly articles, she learned that Christians and Muslims in Ethiopia had long considered Jews capable of acquiring Buda, a kind of mysterious malign power. If you possessed Buda, you could enlist this power to cast an evil eye on your enemies. Because Jews in Ethiopia had been denied the right to own land for five centuries, non-Jews believed that they had come to envy their propertied neighbors. Envy had led to malice. And malice, to witchcraft. To gain power over their enemies, Jews had sold their souls to the devil. Like zombies, they consumed Christian and Muslim corpses. At night they transformed themselves into hyenas. In the guise of these "were-hyenas," they set upon their victims, afflicting them with wasting sickness, accidents, infertility, bad luck, sick herds, and blasted harvests. Sometimes they literally scared their victims to death. Of course, modern medicine tried to explain away such psychosomatic deaths as "vagal inhibition," a physiological syndrome causing the nervous system to stop the heart. But those who believed in the power of Buda knew otherwise.

Maya shuddered as she read these articles. Were these Ethiopian superstitions much different from the vicious Blood Libels that had damned Europe's Jews to recurrent pogroms for centuries? Up until modern times, anti-Semites periodically accused Jews of killing Christian boys and using their blood to make matzah. Although Ethiopian superstitions about Buda had not proved as devastating for the Beta Israel as the Blood Libel had been for European Jews, it had certainly made them plenty of enemies.

When she turned her attention to the subject of the Zar, another popular African folk belief, she discovered an even more bizarre notion. According to an Ethiopian legend passed down by all three Abrahamic faiths, Adam and Eve had originally given birth to thirty children, not just two as the Bible claimed. Eve tried to hide her fifteen most beautiful children to protect them from God's envy, but of course, this was impossible to do. God punished her for this deception by rendering these fifteen beautiful children invisible forever. They became the ancestors of a race of envious and capricious spirits known collectively as the Zar. As for the fifteen children that Eve didn't hide, they became the ancestors of the human race. Since that primeval time, so declares this legend, humanity has been tormented by the invisible Zar spirits, forever driven by insatiable envy.

Unlike Buda, which non-Jews regard as the Jews' secret weapon, Zar afflicts people of all faiths, especially women. Especially women who shed blood. That's why there are so many taboos around menstruation and childbirth, around women who lose blood yet do not sicken or die. Maya had never been able to wrap her head around her own religion's antiquated rules concerning such completely natural events. Why hadn't Jewish women rebelled centuries ago against this form of social control?

Maya laughed out loud.

"Why are men so afraid of women's blood?"

A sudden knock on her office door startled her. Masha's square-featured face appeared in the glass window. She smiled waggishly; her honey eyebrows arched.

Was it her boisterous laugh that had drawn her friend, or had she been talking to herself again?

She winked at Masha and waved her away, pointing to her desktop. Masha gave her a thumbs up and returned to her cubicle. Maya scolded herself. She needed to be more guarded. There were enough rumors floating around headquarters about her odd behavior.

As she continued her probe into the uncanny world of the Zar, Maya learned that there were many ways to appease these restless spirits: by wearing certain tattoos, performing prescribed rituals, engaging in mystical music and dance, even carrying decorated umbrellas—the latter had made Maya laugh out loud a second time—and by participating in *bunna*, the stylized coffee ceremony that Maya had shared at Fewesi's.

She was surprised to discover that Zar spirits could be befriended, even recruited to help cure illness or infertility. What didn't surprise her was finding out that most modern scholars discredited the Zar as "primitive superstition." One charitably tried to reframe it as a method of coping with disruptive social or cultural change. Another, a psychology professor at Tel Aviv University, proposed that "Zar possession" should be classified as a psychiatric illness. Maya resented their patronizing dismissal. Had Western medicine, especially psychiatry and the talking cure, proven any more effective at alleviating human pain and suffering?

Maya recalled something Fewesi had said when she'd explained the *bunna* ceremony to Maya. *Pleasing to Zar also.* At the time, Maya hadn't paid much attention. She'd dismissed the comment as a non sequitur. Or thought that she'd maybe misunderstood what Fewesi had said. Her new neighbor's Hebrew was often hard to decipher.

But now Fewesi's remark struck Maya as a potential clue. She suddenly felt a familiar prickle on the skin of her arms, the pale red hairs rising on pimpled flesh. Maya had learned to pay attention to such *frissons* when she was working a case. She'd always had a sixth sense when it came to solving puzzles—or crimes.

29

MAYA FOUND HERSELF SPEEDING ON the drive home. She parked in her usual spot and took the stairs two at a time, despite her considerable fatigue. When she reached the fourth floor, she stood for a moment in the dark hallway, replaying what she'd read over the past few hours. It made her shiver.

She debated taking a shower. Despite the strong deodorant she used, her body smelled of sweat. Her stomach rumbled with hunger. But she just couldn't wait.

She pivoted on her heels and trotted over to Fewesi's front door. She rapped on the wooden door a few times with her knuckles. No answer. She pressed her ear against the door. No sound of a television or of music playing. She rapped again, louder. The door opened a crack. The chain of the slide bolt snapped taut.

In the escaping flash of pale light, Maya caught sight of her daughter, looking out with a wary green eye.

"Where's Fewesi?"

The six-year-old unlatched the chain lock and opened the door wide, revealing Fewesi's brightly colored living room. Maya noted a brass tray on the low table, the delicate clay *jebena* perched at one end, the giant wooden mortar on the floor.

"She went back to the playground. I left Merida there."

Maya was annoyed. Her neighbor had left Vered alone in the empty apartment! Not that there was anything to fear. Vered had been thoroughly schooled to look out for herself. But as an intelligence agent, Maya knew you could never be too careful.

"Okay, lock the door and wait for me to come back for you. I'll go get your doll from Fewesi. I was thinking about pizza tonight. Okay with you?"

Vered's face lit up. She smiled, exposing three dark gaps where teeth were missing. She slammed the door shut with a vigorous push.

Maya waited until she heard the chain slide firmly into place. Then she hurried down the four flights of metal stairs and out the building's side door into the dying evening light.

Her heart fluttered with dread. Maybe it had been a bad idea to leave her daughter with Fewesi. What did she know about the woman other than her sorrow? How could she have left her young daughter alone with a stranger? What if...? But there was no "what if," was there? It was only her own guilt speaking. After Rafi had gone to prison, Maya had promised herself that she'd spend more time at home with Vered. Play the part of two parents. Put her work second. But she hadn't kept her promise, had she? This new murder case was already consuming her.

She rushed along the paved walk leading toward an open field behind the apartment building. In the gray light she could just make out swings, a climbing gym, a wooden merry-go-round, and a large sandbox. The playground was empty.

Then she noticed a small, dark form in the distance, lit by an unsteady flame. The fire suddenly winked out. The dark form scurried toward her. Bright light from a three-quarter moon glinted off a pair of glasses like fireflies.

Maya quickened her pace, reaching Fewesi in the empty field midway between the playground and the apartment building.

In her hands Fewesi carried Vered's beloved doll, Merida. In the feeble light of the yellow bulb that hung above the building's side door, the doll's porcelain face looked dirty. Her thick skein of artificial red hair had long ago lost its shape. Patches of white porcelain skull shone in the moonlight.

"How could you have left her all alone?"

She'd intended to go easy on her. Fewesi was young. And she was still in the early throes of grief, perhaps not used to taking care of children. But as soon as Maya had caught sight of Vered's doll, all she could think about was how vulnerable her daughter was. And hear the echo of Camille's warning.

"Only for short time, Miss Maya. Few minutes." The young black woman thrust the doll into Maya's hands. "Vered she seem so upset doll left in playground. She say Merida afraid of dark."

A wave of shame washed over Maya. She smiled at Fewesi.

"Yes, Vered does think Merida's real. Thank you for being so sensitive to her feelings."

As the two women headed back toward the four-story building, Maya brought the doll closer to examine it. The dark smears on the doll's face were not dirt as she'd first supposed but smudged ash. Did the ash come from the fire she'd seen as she approached the playground? Why had Fewesi made a fire there? And why was ash smeared on Merida's face?

Fewesi had walked on ahead and was struggling to wrench open the reinforced steel door on the side of the building. For the first time, Maya noticed tattoos banding the young woman's neck. Three inky necklaces made up of chained links. Were they just decorative or did they mean something? She remembered reading that certain tattoos were considered effective in controlling the Zar. Was that what these were? Then she recalled the billawa hanging on Fewesi's wall. Was her neighbor a witch?

"Come," said Fewesi.

She had succeeded in pulling open the heavy door. With one of her small hands, she beckoned Maya into the dark hallway inside.

"Vered be happy to see her doll okay."

Maya followed Fewesi into the building, letting the door bang shut behind her. As she made her way up the metal treads behind Fewesi, she forced herself to shut out her mother's heckling words and the voices of the derisive scholars. She shouldn't jump to conclusions.

She felt a kinship with this young, bereaved woman. Both of them were mothers, weren't they? How could any mother seek to harm another mother's child? It was simply against nature! She would not let herself be bullied by superstition or prejudice. Fewesi would continue to watch Vered. Camille and the scholars be damned!

DAY 5

Friday

30

THE NEXT MORNING MAYA ARRIVED early at Service Headquarters. In place of her usual navy slacks or pencil skirt, she wore dress blues, low navy pumps, and a crisp military-style cap. In her ear lobes were diamond studs, a gift from her parents when she had been inducted into the Service. She'd even applied a bit of makeup. A smudge of blush and a glaze of Ruby Sunset lip gloss to complement her coppery hair.

It was the first time in ages she'd worn her dress blues to work. But as she made her way to her office, very few of her colleagues looked up from their screens to raise an eyebrow or tease her. It would take more than pressed clothes or rare punctuality to reverse her reputation as someone who broke the rules more often than not.

She sat down at her desk, being careful not to crease her skirt. She turned on her desktop and logged on. As always, she checked her in-house emails first. No political brush fires to put out yet. No red flags from Roni. She breathed a sigh of relief. Next, she pulled up her calendar. Nothing on her docket until the Aklilu funerals.

Then she skimmed through Facebook, Twitter, and Instagram to take the pulse of Israeli social media. Her eye was immediately caught by a short Facebook post that mentioned Moshe Aklilu by name. But it had nothing to do with the recent murders of his wife and daughter. Instead, the brief message written in bold black letters warned:

> Your days in office are numbered, Aklilu!
> Your dirty crimes are about to be expozed!

Maya clicked on the name of the person who'd posted the message. It was someone named "Haim Vital." She vaguely recalled this name from a college course she'd taken on Jewish mysticism. Obviously a pseudonym. This Haim Vital's profile offered almost no information—no picture, no biographical data, no photo array of friends. Only: "Joined Facebook in 2016."

She scrolled down further and found several similar posts. One of them, put up by an organization called "Beta Israel Now and Forever," claimed to speak for "all Ethiopian Jews in Israel who have suffered because of the government's failed policies." Under this message, which pointed a finger at Moshe Aklilu in particular, was a photograph of a large group of Ethiopian men, most of them dressed in white *shammas*, raising their fists to the sky, their mouths wide open in protest. The men stood in an open field with mountains in the background. Maya guessed that the photograph had been taken in Ethiopia, not in Israel.

Like the bogus "Haim Vital," this organization provided little information about itself. She would check into both later. Like most intelligence agencies, the Service had amassed large files on malicious trolls and bots.

A third post finally gave Maya some useful information. Although the text didn't mention Moshe by name, it wasn't hard to figure out that the Ethiopian MK was the intended target. In large, bold caps the message read:

> *Benny Tzagai Is The Only True Voice Of Ethiopian Jews!*
>
> *Unlike Others He's Not In The Pocket Of The Whites!*
>
> *Black Jewish Lives Matter!*

Maya didn't know much about Benny Tzagai except that he and Moshe Aklilu had long been bitter political rivals. She Googled him. A profile of Moshe Aklilu published in *Yedioth Ahronoth* three years ago revealed that the two men had been vying for the single Knesset seat in their tiny party in every Israeli election for the past ten years. Tzagai had never garnered more votes than Aklilu. After each defeat, he'd accused his successful rival of corruption and dirty tricks. But Moshe had always been cleared of any wrongdoing. Was Tzagai somehow connected to the Aklilu murders?

Maya swiveled away from her computer screen and grabbed the single sheet of white paper lying in her wire mesh in-box. It was a summary investigation report from Chief Inspector Sarit Levine.

Maya skimmed Sarit's brief report. She found what she was looking for in the second paragraph: "MK Aklilu alleges that his political opponent, Benny Tzagai, is behind the recent graffiti attack on his house. However, the MK could furnish no evidence to substantiate this claim. No further action is required."

No further action is required?

Ever hear of due diligence, Sarit? That's your problem. You move too goddam fast, always so eager to make the kill. As brilliant as you are, you always miss something. That's why I landed this job, not you.

Maya sat back in her chair and closed her eyes. If she told Roni about the posts she'd just found, he'd no doubt warn her: *steer clear of politics!* He would dismiss the online threats as typical partisan sniping before a national election. He'd point out that Moshe Aklilu was only a bit player in these elections. But Maya wasn't so sure. Since neither major political party controlled a ruling majority in the Knesset, the smaller extremist parties would play an outsized role in forming a new government. Although Moshe possessed only a single vote, the major parties would be actively courting him. Maybe the Ethiopians couldn't yet be kingmakers, but they could no longer be barred from the throne room.

Benny Tzagai was certain to be sidelined again in this election. He would obviously resent Moshe's inflated position in the electoral lottery. But would such resentment push him to murder his rival's family? Or was he simply trying to intimidate Moshe, to drive him out of politics? It didn't quite add up.

But it was an angle worth pursuing. Perhaps something more sinister lay behind these men's antagonism, something whose roots extended back decades, maybe to Ethiopia. Wasn't there some proverb about revenge being a dish best eaten cold? Who knew how long someone might be willing to wait to pluck out an eye for an eye?

She clicked open the file she'd created on Moshe Aklilu and reviewed the fragmentary biography she'd put together.

According to official government records, Moshe had been born in the Ethiopian village of Sagade in 1972. When he was six his family had moved to Wolleka, one of the largest Jewish villages in northwest Gondar province. Soon afterwards his father had died in an accident. By the time Moshe was ten, his mother and two sisters had succumbed to cholera. He'd then been adopted by another Jewish family in Wolleka. This family had fled to Sudan in 1993, where they'd found refuge in a United Nations camp. But within a year of their arrival, his adoptive family had all died of malnutrition and disease, leaving Moshe an orphan for the second time. In 1995 Moshe had been airlifted to Israel along with a group of other Jewish refugees.

Maya stopped reading and took a drink of water from her aluminum thermos. *What a nightmare*, she thought. *To lose two families!* She'd heard similar horror stories about other Jews who'd arrived from Ethiopia. Still, something about Aklilu's story troubled her. It was rather convenient that everyone who had known Moshe in Ethiopia was now dead. There was no way to corroborate his story.

She chided herself for being so suspicious. But that's how she'd been trained. Never to believe in coincidence or luck.

When Moshe had reached Israel, he'd been placed briefly with an Ethiopian foster family. After completing high school and a three-year stint in the Israeli army, he'd returned to Beersheva and gotten a job as a low-level recruiter for an employment agency run by Ethiopian Jewish immigrants. The agency trained and placed Ethiopian women as house cleaners, caregivers, and nannies. Over the next ten years, this ambitious young man had advanced through the ranks and become a top manager at the agency. Then he'd left to set up his own agency, branching out to enlist new temporary workers from Eastern Europe, the Philippines, and other African countries in addition to Ethiopia.

Soon after moving to Beersheva, Moshe had married his first wife, Esti, an Ashkenazi woman whose family had originally come from France. Their marriage had produced two children: a son, Gidon, aka Elvis, and a daughter, Hagar. Moshe became an MK in 2012. He had then divorced Esti and moved to Jerusalem. A year ago, Aklilu had married for the second time. His new wife, Titi Akilu, was a twenty-three-year-old beauty queen. For the past seven years, Moshe had lived in his opulent mansion near the Knesset, with his unmarried daughter, Hagar. Recently, Elvis, his wife, Shulamit, and their eighteen-month-old son, Bekeli, had moved in with them.

What else do I need to know about the honorable MK? What was he hiding? Why did someone want to visit such misery on him?

Maya skimmed the next few pages, which chronicled Moshe's political record in parliament. She slowed down when she reached the section about his civic activities. According to local newspaper accounts, he was well-respected in the Beta Israel community. Over the past two decades, he had contributed generously to charities, especially those benefiting Ethiopian Jews. He'd funded a new clinic in Beersheva to treat poor Ethiopians suffering from HIV/AIDS. He'd recently announced a magnanimous award for the researcher who made a significant contribution toward finding a cure for this disease, which afflicted so many in their community.

Maya knew that the man was no saint. Although Moshe had never been indicted for any crimes, he was probably good for many.

Everyone had secrets, especially those with political power. He had risen high fast. Too fast. She needed to dig deeper.

She stood up and stretched her arms toward the ceiling. Roni had finally acceded to turning on the air conditioning, but the antiquated system was in one of its peevish moods, freezing one side of the floor and roasting the other. The ceiling fan overhead stirred the heavy air, rattling in contrapuntal rhythm. With the back of her hand, Maya wiped the beaded moisture from her forehead. Some of the salty residue dripped down and stung her eyes. She could feel sweat trickling down her blouse into the waistband of her skirt. She hoped her dark blazer would cover the stains.

She closed down all her computer files and exited her office.

31

As Maya hurried to the back of the large first floor room, she noted that the air circulating among the cubicles in the center space was much cooler than the air inside her small room. Her office was a steam bath today.

Roni's door was closed, the white blinds drawn.

When she neared his office, she heard him talking on the phone. She leaned forward but couldn't make out any of the words. They sounded slurred, uncharacteristically loud and hurried.

Without knocking, she pushed open the door, startling Roni. He let out a surprised grunt and slammed down the black receiver in his hand. Abruptly, he bent down behind his desk and disappeared. Before he did, Maya glimpsed something in his hand. A light brown bottle with an elegant neck. She recognized the label. Lagavulin 16. He shoved the bottle into a bottom drawer and slammed the drawer shut with a loud thud. When he sat back up, his tawny face was flushed. The large ugly port-wine birthmark disappeared as dark blood dyed his cheeks. His close-set eyes, dark like burnt olive pits, glared at her.

"Ever hear of knocking, Rimon? It's what normal people do before entering a room."

"I wanted to bring you up to speed on the Aklilu case."

"Have a suspect yet? A motive?"

Maya hesitated. Roni was always looking for ways to shoot her down. If she shared her half-baked hunches—that the killer was an Ethiopian sorcerer or a vengeful political rival—he'd stomp all over her. But if she told him she still had nothing, he'd pull her off the case. Not for the first time she found herself pinioned in one of Roni's no-win traps.

"Closing in on both," she lied. "I'm expecting the killer to show himself at the funeral today."

To her surprise, Roni didn't press her further.

Maybe he suspects I'm onto his drinking. And maybe he's admitted to himself that his judgment's becoming impaired. That he's making rookie mistakes. Such knowledge gave her leverage. She'd wait for the right moment to use it.

"I'm heading out to the cemetery now," she said. "Want to get there early, find a good spot to surveil the scene." She wrapped her fingers around the doorknob, then turned back. Roni was eyeing the black phone on his desk. "I'll let you know what I find out."

Roni nodded, not taking his eyes off the phone. His dark pupils then drifted down to the bottom desk drawer and lingered there.

Maya smiled. Leverage. The notion went to her head like a shot of strong whiskey. *Or tej.* Letting the door slam shut behind her, she strode out of Roni's office with a bounce in her step.

32

"LET GO ME! I NO do nothing!"

The two cops held the young woman tightly by her skinny arms. She flailed wildly to escape their grasp. Without handcuffs to restrain her, she soon broke free and dashed toward the front door of the police station, knocking over a heap of manila files that teetered on the edge of a desk. Trying to catch her, her pursuers skated on the paper spill and tumbled to the floor.

At that moment a third cop entered the station. He was so tall that he had to duck under the lintel. He immediately sized up the situation and tackled the fleeing girl. For a moment he lay on top of her like a beached whale. Only the girl's bare painted toes and a few tufts of pink hair poked out from under his heavy frame. Then he struggled to his feet and looked down. The young woman lay still, the wind knocked out of her.

Hearing the commotion Sarit emerged from her office and walked rapidly down the hallway, coming to a halt at the edge of the station's large front room. She noted the two officers sprawled on the cement floor, the lurking figure of Golyat, the motionless body of the young woman, and the rest of the squad, staring at them, frozen in place.

"Okay, anyone going to tell me what's going on?"

Golyat shrugged his colossal shoulders and held out his palms toward her. The two officers on the floor scrambled to their feet, their faces flushed red up to their ears, but said nothing. The young woman suddenly sprang to life, leapt to her feet, and jerked her head from side to side, her one good eye bobbing in its socket like a pinball.

She looked up at Golyat's towering figure and shook her head. Then her eye fastened on the petite figure of the Chief Inspector, dressed smartly in her dress blues, standing, arms akimbo, staring down at her.

"I no do nothing! Let go me!"

Narrowing her eyes, Sarit studied the young woman. She looked as though she'd just been through a war. Her short denim skirt, barely covering a pair of lacy underpants, was ripped at both side seams. Her frilly peasant blouse exposed so much cleavage that it was obvious she wasn't wearing a bra. The two halves of her white blouse were held together by a few inches of skimpy fabric. In her navel glittered a rhinestone. Much of her skin, from her ankles up to her neck, was mottled with purple and yellow bruises. Her right cheek was strafed with bloody scratches, made with fingernails or a sharp instrument, possibly a fork. Black blood clogged both her nostrils. Her left eye was bruised shut. The girl was lucky to be alive.

"Who did this to you?" Sarit asked.

"I do nothing wrong."

The young woman suddenly began to shake. First her shoulders started quivering and then her hands. Her undamaged eye filled with tears. Then her whole body began trembling, and she dissolved into sobs.

"No one will hurt you. I promise. You're safe here."

Sarit kept her voice low and calm, although she doubted the girl derived much comfort from her words. She'd once been told that her voice was closer to a rottweiler's than a cocker spaniel's.

"Just tell me what happened. We'll get you help."

Walking with slow, measured steps, one of the policewomen rolled a chair to the front of the squad room. Then she let go of the chair and stepped back. The young woman shuffled over to the chair and sank down on the cracked dark green Naugahyde seat. Slowly, her sobs modulated to sniffles and gasps.

Sarit approached her slowly. She pulled over a second desk chair and sat down a few feet away. She leaned in until she was only inches away from the young woman's ravaged face. Gently she placed her hand on the girl's forearm. She flinched, and Sarit quickly drew her hand away.

"What's your name?"

"Amila." She suddenly grabbed hold of Sarit's wrist. "Please! No send me back!"

"Don't be afraid, Amila. We'll protect you."

Drawing in a deep breath, the young woman turned her good eye toward Sarit and smiled sadly.

"They promise we marry rich Jewish man in Israel. Big house with maid. Happy life. No more worries."

From her accent, Sarit pegged her as Central European. Maybe the Balkans or Albania. Recent reports told of more women from this region being smuggled by organized crime into Israel. Most of them never showed up on official radar. These poor girls, some as young as eleven or twelve, were willing to trust anyone who promised them a way out of their dead-end lives. If only they knew there were worse fates.

"Can you tell me anything about the people who brought you here? Describe the house where you were kept? Remember a name?"

Amila shook her head. Sarit looked at the girl's hands. Every glossy red nail was chipped. Had she tried to claw her way out of captivity? Had she broken her nails attacking her abusers? Or had she taken to harming herself in order to dull an even more terrible pain?

"Please, Amila!" Sarit pleaded. "Don't let these bad men get away with this. Help us! Help the others who didn't get away!"

Amila stared off toward the ceiling, lost in some memory. Then she hung her head and sobbed again. Sarit waited patiently until her body quieted.

"Dark house. Windows cover up. Smell like ocean. Bad smell. Dead fish."

They could have been unloaded at any of a half-dozen port cities on Israel's Mediterranean coast. Hadera, Jaffa, Ashdod, Ashkelon. Or dropped off at one of the smugglers' landing sites along the shore. Sarit needed something more specific.

"Did you ever hear them call each other by name?"

"One time. One man get angry at big boss. Say he no pay enough for girls."

Sarit could feel her heart speeding up, her nerves tingling. If she succeeded in breaking up an international sex trafficking ring, it could catapult her into a position in Lahav. Make her career.

"The name, Amila! What was the name?"

Amila hesitated, swallowed hard. She leaned in closer to Sarit, whispered into her ear.

"He kill me if I tell."

Sarit placed her hand firmly on Amila's arm. This time the girl didn't pull away. Sarit waited.

"Aklilu."

Had Sarit heard her correctly?

"Can you repeat that?"

"Aklilu."

Impossible! Moshe Aklilu had never been connected to the sex trade. His preferred MO was long financial cons—money laundering, illegal real estate deals, currency manipulation, tax fraud. That's why he'd never been convicted. These crimes were much harder to prove. It had to be Elvis. He was reckless and impulsive. Trafficking young girls would appeal to a young wannabe gangster. All that young flesh to fondle and bully. Sarit was no psychologist, but she'd always wondered what Elvis thought of his father's marriage to the young, nubile Miss Beersheva. His new stepmother was six years his junior! Did he hate Daddy for robbing the cradle—or did he envy him? What better revenge than to shanghai naive young girls into sex slavery! One-up the old man.

Sarit recalled her most recent conversation with Maya Rimon about this case. The intelligence agent had quickly dismissed Sarit's suspicions about Elvis.

"He might have killed Titi," Maya had said, "but he would never have harmed his sister. By all accounts, he was very attached to Hagar. Considered himself her protector."

"Maybe she stumbled onto something he couldn't let anyone know about. Gave him no choice but to silence her. You know, they're not the cleverest criminals, these Ethiopians. Raised to be potters and blacksmiths. Not like the Russians."

At the time Sarit had known she was grasping at straws. But she was certain that Elvis harbored his own dark secrets. Now she knew what they were. It was obvious he'd murdered Titi to punish his father, who'd thrown over Elvis's mother for a young trophy wife. His second secret was right in front of her: Elvis sold young women into sex slavery. Whether he'd want to admit it or not, that made him no different from his father. Both men liked their women young and unspoiled. Maybe Hagar had discovered this secret and then had to pay the ultimate price. There was more than enough motive here to make Moshe's son her prime suspect.

From the moment she'd met Elvis, she'd known that the boy was a bad seed.

33

Elvis drove to southwest Jerusalem in the late afternoon. The weather had turned. The raw chill augured the late autumn rains. He parked his Miata near Mexico Park, securing the steering wheel with a club and activating the car alarm. Kiryat Menachem was dicey. The neighborhood was largely home to immigrants from Ethiopia and the former Soviet Union. Many of them were petty criminals and gangbangers.

As he was walking toward their usual meeting place, he saw a group of black teens huddled in the shadows of a two-story building. By their hunched-up shoulders and lowered caps, he guessed it was a local gang, planning some mischief. One of them noticed Elvis looking over at them. Scowling, he flicked his thumb against his upper teeth, then turned back to his pals. Elvis grinned and continued on his way.

He met Golyat in the small community garden two blocks away. The big, burly cop was already seated on the iron bench.

This time it was Golyat who was nervous. He puffed aggressively on his cigarette, swinging his massive head left and right before settling his icy blue eyes on Elvis.

"I don't think we should meet here anymore," he said. "Levine's compiling quite a file on your family. It's only a matter of time before she figures out that I'm the leak. You're not paying me enough to risk my job."

"Relax! I just left her an anonymous tip about the murders. It'll definitely throw her off my scent. And yours."

Elvis laughed. He tossed his head to one side, causing his sandy forelock to fall over his right eye. He brushed the hair aside with his hand, then reached into his shirt pocket to snag a cigarette. He lit up and tilted back. With pursed lips, he blew out a series of three perfectly round smoke rings. A gust of cold air immediately tore them to shreds.

"Oh, yeah? What about the drugs they found on Titi? Don't you think they'll lead directly to you? At least I managed to snatch Hagar's stash before the cops found it."

Elvis choked on the smoke he'd just inhaled. He coughed, then spit out a glob of charcoal saliva. It landed on a pair of withered leaves plastered to the pavement.

"I never sold any of that shit to Hagar! Maybe to Titi now and again, but never to Hagar. It's obvious that the police planted it on her. To frame me or my father. My sister's as straight as a *dula* stick." He stopped, blinked hard, then inhaled deeply. "Was."

A lump formed in his throat, like wet pulp. Combined with the trapped smoke, it made Elvis gag. He leaned over and threw up. The vomit landed on top of his spittle, burying the dead leaves. He wiped his hand across his mouth, then straightened up.

"They're not gonna pin these killings on me, no way!"

Golyat reached inside the pocket of his dark pants and drew out a few sticks of gum. He quickly unwrapped them, wadded them together, and stuffed the wad into his mouth. He chewed vigorously, like a happy cow.

Elvis stood up to leave. He glanced down at the mustard-hued splatter and shuddered.

"One more thing," said Golyat.

He twisted around and hawked the sticky wad of gum into the grass behind the bench.

"Some girl showed up at our district station earlier today. Beaten to a pulp. Probably trafficked from Eastern Europe. Levine got a name out of her."

"And?"

Elvis returned to the bench and sank down on the hard iron slats. His shoulders slumped.

"Couldn't make it out, but it sure turned Levine on. She ran back to her office and slammed the door. Was there for at least an hour."

"Find out the name." Elvis leapt up and stamped his foot on the pavement, careful to steer clear of the lumpy puddle. "I'm not goin' down for any of this."

"What're you gonna do?"

"Make a phone call."

He rushed out of the park and made a beeline for his car.

When he got to the Miata, he saw that the antenna had been snapped off. They'd taken his new stereo system and the CDs in the glove compartment. Probably the teen gang he'd passed on his way to meet Golyat. *Karma*, he mumbled to himself. *Just goddam karma.*

DAY 6

Sunday

34

"I CAN THINK OF A hundred other things I'd rather be doing on my day off," said Maya, "than fighting with you."

Sitting next to Maya in the passenger seat of the silver Corolla, Sarit Levine made no response. Maya had meant the comment as a joke but maybe Sarit didn't agree with her judgment.

Flicking on her right blinker, Maya turned off Highway 1 to follow Highway 6 further inland, avoiding the Saturday beach traffic heading toward Tel Aviv. The weather was raw for early November. No sun, a brisk wind, but it was always warmer at the beach.

Still not speaking, Sarit pulled down the visor on her side and checked her makeup. A light smear of matte coral to go with her sandy hair. A hint of black mascara and eyeliner to highlight her dark brown eyes. Both women were wearing civilian clothes today—jeans, light-colored tee shirts, and sandals. Sarit's hair was pulled back in its customary ponytail. Maya wore a yellow sweatband to push her unruly auburn curls off her face. Unlike Sarit, she wore no makeup.

"I don't know," said Sarit, snapping the visor back into place. "I'm kind of looking forward to sparring with you, Maya. It's good to keep up our hand-to-hand skills, maybe even try for a green belt and G-2 rank. You never know when you'll need to flatten a bad guy with your bare hands."

"When was the last time you used krav maga in a real fight situation, Sarit? I thought that's what Golyat was for."

So, the sparring between the two women had already begun. The two were as deadly with words as with clenched fists. In a few hours, one of them would draw first blood in the workout room.

Krav maga was known throughout the world as one of Israel's secret weapons. A mix of boxing, wrestling, judo, aikido, and karate, it was closer to street fighting than battlefield combat, notorious for its aggressiveness and use of brute force. Maya and Sarit, like all Israeli military recruits, had been trained in this martial art when they'd entered the army at eighteen. It was also taught to most police, military, security, and intelligence forces. Maya especially liked krav maga because there were no rules.

It had been Sarit's idea to drive up to the Wingate Institute for the day to spar. *Letting off some steam*, as she put it. Located south of Netanya on the Mediterranean coast, the Orde Wingate Institute for Physical Education and Sports was Israel's training facility for various national teams as well as a military training base. Ex-military and security people sometimes went there to keep up their skills or up their game.

Maya had agreed to accompany Sarit more as a gesture of solidarity than because she wanted to sharpen her form. The truth was that the two women investigators needed to start working together more closely if they hoped to solve the Aklilu murders quickly. Their parallel investigations were both now hitting brick walls. Sarit was still targeting Moshe or Elvis as her prime suspects, despite the lack of credible proof. Maya, on the other hand, suspected that there was much more behind these killings than political ambition. From what she'd learned in her research and from talking with Dani and Fewesi, she believed that these bizarre crimes traced their roots back to Ethiopia. She hoped that Sarit would take her ideas seriously and not dismiss them as wild speculation.

They stopped for gas and sandwiches at a rest stop and finally reached the Wingate Institute just before 1:00 p.m. The parking lot was almost full. Maya noted many police and army vehicles in the lot. There were always training courses and demonstrations going on here.

The two women quickly changed into loose-fitting clothes and made their way to their reserved workout space. After a brief warm-up, Sarit suddenly lunged full force into Maya's chest when the latter swung a fist at the other's head. Within seconds, Maya was flat on her back, her chest heaving. The pain that burned her with each breath suggested that Sarit might have broken her rib. From that moment until they quit, exhausted and winded, thirty minutes later, the two women attacked and parried, kicked, and chopped, using their fists, legs, heads, shoulders, elbows, and feet to knock each other onto the padded mat. Before they'd begun, they'd agreed not to use weapons and not to go for each other's faces. But their weaponized limbs did plenty of damage, nonetheless. Their arms sported several raised purple and yellow bruises. And when they changed back into their street clothes, they'd be sure to find more battle scars.

After showering and changing, the two made their way to the cafeteria to have coffee and a sweet. Despite all the pain they'd inflicted on each other, their mood seemed much lighter than it had been on the drive up. They had indeed let off steam.

Maya decided that now was the time to open up about her investigation.

"Ever hear of Buda, Sarit? Or Zar?"

The petite police inspector froze, her teeth clamped on a chocolate croissant.

"What?"

"They're folk beliefs, superstitions really, held by a lot of Ethiopians, including Jews. I've been doing a lot of reading. Apparently, back in Ethiopia, Christians and Muslims believed that Jews could turn themselves into hyenas at night and harm them. They called the Jews 'hyena-people.'"

Sarit chewed slowly on her pastry but said nothing. She took a long sip of her Turkish coffee, then another bite of the croissant.

Maya rushed on, afraid that Sarit would interrupt her, not give her a chance to get everything out.

"The gentiles believed that Jews had Buda, an ability to give their enemies an evil eye and curse them. And there's another superstition that might play a role here. Many Ethiopians, Jews included, believe that there are invisible spirits called Zar, who can possess people, make them physically ill, even kill them."

"And what does any of this have to do with Titi and Hagar Aklilu's murders?"

Sarit glared at Maya, then narrowed her eyelids, as if to give the other woman an evil eye. Maya pretended not to notice.

"Hagar had the image of a hyena carved into her forehead, right? And the graffiti on the Aklilus' house also included a picture of a hyena." She paused. *Just get it over with.*

"And the double-edged blade used to kill both Aklilu women must be a billawa, an Ethiopian ritual knife sharpened on both sides. Don't you see? Everything points back to Ethiopia. Either it's a Beta Israel doing the killing or someone who knows enough about their customs to frame someone else for the murders."

Sarit washed down the last bite of her croissant with the dregs of her coffee, then gently placed the small white cup on the metal table. She dabbed both sides of her mouth with a napkin, wiping off the remnants of her lipstick.

"It all sounds rather fantastic and far-fetched," she said. "But given that we're nowhere near solving this case, why shouldn't we consider every angle? If it's all right with you, Maya, I'll let you chase down these leads, as long as you keep me in the loop. My money's still on Elvis or Moshe. If you want to go in another direction, I wish you joy."

Maya couldn't tell whether Sarit grinned as she finished that sentence. Retrieving a tube of lipstick and a compact mirror from her shoulder bag, the police inspector turned away to paint her lips. Maya decided not to push it. She had shared her intelligence in good faith. The rest was up to Sarit.

35

MAYA WAS AMONG THE LAST to arrive at the cemetery.

The weather had turned a bit warmer after the recent cold snap. Today the sun shone like a xenon headlight, momentarily blinding Maya as she stepped out of her silver Corolla and scanned the vast expanse of white graves that covered the hilltop like mounded snow. Har HaMenuchot was the largest of Jerusalem's cemeteries. These 150,000 souls would be first in line to enter heaven when the Messiah came.

Maya glanced down at the black-and-white map they'd given her at the gate. She didn't need it to locate the gravesite. She spotted the dense crowd, mostly dressed in white, perched farther up the hill. Near them, parked along the road, was a long line of cars, many of them large black sedans. She drew in a deep breath and began the long tramp up the hill.

She wasn't surprised to see so many government officials at this funeral. Moshe Aklilu was a prominent member of the Knesset, a very public voice for his community, and a successful businessman. To show up to honor his dead was the respectful—and politic—thing to do. As she came closer, she noticed that the mourners had divided themselves into several distinct groups. Close to the two open graves stood family members, the elders among them wearing white *shammas* with white scarves draped around their necks and shoulders. Surrounding them were other members of the Ethiopian community. Neighbors and friends, business associates. She couldn't make out any of their words, but from the gaping mouths and contorted faces, she guessed many of them were wailing. She'd read about the theatrics displayed at Beta Israel funerals. Not very different from the way Arabs mourned their dead.

Behind this group stood the non-Ethiopians. Mostly Ashkenazim, judging from their fair complexions and the women's stylish hats. Parliamentary colleagues, business associates, the white literati and glitterati. Possibly some of Moshe's partners in crime as well. In the outermost ring stood members of the press and the police. Maya noticed among them a few dark-clad men with plastic corkscrews sprouting from their ears and bulges under their jackets. Private security.

In this outside ring she spotted Roni, squirming with impatience, smoking a cigarette. Beside him stood Arik Ophir, the Israeli Minister of Security. A few steps away stood Sarit, craning her neck to see over the crowd. She finally gave up and cocked her ears. Next to her loomed her giant sidekick, Golyat, staring straight ahead, his height giving him an advantage over his petite boss. The dark-clad security men paid no attention to the activity near the graves. Their mirrored eyes swept over the crowd, watching.

As Maya drew closer, she heard the keening. Like police sirens throttled by trumpet mutes. Yowling horns of grief. She walked around the outer perimeter until she found a gap through which she could see the graves. When he caught sight of her, Roni eyed her balefully, but she ignored him. Peering through the thicket of mourners, she saw Moshe, seated in a plastic folding chair. Near him stood an Orthodox rabbi, a black-coated, gray-bearded man wearing a broad-brimmed hat typical of Haredi Jews. Unlike the other Ethiopians, Moshe wore a dark suit and tie. On his balding head he wore a large white kippah embroidered in gold. His face was drawn, making him look much older than his forty-three years. His face bore an expression midway between consternation and grief.

Pinned to one of his lapels was a small, shiny black ribbon attached to a black silk button. The ribbon was slashed diagonally as a symbol of mourning. *K'ria*, a heart torn by grief.

Maya ran her eyes past Moshe to the other mourners.

Next to Moshe sat Elvis. His wife, Shulamit, was not with him. The woman seated next to Elvis was someone Maya didn't recognize. Probably Moshe's first wife, Esti Yitzhaki. Mother of Elvis and Hagar. The light skin of her face, neck, and hands, set against the two black men, seemed pallid. She wore a tailored black two-piece suit with an elegant wide-brimmed hat. Her eyes were hidden by large sunglasses. She, too, wore a black *k'ria* ribbon on the lapel of her jacket. But not Elvis, Maya realized. No black ribbon was pinned to his lapel.

On the hard ground to Esti's left sat a toddler. Maya recognized Bekeli, Elvis's eighteen-month-old son. He was playing with a stick, making lines in the dirt. Esti paid no attention to the little boy. She stared straight ahead through her opaque lenses. Near the child hovered a dark shape, draped in black, its hooded eyes fixed on the boy. One of the Aklilus' dwarfish maids.

The Orthodox rabbi cleared his throat. The wailing of the crowd subsided to a low moan. In a few moments the words of the 23rd Psalm rang out in a plaintive Eastern European melody:

> A psalm of David.
> Adonoy is my shepherd. I lack for nothing.
> Adonoy leads me beside still waters
> And restores my soul.

Suddenly, a second voice joined the rabbi's tremulous tenor. Or rather sang over it. The new voice, a deep baritone, intoned words in an unfamiliar language—Amharic or Ge'ez. The tune was unfamiliar. Maya found it quite haunting. Most of the black mourners joined in. The keening resumed, strangely harmonizing with the melody. Peeved, the black-hatted rabbi held up his pale, wrinkled hands, but the singing didn't stop. He reached up his right hand and clamped it down on his broad-brimmed hat, which threatened to fly off in a sudden gust of wind. Then without a word, he stomped through the crowd of mourners and disappeared.

Now a tall, white-bearded black man stood beside Moshe. It was the Qes, looking regal in his flowing white *shamma* and white turban. In his resonant baritone, he sang to the end of the psalm and then stood silent. All other sounds ceased. After waiting several moments, he began to speak in Amharic. Maya recognized the names, "Titi" and "Hagar." And the words, "jib" and "billawa." She kept her eyes focused on Moshe and Elvis. The former sat like a stone, unmoved and unmoving, his eyes staring ahead. Elvis fought back tears, especially when the Qes mentioned Hagar's name.

When the Qes finished speaking, the wailing resumed, even louder than before. Esti shook her head and mumbled. She unsnapped the purse on her lap, rummaged around inside, withdrew something white, then snapped the purse shut. She dabbed the corner of each eye with the lace handkerchief, delicately blew her nose, dabbed at her ashen cheeks, then thrust the white square of cloth back into her purse. She looked over at her ex-husband, who sat ramrod-straight, blankly staring. Elvis reached over and patted his mother on her arm. She threw his hand off and looked down at her lap. He thrust both his hands into the pockets of his dark suit pants.

Suddenly, Maya noticed movement out of one corner of her eye. A slim figure, dressed in a white *shamma* and white knit kippah, drew near and stood beside her. She noticed that the skin of his face and hands appeared even darker against the dazzling white of his tunic. Like charred bark.

It was Dani.

"I'm surprised to see you here," she said. "I'm here trolling for a killer. What's your excuse?"

Dani laughed. The lines at the corners of his dark eyes fanned out like a fine tracery of gossamer.

"I've come to give you moral support," Dani said. "Funerals are never easy, even if it's not your own family. Especially if you don't know the customs."

Maya saw Roni looking her way, sizing up Dani. He raised his sharp eyebrows, then thrust his cigarette in her direction. She stared at him until he looked away. Sarit also took note of the tall, young black man standing next to Maya. She grinned, raised one sandy eyebrow, then poked her pointed chin at Dani. Maya narrowed her eyes until Sarit, too, averted her gaze.

Maya redirected her focus back to the gravesite. Standing at one end of the two open pits, an elderly man was giving a eulogy in Amharic. He leaned unsteadily on a wooden cane. Moshe listened attentively. Elvis picked dirt off the bottom of his shoes.

The eulogy ended, and the keening resumed.

Dani grinned.

"Hired mourners, no doubt. The more important the deceased, the louder the wailing."

"It's giving me a headache," said Maya.

Dani reached up his hand and lightly stroked her temple, brushing back an auburn curl. His touch sent a thrill down her spine. She waited a moment before speaking.

"Obviously, the killer hasn't shown his hand," she said, her voice once again steady. "I'm going to leave."

"If you want to show respect, you should help fill in the graves. Shovel some dirt in."

"They won't notice my absence, believe me. Must be several hundred people here."

Maya turned her back to the graves and began trudging down the hill. She heard footsteps behind her. Dani touched her elbow, then walked beside her. His long legs could have reached her car in half the time, but he slowed down to keep pace with her. She didn't dare look behind her. She could almost feel Roni's eyes boring holes into her back.

36

MAYA DIDN'T STOP FOR LUNCH on her way back to work. She drove straight to Headquarters, not even stopping for a coffee. She wanted Roni to find her working at her desk. Too busy for his prying questions.

But it was almost one, and she was famished!

She felt a drop of sweat trickle down the side of her cheek. The damn A/C must be pumping hot air directly into her office! She wiped the sweat away with the back of her hand but stopped short of wiping the hand on her skirt. She could probably get at least one more wearing in before sending her dress blues out to clean.

She leaned back in her chair and stared at a meandering crack in the ceiling. Why had Dani shown up at the Aklilu funeral? Up until now she'd enjoyed keeping him a secret, even from Masha. It was bad enough she had told her mother. Now Roni would start hounding her for his name, the status of their relationship. It would give him another barb to needle her with.

Her desk phone rang.

"Maya Rimon?"

"Speaking."

"Stop spy on Moshe Aklilu!"

The man had an accent as thick as hummus. She couldn't place it, but it was definitely not European or American. Didn't sound Ethiopian, either.

"You punch the moon. You be sorry!"

Before Maya could say a word, the man hung up.

From his brusque tone, she could tell that this call was meant as a threat. Her investigation had clearly touched a nerve.

She knew that Moshe had plenty of enemies. But who were his friends? Who would risk raising the hackles of the Service to protect him?

The caller had used a peculiar phrase—"punch the moon." It was not an Israeli idiom. Then she remembered seeing this same expression in an interrogation transcript she'd scrolled through during a previous investigation. That case had involved a sex trafficking network. The ringleader had been Filipino. What was his name?

Maya's ears chimed like a carillon as the name suddenly came back to her. Joey Villanueva! He'd been on the Service's radar for almost ten years. His formal name was Jejomar Hernando Villanueva.

Maya swiveled around to her desktop and pulled up the man's file. He was certainly one of the most unusual criminals she'd ever come across.

Villanueva had first come to Israel as a temporary contract worker, caring for an elderly Jewish man with diabetes and other ailments. He was one of thousands of Filipinos who had poured into the country in the 1990s to serve as caregivers for Israel's steadily aging population. A small number of these temporary workers were men like Villanueva, who were in the process of transitioning to women. Unwelcome in their conservative Catholic homeland because of their unconventional lifestyles, they found an opportune niche for themselves caring for old Orthodox men who according to Jewish law could not be physically tended by women outside their families.

Villanueva hadn't stayed long in his caregiving role, however. He set his sights on greener pastures. When his visa had expired, he'd gone underground, opening a club in Tel Aviv with two other Filipinos, featuring drag queens as entertainers. From there it hadn't been too much of a leap to start trafficking women and transgender people from Eastern Europe and Asia to Israel. His client list included some of the richest men in the country as well as some of the dirtiest. And he had also been linked to several real estate scams in Tel Aviv, possibly involving the Russian mob. The man was as crooked as a shofar.

Maya's mind was racing. Drag queens. Sex trafficking. Organized crime. Real estate scams. What did any of this have to do with the murders of the two Aklilu women? Were Aklilu and Villanueva working together? Had a falling-out between them prompted a vendetta against Aklilu's family? And what about the double-edged knife and the hyena sign carved into Hagar's forehead? Was this disturbing symbolism meant to throw them off the scent or were they vital clues?

Over the past decade Villanueva had been arrested half a dozen times. Each time he'd gotten away with a suspended sentence and a hefty fine. The Tel Aviv authorities had been keeping tabs on him for sex trafficking, but they didn't have enough yet to shut him down.

As she scrolled through the many pages in the electronic file, Maya kept looking for Moshe Aklilu's name, but it never appeared. Either he was not involved in these crimes, or he'd managed to keep his head down better than Villanueva. She doubted whether any of this would lead her to her killer. She still needed to find a motive for these murders. Who benefited? What was she not seeing?

She stood up and stretched her lean arms toward the ceiling. Her stomach grumbled. She pulled open the middle drawer of her desk and poked around until she felt a hard oblong shape wrapped in foil. Alternating between gulps of cold water from her thermos and mouthfuls of the energy bar, she finished her meager lunch in three bites. Moments later she was in Roni's office.

"Come in!"

Roni shouted the words into her face when she was already standing in front of him. Was it her imagination or had he again quickly shoved something into his desk drawer? His breath smelled sour. His dark, close-set eyes refused to meet hers.

"What is it now, Rimon?"

"Wanted to bring you up to speed with the case. Just got a threatening phone call. I'm pretty sure the caller was a Filipino."

Roni stared at her. His cigarette dangled from his thin lips like a broken branch. He took it out of his mouth and balanced it precariously at the edge of his desk.

"I'm thinking the caller might have been Joey Villanueva."

Roni slammed both hands down on the wood surface of his desk.

"That trans guy who runs the night club starring drag queens? You gotta be kidding!"

"The caller warned me to drop my investigation of Moshe Aklilu. I'm thinking there might be a connection between the two. Villanueva and Aklilu. A new lead."

Roni opened his mouth, revealing rows of tea-stained, crooked teeth. He grabbed his cigarette just as it began to teeter at the edge of the desk. The long shaft of ash flew into the air and rained down like a swarm of midges. He tossed the butt into the small metal can next to his desk. Then he reached into his pants pocket, drew out a fresh cigarette, and thrust it between his dark lips. He flicked his lighter and sucked in a long drag.

"Do yourself a favor, Rimon. Find the killer, and make an arrest. Stop chasing phantoms! Ophir is up my ass about these murders. And I'm sure Aklilu's up his. Just do your job!"

With a brisk swipe of his hand, Roni shooed Maya out of his office. As the door closed behind her, she heard the squeak of a wooden desk drawer, the thump of a solid object landing on the desk, and the clink of ice.

37

With a gentle shove, Maya pushed open the unlocked front door of the Aklilus' grand villa and walked in. The front hall was packed with visitors. They talked quietly among themselves under the massive cut-glass chandelier. The living room off to the left was also packed. Most of the guests stood in small clusters of two or three. Others sat silently on the plush white couches.

The pair of official mourners—Moshe Aklilu, still dressed in his dark cemetery suit; and Elvis, now clad in bleached jeans and a white short-sleeved shirt—sat at one end of the large room, side by side on low wooden stools. A few feet away from them sat a young Ethiopian woman wearing a white, floor-length tunic, a long white scarf draped around her hair and neck. Maya guessed it was Shulamit, Elvis's wife, who hadn't shown up at the funeral.

Maya scanned the crowd before stepping into the plush-carpeted living room. She was surprised to note that everyone in the room was white. Except for the mourners, father and son. And Elvis's wife.

Weaving between the guests, Maya slowly made her way toward the mourners. When she stood in front of them, she bowed her head and waited. Finally, Moshe looked up and frowned. A moment later, Elvis did the same.

Maya cast her face into a vacant mask. Her voice was equally without expression.

"May God comfort you among all those who mourn in Zion and Jerusalem."

She pronounced the traditional Ashkenazi formula of condolence in a monotone, as though she were speaking to a bank clerk.

The elder Aklilu nodded perfunctorily, then looked away. Elvis stared at Maya. He tossed his head carelessly to one side. A thick sandy curl flopped over one dark eye.

"I'm sorry for your loss," Maya said.

She tried to make herself sound sincere. Elvis sneered at her. He then turned to his father, whose gaze was still averted.

When Moshe turned to look at her, Maya noticed that the bright whites of his eyes were shot through with spidery veins. His left leg, which rested on his right knee, began to jiggle. It was soon joined by his hand, which drummed steadily on the side of the black mourning stool.

And then she saw the scar on one side of the MK's neck. She hadn't noticed it in any of the photos in his file or in his appearances on TV. A curving sliver like a crescent moon.

Or like a billawa.

At that moment, the older Ethiopian maid appeared, carrying a silver tray. She was dressed all in black, with a black scarf wrapped tightly around her head. She walked over to the low glass coffee table in front of Moshe and gently set it down. On the tray stood an elegant vessel made of highly glazed black ceramic, with the same curved neck and spout that Maya had seen at Fewesi's. She remembered the Amharic word. *Jebena*. In addition, there were two matching cups without handles, a blue bowl filled with sugar, and two small silver spoons.

Maya inhaled. The aroma of freshly roasted beans was intoxicating.

"You stupid donkey! I told you—no coffee until the third day of mourning."

Maya walked over to the second couch and sat down not far where the maid stood. She strained to hear what the old woman was saying. But she could only make out two Amharic words that she already knew: *Buda. Jib.*

The maid abruptly ended her mumbling and fell silent. She glanced across at Shulamit. Elvis's wife stared back at her, her amber eyes glowing like burning coals. The maid shuddered, muttered a few more words, then ran back into the kitchen.

"That idiot woman and her idiot daughter!" said Moshe, his voice wheezy in exasperation. "Should have gotten rid of them a long time ago."

Maya glanced down at the old Poljot on her wrist. 3:00 p.m. She'd been here almost thirty minutes.

She rose to leave.

Moshe bent forward and beckoned to her. She walked over to him and seated herself at the end of the couch a few feet away. He leaned closer until she could smell his pungent aftershave. Something European and expensive.

"I didn't want to say anything in front of my son, but I've begun to worry that he might somehow be mixed up in these terrible crimes. I know he was selling drugs to my wife. Maybe my daughter too. I probably should have said something about it to the authorities instead of looking the other way." He hesitated. "You should know that he very much resented my marriage to Titi. He and his mother have remained quite close over the years. I would never have thought him capable of such a heinous act, but maybe..."

He let his deep bass voice drift off, then resumed.

"However, I can say with complete confidence that he did not murder his sister. Those two would have done anything to save each other's necks!" He hesitated again, then sighed. "Despite all my efforts, he's fraternized with some pretty questionable types over the past few years. The killer could have been any one of them."

Maya let Moshe's words hang in the air until he looked away from her. From past experience she knew that families who were under investigation often turned on each other. Even if they weren't guilty of the crime under investigation, they were often guilty of something else, enough for them to betray their nearest and dearest.

"I know how hard this must be for all of you," Maya said. Her words were flat, fooling neither of them.

"Please go now," Moshe said. He sank down on to the black stool, his shoulders sagging. "Leave us to our grief."

Maya looked around. They were now alone in the large living room. She took a few steps toward the back patio and peered through the double glass doors. The back lawn was almost completely covered by a large white tent. Through its translucent plastic sides, she saw people—black and white—talking and eating. The back walls of the tent were lined with tables heaped with platters of food and rows of plastic bottles.

She turned to leave. When she stepped into the foyer, she was accosted by the elder maid. The woman grabbed Maya's arm and squeezed hard.

"What do you want?"

The woman apparently did not understand Hebrew. Maya held up both hands, palms up.

The maid pointed to the black robe she was wearing, then to her head covering. She grabbed the lapel of Maya's blazer and tugged at it.

"My clothes?"

Maya mimicked the maid's gestures, first pointing to the small woman's robe, then to her own clothing. The woman nodded her head. Then she dragged Maya over to an array of family photographs hanging on the wall of the foyer. With a withered finger, she pointed to Titi, then to Hagar.

Maya shrugged her shoulders. What did the maid want with the victims' clothing? They were being held in evidence until the case went to trial. She shook her head.

The maid turned her face up and reached her hands toward the ceiling. Then she began to wail. From the living room Moshe yelled at her in Amharic, but the wailing only grew louder.

Maya headed toward the front door. She had a lot to ask Dani about.

38

SHULAMIT ROSE FROM THE COUCH and walked quickly to the front door. Through one of the long glass panels framing the wooden door, she watched the white female agent proceed down the tiled path to the street where her car was parked. Though small-boned and lean, the woman's stride bespoke formidable strength. She got into her car without looking around to see if anyone was watching. When the car disappeared from view, Shulamit left the house and got into her own car, a white Smart Car that Elvis had bought her last year. She looked back at the house before driving off, then followed the silver Toyota.

The drive took longer than she expected. She had assumed that an intelligence agent would live in one of the city's better neighborhoods, but she'd been wrong. The silver car kept traveling south, almost all the way to Rachel's Tomb. Who would choose to live so far from the city center if they didn't have to? Maybe the agent wasn't on her way home. She was on assignment, chasing down suspects. When the silver car turned off for the low-income settlement of Givat Ha-Matos, Shulamit kicked herself for being so foolish. No way that woman lived here! She'd taken a big risk for nothing.

Yet Shulamit wasn't yet ready to give up. She stayed back a good distance while the agent parked her car in front of a four-story apartment building. Across from the building, a few mangy dogs raked through a pile of trash, fighting over scraps. The ground surrounding the apartment house was covered with patches of withered grass, but mostly it was just bare dirt. Behind the building was a playground, but no children played there.

She waited until the agent had entered the side door of the apartment house. Then she turned off her engine, strapped the yellow club to the steering wheel, and locked the car. She hurried over to the side of the building and took a few deep breaths.

Luckily the steel door wasn't locked. When Shulamit yanked it open, she found herself staring into a black void. The darkness thickened once the heavy door clanged shut behind her. With her fingers she felt around the rough concrete walls until she found the stairwell light. She pushed in the black plastic button and waited for the lights to come on. In the harsh light she stared up through four flights of metal treads. No one moved on the stairs or any of the landings. The heavy silence was disturbing.

She quickly made her way up the stairs, stopping at each landing to peer at the nameplates on the doors. Twice she had to punch in stairwell buttons on the landings when the hallway lights suddenly winked out, leaving her blind.

By the time she reached the top floor, she'd lost hope. This was nothing but a wild goose chase. The agent obviously didn't live here. She was just pursuing her investigation. But Shulamit decided she would look at these last nameplates anyway. Maybe she'd learn something that would prove useful.

The first nameplate on the fourth four landing was carefully scribed on colorful Armenian ceramic tile. Cohen. The most common name in Israel. The name on the second door was unpronounceable, Russian or Polish. But the third name was definitely Ethiopian. Ingedashet.

Before she could read the fourth nameplate, she heard that door's deadlock slide out of its socket. Quickly she pulled off her flipflops, raced to the stairwell, and ran down to the landing on the floor below. Her bare feet made no sound on the stone steps.

The fourth door opened. Shulamit squinted up through the narrow opening between the stairs. She saw a pair of white legs walk over to the door labeled "Ingedashet" and knock. Moments later a young woman's voice spoke through the closed door.

"Who dere?"

She recognized the accent immediately. The tenant in the third apartment definitely came from Gondar Province.

"It's me. Maya."

The intelligence agent! So, she did live in this out-of-the-way rathole full of immigrants and relocated homeless families. Government jobs must pay as poorly in Israel as they did back home.

"Listen, Fewesi, I have to go out later this evening. Can you watch Vered for me?"

"No problem. Bring her. I watch."

The young Ethiopian woman still spoke through the closed door. Was she afraid of her neighbor? Afraid to be seen? Afraid in general?

The agent turned to go, pivoting on her heels. The leather soles of her sandals scraped against the hard stone floor. Then she reversed course and pivoted back.

"Can I ask a favor, Fewesi?"

The third door finally opened. Shulamit heard the bolt slide out of its socket, the wooden door creak.

"Not understand. You want from me a *tovah*? A goodness? What goodness I can do?"

Maya Rimon laughed. Shulamit bristled at the agent's condescension. So typical of Ashkenazim.

"What I meant," said Maya, still chuckling, "can you do something to help me out? I'm sorry I don't know the Amharic expression."

The Ethiopian woman laughed. It was a meek sound, tentative. Obviously, she still didn't understand what Maya Rimon wanted from her.

"I try. What goodness I can do for you?"

"I've been feeling kind of anxious lately." The agent hesitated. "Worried. Not able to sleep."

"Ah, I know how dat feel."

"You told me that you know something about herbal medicine. Plants that heal and take away pain. Do you have anything that can help me relax and maybe get a decent night's sleep?"

The Ethiopian woman pivoted on her bare feet, a soft, swishing sound, then padded back into her apartment. She returned moments later.

"Put in hot water and drink. Very slow. Eat food at same time. Bread or t'ing like dat. It help."

"Thanks so much! I'll bring Vered over after dinner."

The two women returned to their respective apartments and closed their doors.

Shulamit listened until she heard the two chains clank shut. Then she walked barefoot down the stairs in the dark until she saw a glimmer of light leaking in under the metal door that led to the outside. She pushed open the heavy door and exited the building.

So, Maya Rimon's neighbor was a witch!

Shulamit released a deep sigh. They'd soon find out which of them wielded the more powerful magic.

DAY 7

Sunday

39

Maya called Dani as soon as she got home from the Aklilus' house. He answered on the first ring.

"Dani Solomon."

He sounded so proper, even at home. She considered hanging up. But she liked hearing his gentle voice, those unhurried British vowels.

"It's Maya."

"Oh." A slight pause as Dani cleared his throat. "Hi."

Was he pleased to hear from her? Or peeved?

"Why did you show up at the funeral?" Maya asked.

"He's an important man, Moshe Aklilu. And he's been quite generous to JEJI. It was a sign of respect."

She dove right in and began peppering him with questions: Why wasn't Elvis wearing a *k'ria* mourning ribbon like his parents? Why hadn't his wife shown up at the funeral? Why did their servant insist on having the victims' clothes returned to the family?

She paused, winded, almost out of breath.

There was so much else she wanted to ask him. But would any of it prove relevant to her investigation? Or was it all just an excuse to keep him on the phone?

"I don't want to miss something that might bear on my case. Just because I'm unfamiliar with your...peculiar customs."

"Peculiar, eh? Less peculiar than your customs of covering all the mirrors in the house and going shoeless during shiva?"

Was he teasing or had she insulted him? Maya felt warm blood rush to her cheeks. She was glad her discomfiture wasn't detectable over the phone.

"And let me assure you, Agent Rimon, if you think *these* customs are peculiar," Dani's voice was unabashedly sarcastic, "you should have seen the whole minstrel show we used to put on back in Ethiopia. It would have made an anthropologist swoon." He paused, his voice more dispassionate. "But not to worry, we've cleaned up our act since coming to Israel, become less of an embarrassment."

Maya's cheeks were burning. She tried to imagine the impish grin on Dani's handsome face.

"To be honest," Dani continued, his tone now somber, "most Ethiopian Jews can't wait to abandon their primitive ways and become *real* Israelis. To change their spots, so to speak."

How's that for a colonialist metaphor, she imagined him chuckling to himself. *What a sharp wit the man had.*

"Sorry, Dani. I didn't mean to be insulting."

A long pause. Dani cleared his throat. When he resumed speaking, his voice was formal. All business.

"Okay, let me try to answer your questions. I assume they're important to your investigation. First, about tearing your clothing when someone dies. Unlike you Ashkenazim, we never did this in Ethiopia. That's what the non-Jews did. But when the Beta Israel first arrived in Israel, they saw that's what 'real' Jews did, so they copied them. They didn't want to be considered 'peculiar.'"

Maya pictured Dani's grin stretching wider, exposing brilliant white teeth.

"That was the first immigrant generation. But more recent arrivals have become less submissive. They prefer to hold on to their heritage. Go back to the old ways."

A whoosh of breath. Dani sighed.

"It's a losing battle, of course. Most of the old ways are already gone. Happens to all immigrant groups."

Another whoosh of breath. The sadness in Dani's voice was almost palpable. Maya began to regret calling him.

He pressed on.

"As for your second question—why Elvis's wife wasn't at the funeral—I have no idea. It's very bad form." Dani had unconsciously slid back into his Oxbridge diction. "We have a saying: 'Better to be seen with unwashed feet or to bed an in-law than miss a relative's funeral.' Elvis's wife had better have a good excuse for not showing up today."

"What about their old servant demanding that the police return the murder victims' clothes?"

A snort of disdain hissed from the other end of the line.

"Just an ignorant superstition popular among country people. The maids probably aren't even Jewish. Managed to slip in illegally. Many Ethiopians, especially from the mountains, don't believe that a person is really dead until they hold his clothes in their hands. That's especially true if someone dies under mysterious circumstances."

Maya visualized the two stunted servants, mother and daughter, shrouded in black, always skulking in the shadows.

"Any other questions for me, Agent Rimon?"

Maya was glad to hear that the teasing tone was back in Dani's voice. His mood had lightened. All seemed forgiven. Her pulse quickened. She wished she had more questions to ask. And the brightness in Dani's voice revealed that she wasn't the only one who felt that way.

Then she thought of something Dani might also know about. *Gultosh.*

"Do you know anything about the village of Gultosh, in Gondar Province? Moshe Aklilu told me he comes from there. But his official bio lists Sagade as his birthplace. Why would he lie about where he was born?"

A long pause.

"I'd rather not discuss this over the phone. Come see me at my office tomorrow."

"I'd rather talk about it now. Tonight. It's pretty urgent."

An even longer pause.

He didn't want her to come to his apartment. That was obvious. But she pushed—and he yielded. She hung up before he could change his mind.

***

Vered gave her a hard time about going next door to stay with Fewesi.

"I don't want to go to that lady's house! It smells funny. And it's boring. She doesn't even have a TV!"

Maya turned to face her six-year-old daughter, who was sitting beside her on the sagging orange loveseat. She threaded her fingers through Vered's wild mop of auburn curls.

"I have to go out tonight, *motek*. For work. It's only for a few hours. Please don't make this difficult."

Vered screwed her face into a scowl. She shook her head free, crossed her arms, and scuffed one sandal back and forth on the cement floor.

Maybe she should drop the idea of going to see Dani tonight. Wait until tomorrow like he suggested. But that would set a bad precedent. She needed to put her foot down with Vered. It wouldn't kill her daughter to be bored for a few hours.

But there was another reason she wanted to see Dani tonight. She was loath to admit to herself that she was willing to put her own needs before her daughter's. Was that so terrible? Suddenly, in her mind's eye the image of Dani's handsome face morphed into Merida's ashy porcelain features. Like a sinister omen. Quickly, she banished the image from her mind.

"That's enough, Vered Nehama!"

Vered quickly sprang up from the couch. Her mother only used her middle name, chosen in memory of Maya's feisty kibbutznik grandmother, when she was at the end of her rope.

They walked briskly across the hall. Maya knocked on Fewesi's door, which opened immediately. The young Ethiopian woman smiled warmly at Vered. The young girl averted her eyes, staring at the floor. Maya raised her sandy eyebrows and shrugged. Fewesi's toothy smile broadened. She squatted down on her haunches, inches away from Vered's chest.

"We bake cookies, Vered. Wit' raisins and honey. Taste very good. I teach you how to make."

Vered looked up and peered at Fewesi. Her freckled nose wriggled. Maya smelled it, too, the sweet fragrance of fresh baked dough mixed with the familiar aroma of roasted Ethiopian beans.

Fewesi held out her hand. Vered took it. Together they walked into the apartment. The door closed softly behind them.

40

Maya knew it wasn't a good idea, meeting with Dani in his apartment at night. Roni would consider it a breach of protocol. But as she drove north in the waning light, she told herself that it was necessary. Dani had intimated that he had some useful information for her. Obviously, it couldn't wait. Who knew when the killer would strike again?

She rounded a bend in the road and saw the lights of Mevaseret Zion. The white stone buildings sparkled in the distance.

Dani's neighborhood was located between the Police Station and the Harel Mall. His street was lined with identical two-story apartment houses constructed of Jerusalem stone. Almost all the red tiled roofs were punctuated with skylights. It was already after seven, so the area was lit up with streetlamps and glowing windows, the glass panes flickering with blue light from flat-screen TVs.

Maya parked her silver Corolla in front of his building. She locked her car and walked briskly toward the front double-doors.

Dani's apartment was on the first floor. He answered the door dressed in shiny blue running shorts but not wearing a shirt. Maya noted that his chest, firm but not heavily muscled, was almost hairless. The smooth, ruddy-brown skin shimmered with beads of water. His wet hair, cropped close to his skull, resembled knapped shale.

"Maya! You're early!"

Under his dark skin, Maya detected a flush of embarrassment.

"I just got out of the shower after a run. Give me a minute."

He disappeared into the apartment's other room. The brief pause gave Maya time to regain her composure. Seeing Dani's bare chest, not powerfully built like a boxer's but hard and ropy like a gymnast's, had robbed her of breath. Had he meant to show himself nearly naked to her, or was she, in fact, early? She shook her head to clear it, then walked into the large central room and sat down.

The room was more austere than she'd imagined. Hardly any furniture. No art on the walls. No decorative pottery or culinary appliances on the kitchen counter. As if he were only staying for the night. No sense of permanence or ownership.

Dani came back into the room, wearing jeans and a white button-down short-sleeved shirt. His feet were bare. He sat down next to her on the yellow vinyl couch. Almost immediately his hands began grappling with each other between his knees. Maya glanced over at the pink scar tissue covering most of his left palm. He followed her gaze, then quickly thrust his right hand under his thigh.

"Sorry for the indecorous welcome."

Maya giggled. Dani grinned.

"My mother would have been horrified," he said. His grin widened.

"And my mother would have had you arrested!"

Maya meant to laugh, but her voice stuck in her throat like a bone.

"Can I offer you something to drink? Cold water, juice?"

"Maybe something a bit stronger?"

Dani raised his dark eyebrows, releasing a spill of wrinkles at the corners of his eyes. He rose and walked over to the small refrigerator in the kitchen area. He opened the refrigerator door and disappeared behind it.

"White wine? Beer? I have some homemade tej. My mother's secret recipe."

"Not tej!"

Now it was Maya's turn to blush. She remembered how intensely that potent honey wine had affected her a few nights ago at the fundraiser. Her head floating away. Her body drawn toward Dani like iron to a magnet. Her will robbed of its brakes. No tej!

"White wine would be great."

Dani filled two glasses from a half-empty bottle and carried them over to the couch. He sat down in the same spot and set the glasses down on the coffee table. Then he reached his right hand over the couch's armrest to retrieve the battered briefcase sitting on the floor. He placed it between his legs, pried it open, and withdrew from its dark interior a slim manila folder, which he placed on the low wooden table in front of them.

He stared down at the folder. The skin of his face became taut, stretching over his angular cheekbones and sharp chin. His lids hooded his dark eyes.

"You asked me about Gultosh." His voice sounded strained.

"What about it?"

"We have a strict policy at our agency. We're firmly committed to protecting our clients' confidentiality. Many of them have experienced severe trauma. We've promised them that we won't disclose their pasts, that we'll let them get a fresh start here. I want to help you, Maya, I really do, but I owe it to my clients not to betray their trust."

Maya listened to Dani's speech with growing impatience. Two young women were dead, slashed by a cruel killer. Of what value were such high-minded scruples if they shielded a monster from justice? There were always going to be trade-offs in an imperfect world.

"I hear you, Dani, but I'm asking you just this once to make an exception. Stop thinking like a bureaucrat. Help me stop a killer before he takes another life. If you know something, you have to tell me. So, what do you know about Gultosh?"

Dani bent forward and grasped the folder in his right hand. He placed it on his lap and lifted the thin off-white cover.

"As far as I can recall, I've only come across this name once before. It was in connection with a small group of Ethiopian Jews who fled this village in 1995. All but two of them died en route."

He fell silent. Maya waited.

"Only one woman and her young daughter made it to the UN refugee camp on the Sudan border."

Maya felt a nervous excitement roiling her chest. This woman might have known Moshe Aklilu back in his home village. If he'd left any secrets behind, she might know what they were.

"Where are these two women now? How can I get in touch with them?"

"You can't. We contacted UNHCR when we first learned of this case. The mother died shortly after arriving at the camp."

Maya slumped backward. The stiff cushions of the yellow couch let out a breathy sigh.

"What about the daughter?"

"The aid workers lost track of her. You have to understand that these camps are fairly chaotic. Too many people, not enough space. Many refugees are undocumented. Some are fleeing the authorities back home. And there's so much disease and malnutrition, not to mention petty thievery and sexual assault. It's a wonder so many of them do survive. In all likelihood the daughter died soon after her mother. They had several bad outbreaks of cholera at that camp."

Dani leaned forward and reached into his briefcase again. He pulled out a small leather book. Its brown cover was worn and stained.

"In 2005 an Ethiopian refugee newly arrived at the camp found this buried in the dirt. It's the mother's diary. The UN authorities sent it to the Jewish Agency, and they passed it on to us. My predecessor made little effort to follow up. But the caseworker who worked the case is still at JEJI. She recently brought it to my attention, hoping that I'd reactivate the search for the missing daughter. When I recently reviewed the file, I discovered the diary. I've been reading through it the past few days."

He handed the small journal to Maya, who eagerly opened to the first page. Her eyes swam as they encountered the eddying squiggles of the Amharic alphabet.

Dani laughed.

"Makes Hebrew look pretty simple, doesn't it?"

Maya handed the book back to him, then took a sip of her wine. Her mouth tingled with pleasure. It was a surprisingly good pinot grigio. The man knew his wine.

"The writer mentions Gultosh right at the beginning," he said. "It seems like a few families from this village left together. The eldest son of one of the families volunteered to serve as their guide. He said he knew the way to the Sudanese border, that he could get them there safely."

"But he didn't, did he?"

"No. But not because of the usual dangers that Jewish refugees faced—hunger and thirst, bandits, venomous snakes, jackals. No, their so-called guide betrayed them. A few days out, he stole all their food and water and took whatever valuables they'd brought with them. Then he left them there to die. And disappeared without a trace."

"Does she mention his name?"

Dani nodded.

"Negasi. But no last name."

Maya leapt to her feet, fists clenched by her sides. The skin of her arms shivered with goosebumps. She recognized the telltale *frisson* that told her she was on the right track in her investigation. Somehow this woman's story was tied to her murder case. But how? Who was Negasi? And what connection did he have to Moshe Aklilu?

"What else does she say about Gultosh? Does Moshe Aklilu's name come up?"

Dani shook his head.

"I've read through the whole diary. Twice. There's no mention of Moshe Aklilu. And there's no further mention of Negasi once he abandoned the group."

Maya's shoulders sank. Not much of a lead to go on.

"Will you help me look for her, Dani? The daughter. She'd be, what, twenty-nine by now."

Dani took a sip of his wine and carefully set his glass back down on the table.

"Twenty-five years is a long time. What are the chances of finding her, especially if she's changed her name or gotten married?"

"But will you at least give it a shot? I really could use your help."

Dani looked at her. His black eyes shone in the muted light of the table lamp.

Maya's mind, already hazy from the wine, drifted. She thought she saw him grin and nod his head, but she couldn't be sure.

41

SUDDENLY LOUD RAP MUSIC EXPLODED over their heads. On the low wooden table, the two empty wine glasses began to vibrate and judder. The apartment's large front window rattled in its casement. Maya covered her ears with her hands and squeezed her eyes shut.

Dani laughed.

"My upstairs neighbors. Momo and Stav. Huge fans of rap, hip-hop, ska, reggae, and most recently, K-Pop boy bands. Just the other day Momo boasted to me that he'd paid sixty thousand shekels for a ten-thousand-watt amplifier and an array of subwoofers. Whatever they are." He grinned. "The police have warned him several times to keep the noise down. He's setting off car alarms on the street."

"How can you stand it?"

Maya found herself yelling, even though Dani was seated only a few feet away.

Dani pointed to a thin shelf suspended under the coffee table. On it sat a small stack of cork coasters in a dark wooden frame, several magazines, a box of tissues, and a pair of sound-blocking headphones.

"I spend most of my evenings swaddled in those." Dani grinned. "But of course, they're useless when I have company. But that happens so rarely..."

Then, just as suddenly as the music had erupted, it stopped. Or rather, it was replaced by something slow and jazzy, playing so softly that Maya first thought they'd shut the music off. Then she heard a loud thump, and shortly after that, the creaking of bedsprings. A man's voice began to rumble and bark, emitting animal noises. She could hear him panting, almost smell his sweat.

C'mon baby yes oh baby that's it don' hold back on me c'mon yes c'mon bitch oh baby that's right!

She glanced quickly over at Dani, whose eyes were fixed on the bare floor. His breathing had become rapid and shallow. A warm flush suffused his ruddy cheeks. She looked away.

Now the woman's voice joined the man's. But her words followed a different script. Maya heard in her voice pain and rage. And something else. Humiliation. The woman's choked words trembled with tears.

Stop Momo please you're hurting me I told you I don't like when you do that no more please baby I can't stand no more I'm beggin' you!

Dani sprang up from the couch and walked into the kitchen area. He grabbed a glass from one of the cabinets and filled it from the tap. He gulped the water down and pitched the empty glass into the sink. The thick glass clanked against the white porcelain but did not shatter. He then leaned over the sink and bent his head. He started gagging but Maya couldn't move to go to him. She felt the gorge rising into her own throat, cutting off her air.

From the apartment above came the sound of an open palm slapping skin. The sound repeated. And repeated. The woman cried out, but the man continued to hit her. She began to sob, loud gulps of air followed by shrill wails. One last slap, and she fell silent. Heavy footfalls retreated into another room. Soft weeping continued overhead, followed by sniffling. Then all sound stopped.

But the music kept playing. A sensuous cascade of jazz rained down upon their heads.

Dani remained at the sink, his back toward Maya. She stared at him, waiting for him to turn around. Suddenly she expelled a loud whoosh of air. How long had she been holding her breath?

Dani pivoted on his bare feet. His face was hard to read. Embarrassed? Shocked? Aroused? His features were void of all expression. She could feel her own face on fire.

"I'm so sorry, Maya."

She shook her head and tried to smile, but her lips were frozen.

"Not your fault, obviously." She took a deep breath. "How often does—" Her green eyes swooped up toward the ceiling, "—*that* happen?"

"When they first moved in about six months ago, *that* never happened." He giggled, then looked abashed. "Well, they did make plenty of noise when, you know, they opened up the sofa bed. But him hitting her? Never."

He shuddered. He turned back around, retrieved the glass from the sink, filled it up again, and drank the water down in two swigs. He held the empty glass out to her. She shook her head.

"Something must have happened recently. Momo has become much rougher with her. I hear her crying when he's not home. Maybe he lost his job. He's a security guard at the mall. I'm thinking I might have to call the cops before he really hurts her."

A memory flashed into her mind.

One night in the living room. Rafi, drunker than usual, yanking her arm as she walked away from him. They were having one of their usual fights about Vered. Rafi was feeding her too much junk food. He countered that she was being overprotective, a helicopter Mom. He was a brute! She was a bitch! And on it went. Furious she finally marched over to their daughter, who was in tears, green slime leaking from her nose, and grabbed the bag of candy Rafi had just bought her at the playground. He grabbed it back and shoved it into his daughter's bony chest. With her open palm, Vered smacked the paper bag toward the floor. Colored jellybeans flew everywhere. Rafi yelled at Vered to stop crying like a baby. Maya yelled at him to leave her alone. Rafi slapped Maya across the cheek. Vered yelled at both of them to stop fighting. A glass vase flew at the wall. Rafi stormed out of the house. Vered ran to her room, slamming the door. Maya ran after her, not realizing she was barefoot. A shard of glass pierced the tender sole of her foot. She yowled in pain. In frustration. In rage. In sorrow.

She was not aware that she had begun to cry. Dani came over to her and sat down beside her. With his hand, he gently brushed the tears from her cheeks.

"Sorry," she said. "Didn't mean to get so emotional."

"Want to talk about it?"

"I'll take that glass of water now."

He brought her the water and sat back down. This time his thigh brushed up against hers. She felt the rough scuff of denim as his jeans rubbed against hers.

"Your noisy neighbors triggered a bad memory," she said. "About my ex. He was like Momo. Often abusive."

"But you got away from him, didn't you? He's no longer hurting you."

Should she tell him about the nightmares, the occasional panic attacks, the awkward questions her six-year-old daughter had begun asking her? The unpleasant visits with Vered at the prison where Rafi was serving a sentence for his white-collar crimes?

Dani noted her hesitation and placed his hand lightly on her arm.

"You don't have to tell me anything, Maya. We don't know each other very well."

Her breathing slowly returned to its normal, steady rhythm. She was enjoying the touch of his fingers, his soft voice, the deep calm pooling in his eyes. She didn't want to ruin things by bringing in the toxicity of her disastrous marriage. Or her recent washout with Hillel Stone.

Dani began stroking the skin of her forearm, sending sparks of energy shooting through her veins. Her whole body began to shiver and pulse. And then she became aware of the roughness of his hand. The burned palm.

"Do you mind if I ask you a personal question?"

Dani smiled. Her body tingled with pleasure. His smile thrilled her. She loved looking at those brilliant white teeth shining against his smooth, dark skin.

"I think I owe you one. Ask away!"

She placed her hand gently upon his and drew it away from her arm. Then she turned the left hand over so that the pink palm faced up. The skin was like a scorched landscape, riddled with craters and angry red lines. Most of the normal tracery found on people's palms—a lifeline, a love line, a fate line—were obliterated by the scars.

"How did *this* happen?"

Dani tried to ball his fingers into a fist, but Maya gently peeled them open.

"My father was a silversmith back in Ethiopia. He used to make the most elegant jewelry and knives as well as sacred vessels for churches, mosques, and synagogues. Once, when I very young, maybe three or four, I watched him shaping a *qāčel*, a kind of gong used in Ethiopian churches. It was so beautiful. The silver glowed brightly in the hot flames. Foolishly, I tried to snatch it out of the fire with my hand. The molten metal burned my palm. It's one lesson I'll never forget."

With the fingers of her other hand, Maya stroked the rough surface of the scarred skin. In some places it was smooth; in others, hard and knobby. Dani curled his fingers around hers and squeezed. She squeezed back.

"I think I'd like to try your mother's tej now," she said.

They both laughed. Maya felt the muscles of her back and shoulders relax. She leaned back against the stiff cushion, her hand still wrapped in Dani's long fingers. Slowly he opened his hand, and she withdrew her fingers from his grasp.

The tej was sweet and even more potent than what she'd drunk at the cultural center. It went straight to her head, giving her the pleasant sensation of floating up toward the ceiling. Her body relaxed even more, and then she felt Dani's warm lips on her mouth. Was it the drink or his lips that set her on fire? She felt his arms encircling her upper body, smelled his fragrant aftershave. It smelled like something just harvested from a green field. Her body, so much smaller than his, rose up to meet his smooth chest. Her hands grazed the tight coils of his black hair. She tasted the honey of the tej, the honey of his mouth, the heat of his father's forge.

Then, suddenly, she pulled herself back.

"I can't, Dani! I'm sorry, but I just can't."

She began to cry. She turned her face away, felt her spine curl up like a drooping plant. Her head sank down into her hands.

"What's the matter, Maya? Is it something I did?"

She shook her head. Her sobs deepened, wracking her thin frame.

"It's been three years already!" She banged her fist on the low table. "Three years! And I still can't let myself feel. I don't know what it is. Maybe there's something wrong with me."

She felt his hand on her head, stroking her hair, then her cheek. And then he drew his hand away.

"Don't pull away! Please put your hand back where it was. Please don't give up on me!"

She sat up and looked into Dani's face. His dark eyes were moist. His mouth, the full lips closed in a half-smile, was sad.

"So, I guess we've both been burned, eh?"

His grin broadened.

She tried to smile, but the tears came again. And again, he wiped them away.

"I think I should head home now," she said. "I left my daughter with a neighbor."

Dani leaned over and kissed her lightly on the cheek.

"I'm not giving up on you, Maya. Or on us. I've got my own issues with letting my feelings out. Next time it'll be me on the hot seat, okay?"

She leaned forward and pulled a tissue out of the box under the table. She blew her nose, then pressed the crumpled tissue into a pocket of her jeans.

"Scout's honor?"

Dani raised his left hand, the scarred palm facing her.

"Scout's honor!"

She stood up and headed toward the front door. Upstairs a door slammed. Moments later loud, raucous music boomed above them like thunder, shaking Dani's windows and rattling the two glasses on the table.

Maya gazed up at the ceiling, which had begun vibrating in a seismic beat, keeping time with the music. She blew Dani a kiss, opened the door, and walked out into the night.

DAY 8

Monday

42

Inspector Sarit Levine had been summoned to some pretty bizarre crime scenes in her thirteen years on the force—a kangaroo sanctuary, a noodle factory, a sewage treatment plant—but never before had she found herself investigating a murder at a children's playground. And she could tell that she wasn't the only one here unsettled by the site. The Medical Examiner, Dr. Selgundo, kept glancing uneasily at the grinning green and yellow metal animals poised nearby on giant coiled springs, probably imagining his own grandchildren rocking on them. And Dahlia, the young female cop who had driven her here when Golyat failed to report to work this morning, seemed close to tears. Sarit knew that Dahlia's three-year-old son had recently broken his arm falling off the monkey bars at their neighborhood playground. Was she visualizing his little body lying broken at the base of the tubular slide in place of the full-grown body that everyone was gazing down at?

Sarit tapped her foot impatiently on the rubber turf as she waited for Dr. Selgundo to finish his preliminary evaluation of the body. Avraham always took his time at a murder scene. And if he felt pressured by the detectives or the press, he seemed to proceed even more punctiliously than usual. But that's why he was the most respected ME in the country. Courts rarely overturned his findings.

"No apparent wounds on the back of the victim's body," continued Selgundo, turning toward the recorder. "No bloodstains on the clothes or exposed skin."

Given the victim's dark skin and the location of the murder site in Mexico Park, Sarit surmised that the victim was probably

Ethiopian. But his bronze complexion seemed unusually light for an Ethiopian. And his hair was the color of desert sand and smooth rather than kinky. He seemed young, judging by the stone-washed jeans, sleeveless denim vest, and drop tail T-shirt hanging below the vest's hem. Probably when Selgundo rolled him over, the shirt would advertise an American rock band or flaunt an obscene slogan.

Her eyes traveled down to the young man's feet. The right foot was clad in a sandal made of tooled leather, unscuffed. High-end European. The other foot was bare, the sandal gone AWOL. The bare sole of the unshod foot was soft and pink. Clearly not a manual laborer. Doubtless just some foolish rich kid, run afoul of a gang or the hapless victim of thieves. Mexico Park could be a danger-ous place, especially at night, which was probably when the murder had occurred.

"Have you checked his pockets, Avraham? Wallet, ID, cash, credit cards?"

Selgundo nodded.

"All gone. No cellphone, either."

"Probably refused to give them what they demanded. The fool. Paid for it with his life."

Selgundo made no response. He never weighed in on possible motives for a homicide, certainly not at the crime scene. He restricted himself to observing, recording evidence, taking notes and photo-graphs. He left speculation to the detectives.

"I'm going to turn him over now."

The ME spoke into a small recorder, which sat on the black, hard-shelled examination case he brought to all his crime scenes.

Sarit gasped when Selgundo rolled over the corpse, exposing the victim's face.

It was Elvis Aklilu!

The skin of his handsome face, half-hidden by a wave of brillian-tined hair flopping over his forehead, was patterned like a Berber rug.

He'd probably been lying face-down for hours on the knobby rubber surface of the playground. His eyes were closed. His thin lips hung slightly open, revealing small, perfectly aligned teeth.

The Medical Examiner bent down to get a closer look at Elvis's chest. The two halves of his denim vest lay open, exposing a broad band of white cotton. An angry slash ran down the shirt like a streak of lightning. Whatever image or words were imprinted on the shirt were too bloody to make out.

"We'll have to wait until I do a full autopsy," he said, looking up at Sarit, who stood peering over his right shoulder, "but my initial impression is that the wound was made by the same weapon that killed the other two victims. A long, curved, double-bladed knife."

With his forefinger he beckoned Sarit to come closer.

"See the jagged edges on both ends of the stab wound."

Sarit bent down, noting that the dried blood looked almost black when viewed against the murdered man's light brown skin.

Gently he placed both his hands under Elvis's head and turned it from side to side.

"No visible blunt force trauma to the skull. No ligatures on the neck or hands."

He laid the head back down. Then he reached into his case for a tongue depressor. Carefully he pried the teeth apart with the flat wooden paddle, then peered into the black cavity of Elvis's mouth. He bent closer until one of his eyes almost rested on the bloodless lips. Then he pulled back and took a deep breath. With his index and middle finger, he reached inside and carefully drew out a small piece of paper. He wiped it clean of saliva, then held it up by one corner.

"Inside the deceased's mouth I have found a small rectangular piece of stiff paper—precise measurements and composition of the paper to follow." He squinted at the black squiggles of writing covering the top and bottom thirds of the paper scrap. "Possibly Amharic or Ge'ez, but I will need to verify that with an expert. Between the lines of script is a drawing in black, red, and yellow ink. Looks like some sort of animal."

"A hyena," muttered Sarit. Selgundo eyed her curiously. "Non-Jews in Ethiopia thought the Beta Israel could transform themselves into hyenas at night and prey on them."

"Ah, yes, like the bloody image carved into that poor young woman's forehead." Selgundo shuddered. "Barbaric."

Sarit held out her hand, palm up.

"Hand it over, Avraham. That paper is vital evidence."

The sun had come up by now, bursting through low, gray clouds. Its pale autumnal glow brightened the red, yellow, green, and blue surfaces of the elaborate climbing apparatus that dominated the playground area. Sarit imagined children clambering over its slides, ramps, and bars, whispering to each other in mock horror about the man who'd been murdered here. Most children found such creepiness tantalizingly delicious.

The ME shook his head.

"You know I can't do that, Sarit. Protocol. I need to go back to the lab and log everything I found on the corpse and then do some tests to find out what I can about them. There might be fingerprints or trace residue that will prove invaluable to your investigation."

Sarit shrugged and let her arms drop to her sides. The ME was right, of course. She'd just have to stay on him to make sure he got the results to her as fast as possible. She had no doubt this was the same killer.

She turned and walked over to the metal perimeter fence surrounding the park. For the first time in months, she craved a cigarette. She stamped her foot on the ground, irritated that the playground's rubber surface deadened the sound of her frustration.

Damn it! Elvis Aklilu had been her prime suspect. She'd had it all figured out. Titi and Hagar had stumbled upon his drug smuggling operation and threatened to report him to the police. He'd had no choice but to silence them. Or maybe he had double-crossed his supplier, one of the black gangs running drugs in Israel's coastal cities. They'd killed the Aklilu women as payback. Golyat had agreed with her that this theory made the most sense. Maybe that's why he'd failed to show up this morning. He was tracking down leads.

But she should call him and let him know he was chasing his tail. She had been wrong. Elvis was not the killer. He had joined his sister and stepmother as victim. What a waste! All of them cut down in their prime.

That left only Moshe and Shulamit as credible suspects. Each certainly had ample opportunity to get to the victims. All three of them lived under their roof.

And as Ethiopian immigrants, they would know all about billawas. Hadn't Sarit seen all sorts of folk objects decorating Moshe's office at the Knesset? How hard would it be for him to lay his hands on a ritual knife, claiming it was for his personal collection? Or for his shrewd daughter-in-law to filch it?

The key piece that was still missing was motive. Why would Moshe or Shulamit murder members of their own family? What would each of them gain by it? Were these the actions of a madman or of a calculating killer?

The most plausible motive, which pointed to Moshe as the likelier suspect, had to be fear of exposure. As the most prominent Ethiopian Jew in Israel—the first and only Ethiopian member of the Israeli parliament and a highly successful businessman—Moshe Aklilu had a lot to lose. He could not afford a public scandal. His unblemished reputation was the collateral that anchored his business and political empires. If he was exposed as a fraud and a grifter, a sex trafficker or worse, he stood to lose everything.

That was motive enough for murder.

But what did Shulamit have to gain by murdering her husband, her sister-in-law, and Moshe's young wife? An inheritance? Not as long as Moshe was still alive. And even with Moshe dead, Bekeli, as a blood relative, was the logical heir. No, this line of reasoning was too far-fetched. Moshe was now her prime suspect.

Sarit spun around on her heels and marched back to the corpse, which was already zipped up in a black body bag.

"Okay, Avraham, I'm done here. Heading back to the station."

She motioned to Dahlia, who stood next to the seesaw, staring down at the ground.

"Get back to me as soon as you do the post. It's high time we stopped this *mamzer*."

Selgundo muttered something under his breath but did not look up. Methodically he returned his tools to their proper place inside his examination case.

Sarit strode briskly toward her car. She was insensible to the happy sounds of children playing in another area of the park.

You're done, Moshe. You've had your run. Should have stayed in Ethiopia with the hyenas.

Chuckling, Sarit yanked open the passenger door and slid into the passenger seat. She could already envision the stunned expression on Moshe Aklilu's face when she slapped the handcuffs on. She was still chortling when Dahlia slipped into the driver's seat and started the engine. The young woman's face was ashen. She didn't ask Sarit what was so funny.

43

SHULAMIT WAS JUST FINISHING BREAKFAST when the doorbell rang. She looked down at her Apple Watch. Not even 8:30. Who would pay a condolence call this early in the morning? And ring the doorbell! No doubt one of Moshe's clueless white friends.

They know so little about us, show so little respect for our dead. And they call us primitive!

Then she heard the hurried shuffling of the old barya, rushing to answer the door.

Moments later came the old woman's shriek, followed by a series of ear-piercing wails.

She ran toward the front hall. Given the barya's alarm, Shulamit expected to see a masked gunman or a blood-covered apparition looming in the doorway. Instead, she found two uniformed policemen, standing stiffly at the top of the stone stairs, dumbfounded. The younger cop carried a large glossy photograph of a faded sleeveless denim vest, its hems and seams frayed. Shulamit immediately recognized the embroidered patches sewn on the vest's two front pockets. Mr. Natural and Juggalo.

Thrusting one wrinkled black finger at the photo, the old housemaid began tearing at her matted pelt of gray hair. The black *netela* on her head tumbled to her shoulders. Her wizened face contorted in grief. Her wailing intensified.

Shulamit addressed her in Amharic, making no effort to disguise her irritation.

"What is it, you old fool? Why are you carrying on like this?"

"Aiiiee, mistress! Look how they come to tell us he's dead. So improper! They will surely bring down a curse upon this house."

She began tearing at her wrinkled cheeks with dirty fingernails. Dark blood oozed from the scratches.

Shulamit glowered at her.

"Surely we are cursed already!"

She turned her back on the old woman and faced the policemen.

"So, what is it that you have come to tell me?"

The older policeman, short and pudgy with ears that stood out from his head like cup handles, cleared his throat.

"Are you the wife of Gidon Aklilu?"

She nodded. The police always used Elvis's formal name when he got into trouble.

The cop glanced down at the piece of paper trembling in his hand and began reading in a toneless voice.

"We regret to inform you that your husband's body was found earlier this morning in Mexico Park in Kiryat Menachem. We are treating his death as a homicide. We are sorry for your loss."

As if she understood the man's Hebrew words, the old maid threw her skinny arms up toward the high ceiling and keened so loudly that Shulamit had to cover her ears with her hands. She looked at the two policemen. They shrugged their shoulders, their eyes opaque.

The younger cop handed her the photo. It was only then that she noticed the rust-colored bloodstains.

For the next few moments Shulamit stood like a statue, mute, staring at the two policemen as if they were speaking a foreign language. Behind her the old maid continued to wail, the volume of her keening subsiding as her strength ebbed.

Shulamit took a few steps back into the dark hallway. She felt embarrassed to still be dressed in her terrycloth robe, with no makeup and barefoot, but they shouldn't have come so early. At least her hair was no longer in curlers.

"What? Elvis—dead? Murdered, you say? Not possible!"

"I know it's a shock, ma'am. Why don't we go inside? You should drink some water, sit down."

Mechanically, she turned and led them into the white living room. As she passed the elder housemaid, she hissed into the old woman's ear in Amharic.

"You're embarrassing me! Go to your room and compose yourself."

"But these men are strangers! Such terrible news should be brought by a suitable messenger!"

With her fingers wriggling in the air, the old barya limped off and soon disappeared into the bowels of the large house.

When she and the policemen were seated on the white couches, across from each other, Shulamit said, "You must forgive the old woman. She's never adjusted to Israeli ways."

Both men smiled uneasily, obviously eager to leave.

"I would offer you coffee," she said, "but we are just at the beginning of *Sevat Ken*."

The men's smiles vanished. They turned their palms toward her, bewildered.

She shook her head, cleared her throat. But she made no effort to relieve their discomfort.

"You call it *shiva*. We don't serve coffee for the first two days. We're mourning two others dead."

They sat together in silence. Shulamit was just as eager for them to leave as they were to escape. She let them squirm for a long minute. Then she looked down at her watch.

"Guests will be arriving soon to offer their condolences. You don't need to stay any longer. I'll have plenty of company."

The two men sprang up. Unsure what to do with their hands, they let them dangle at their sides. She nodded to them. They turned and walked to the door, which had remained open all this time. In a few moments, they were gone. The heavy door closed softly behind them.

Shulamit waited a few minutes. Then she stood up and made her way to her father-in-law's office, her bare feet making no sound on the cool terracotta tiles. She knocked softly, although she knew that Moshe never worked here in the early morning. In all likelihood, he was still asleep, exhausted after yesterday's long day of consolation.

She opened the wooden door, stepped inside, then closed the door gently behind her.

Moshe's imposing mahogany desk was uncluttered as usual, except for the green leather blotter and his precious fountain pen. She walked lightly across the plush carpet and sat down in the large leather desk chair. The seat cushion sighed lightly from her weight.

She began with the top center drawer. As she expected, it was unlocked. He never locked his desk when he was at home, assuming that none of them would dare come into his office while he was in the house. With both hands she began riffling through the jumble of stationery items in the narrow drawer. Not that she knew precisely what she was looking for. She only hoped she'd find something here from Moshe's past that would bear witness to his guilt.

Having found nothing of interest in the center drawer, she moved on to the two drawers on the right. Inside each she found hanging files and ruled ledgers. At the back of the bottom drawer, she found an expensive bottle of *araqe*. She leafed through a few of the manila folders, but they were all related to his businesses. And none of them concerned anything that happened before 1996.

She then turned to the two drawers on the left. The top drawer had more files and ledgers. But the bottom drawer finally rewarded her efforts. It was filled with all sorts of handicrafts from Ethiopia: amulets made of paper, tin, and silver; a beautiful woven *netela*; an engraved silver wine cup; a small, glazed incense pot; bracelets and necklaces made of polished tagua nuts.

And a doll with yellow corn silk hair and real bone buttons. Her beloved Gudit!

Gently Shulamit lifted the doll out of the drawer and clutched it to her chest. Then she laid it down on the soft carpet under the desk and continued her search.

At the very bottom of the drawer, she found a silver hair clasp, shaped like a bird. A giant kingfisher. The silversmith had captured the graceful bird in flight, its fanlike wings and tail banded in alternating rows of black patches and white dots. She noted the realistic details—the diagonal stripe on the bird's neck, the small eye-dot, and the long, pointed bill. The artist had managed to convey the bird's various colors through indentation and delicate lines. She could picture the clasp binding the long hair of the woman for whom it had been made. Her mother. Her father had assured his young daughter that he would never make another like it. It had been his grand masterpiece. Seeing her mother's name, *Kidist*, engraved on the back side of the hair clasp confirmed that it had once been hers. She gently ran the soft pad of her index finger over the clasp, feeling its subtle contours. Then she slipped it into the pocket of her terrycloth robe.

Carefully, she put everything but the doll and the hair clasp back into the bottom drawer, trying to shape the pile so that it resembled the way she'd found it when she'd opened the drawer. It was hard to make up for the missing bulk of the doll, but she worked at it until she was satisfied. She would keep Gudit and the silver clasp hidden in her bedroom among her things. She would need them later. As proof.

44

GAZA STREET WAS QUIET WHEN Maya arrived. Whoever was going to work had already left. She found a parking space close to her parents' apartment building, locked the steering wheel with the club, and rushed into the lobby, waving to the old Algerian receptionist as she headed toward the elevator. He motioned for her to sign in at the desk. She blew him a kiss and pointed toward her watch. The old man blushed, then looked down at the register, pretending to read through the list of visitors. Without looking up, he waved her in.

When she reached her parents' door, she began rooting around in her large shoulder bag, looking for her keys, but she quickly gave up. She pounded on their door, not stopping until her mother opened it moments later.

"Sha! You'll wake the neighbors. Some of them sleep late. Most of us who live here are retired, remember."

With her hand, Maya brushed her mother aside and ran through the living room toward what they all now referred to as "Vered's room." Her daughter lay still on the single bed, her eyes closed. She was still dressed in her flamingo pajamas. Her face was flushed, her breathing shallow.

"How long has she been like this?"

Camille opened her mouth to reprove her daughter but stopped herself. Maya's breathing, too, was irregular, rapid, not slow like Vered's, and her color was just as high. She drew close to her daughter and placed a hand gently on the girl's thin shoulder.

"I told you on the phone, Maya," her mother said. "I came in this morning to see if she was awake and found her like this. She keeps complaining that her head hurts like someone's hitting it with a hammer. And she says that the light's funny when she opens her eyes."

Maya walked over to the bed and sat down beside her daughter's slight form. She placed her palm on Vered's forehead and was relieved to find that it was cool. But the six-year-old's freckled cheeks still glowed with fever. She placed two fingers on her daughter's delicate wrist and felt the pulse, unsteady and slow.

"Vered, *motek*, tell Ima what's wrong."

The young girl groaned.

"My head, my head!"

Vered tried to raise one hand toward her forehead but failed to muster enough strength. The hand flopped back down on the quilt and lay still.

"Can you open your eyes? Please, try to look at me!"

Maya was trying hard to keep the hysteria out of her voice, but she heard the quaver in her words. She took a few deep breaths to calm herself.

"Can't, Ima. The light hurts too much."

Maya nodded toward her mother, who walked over to the switch near the door and flicked off the overhead light. Maya reached over her daughter's body and pulled the cord to lower the blinds over the window. The room was now so dark she could no longer see Vered's face or make out the auburn color of her hair, almost a match to her own. In a few seconds, her eyes adjusted to the dim light.

Her mobile began to buzz. Maya fished it out of her pocket and glanced down at the screen. Sarit. She disconnected the call and shoved the phone back into her pocket.

"Did you hit your head on something? Or strain your eyes reading without a proper light?"

Vered shook her head, then yelped in pain.

"Could it be something you ate or drank?"

Camille snorted.

"There's nothing wrong with the meals I feed her! Last night we had one of her favorites—couscous with oranges."

"Maybe you made it too spicy for—"

"There's no doubt in my mind that my granddaughter gets her taste buds from *my* side of the family! The hotter, the better. She doesn't complain about my cooking like you do."

"Don't start with me, Ima." Maya blew out an exasperated breath. "I'm only trying to help."

Camille thrust her large nose into the air and sniffed. Then she plumped up one side of her steeple of blond hair with her hand and looked over at Maya.

"I talked to her pediatrician while you were driving over. She suggested I give her strong tea. Didn't help at all. I just sent Abba to the pharmacy to pick up the prescription the doctor ordered."

"Ima..."

In a feeble voice Vered mumbled a few words, but Maya couldn't make them out. She lowered her head so that her ear almost touched her daughter's pink lips.

"Try again, *havivati*. I'm listening."

"She...gave me...cake."

Vered's words were barely audible. Maya's eyes filled with tears. She fought them back. She sat up and stroked her daughter's russet curls with her hand.

"I did no such thing!" Camille stood, fleshy arms akimbo, glaring at her granddaughter. "I don't believe in serving dessert except on Shabbat and holidays. And on special occasions."

Vered shook her head. Maya again bent down to hear her daughter's whispered words.

"Not Jeddah. Ethiopian woman." *Etiopit.*

Camille's large mouth gaped like a bottomless chasm. She opened her eyes wide, then narrowed them to glower at her daughter.

"I warned you about that neighbor of yours, Maya. That woman is a witch! How could you trust her with your only child? She's poisoned her or cast a spell over her. That's what she probably did to her own baby to get rid of her. You should report her immediately to the authorities. She shouldn't be allowed anywhere near innocent children!"

Maya felt all her strength drain from her limbs. She sagged down on the narrow bed. What was she supposed to do? Give up her career, her whole life, to care for her child? It was hard enough being a single mother without having Camille blame her every time something went wrong. Vered would be okay. Wouldn't she? It was just a very bad headache. Maya herself had periodic migraines that knocked her flat. Maybe it was genetic. Or had she become too distracted by Dani to notice what was going on with Vered? Had she put her own daughter at risk because of her feelings for this new man in her life? Was she in fact the bad mother that Camille accused her of being?

Her mobile buzzed again. Another call from Sarit. Again, she jabbed the red "End Call" button and repocketed the phone.

Vered groaned and mumbled a few words. Maya bent down to hear her.

"Am I gonna...die, Ima? Oh, the pain! Make it stop!"

The door opened, and Moti walked in, carrying a small white paper bag. Maya ran to him, snatched the bag from his hand, and headed for the kitchen. Moments later she returned with a glass of water. In her other hand she held a small clear plastic bottle of pills. She sat on the bed and began fumbling with the child-proof cap, cursing under her breath. The white lid suddenly popped off, releasing a spray of little blue pills onto the bed. She picked up one of them and brought it close to Vered's mouth.

"Here, *motek*, swallow this. It'll make you feel better. I promise."

Placing her palm under her daughter's head, Maya gently raised up Vered a few inches and placed the blue pill on her tongue. Then she brought the glass of water to her lips and tilted it. Vered gulped a few sips and coughed. It took her a few more tries to get the pill to slide down her throat. Maya then lowered her daughter's head. It barely made a dent in the pillow.

Maya stood up and marched resolutely out of the tiny room toward the front door. Camille spun around on her pink slippers and followed her.

"Make sure you give her a pill every four hours," Maya said, turning around. "And keep her well hydrated. Maybe you should try strong tea again, like the doctor suggested."

Camille smiled. Maya immediately recognized this as one of her mother's rare smiles that revealed her genuine affection for her elder daughter. Maya pretended not to notice. Camille's mouth soon drooped back into its more customary profile, downturned at the ends to indicate only provisional contentment.

"I promise I'll call you if there's any change," Camille said. "Where are you off to now?"

"To talk to my neighbor Fewesi. I need to get to the bottom of this." She hesitated, her hand on the brass knob. "And I have an appointment at headquarters with a CI. I should be back no later than five."

"She needs you, Maya. Now more than ever. Don't disappoint her."

Maya opened the door and entered the hallway. She didn't say goodbye to her mother before the door swept shut.

45

BEFORE SHE WENT NEXT DOOR to speak to Fewesi, Maya decided to grab something to eat. When her mother had called about Vered early this morning, she'd been too upset to think about eating breakfast. Now she was ravenous. She unlocked her front door cautiously, expecting the cat to make a break for freedom as it always did. She'd forgotten to feed it before leaving this morning, so it would be mad as well as stir-crazy.

But Bezoona didn't greet her when she opened the door. In fact, the black cat was nowhere to be seen. She began looking for her in all the usual places—curled up on the beat-up orange loveseat in the living room or basking on the sunny windowsill at the back of the large front room or camped out on Vered's bed. No Bezoona. Maybe she was using the litter box in the bathroom. And that's where she found the cat, stretched out on the black-and-white checkerboard tiles in the tiny bathroom, looking dead. Not even her black tail was twitching.

She crouched down and stroked the top of the cat's soft head with her finger. No throaty purr in response. She picked her up and cradled her in her arms. She was glad to find that the sleek body felt soft and supple. She placed her finger on the cat's throat and felt the whisper of a pulse. Still alive, thank God! Vered would be devastated if her beloved Bezoona died.

She took out her phone and looked up the number of the vet who lived in East Talpiyot, about ten minutes away. She left a message with the front desk for the doctor to call back immediately, that their cat was near death.

As soon as she hung up, her cellphone buzzed. But it wasn't the vet. It was Sarit again. She let it ring until the call went to voicemail. She shoved the phone back into her pocket without listening to the message.

While she waited for the vet's call, she wolfed down some Bulgarian cheese on a piece of bread with butter and some slices of cucumber and made herself a cup of Nescafe. She was still hungry, so she cut up a tomato and washed it down with some mango juice.

Her mobile rang as she was washing up her dishes.

"You say your cat's 'near death'? And exactly how did you reach this conclusion, Giveret?"

The vet's words were clipped. Normally, she was patient and sympathetic with her clients and their animals, but today she sounded annoyed. Well, it just couldn't be helped. Maya didn't have time to bring the cat into the office today, not with Vered so sick and her murder investigation stalled, spinning its wheels.

"It's not rocket science!"

She knew she shouldn't have snapped at the doctor. The vet was doing Maya a favor by treating the animal over the phone.

"She's not moving," Maya said, her voice calmer. "She's hardly breathing. I could barely find a pulse."

"Is her nose wet?"

Maya huffed out a gust of air, then walked back into the bathroom, bent down, and felt the nubby tip of the cat's nose with her fingertip. It was bone-dry. She told the vet.

"OK, a few more questions. Has she been throwing up?"

Maya looked around and spotted a coagulated pool of beige-colored vomit under the sink. She told the vet.

"One final question. Take a look at her paws. Do you see anything unusual adhering to the pads of her feet?"

How do I know what's usual or unusual for a cat to step in?

Maya kneeled down on the hard tile floor and carefully lifted up the cat's feet, one at a time. On two of the soft gray cushions of skin, she found what looked like food crumbs. They could be from food she'd prepared a day ago, or a month ago. She wasn't a very conscientious housekeeper. How was she supposed to know where the food came from? She pinched one of the crumbs and rubbed it between her fingers. It crumbled like a cookie. Or cake! She brought the yellowy powder close to her nose. She smelled cinnamon, cardamom, honey, and something that reminded Maya of the gooey syrup Americans poured on their pancakes. The same spices that she'd smelled in Fewesi's coffee cake. She told the vet.

"I doubt whether homemade cake could poison your cat. But I can't be sure until I examine her in my office. You'll have to bring her in. And make sure to bring some of the crumbs too."

Irritated, Maya told the vet she'd call in a day or two to make an appointment if the cat didn't get better. Then she abruptly hung up. She didn't have time to drive to East Talpiyot and wait for an hour until the vet squeezed her in. Bezoona would just have to take her chances.

***

Five minutes later Maya stood outside Fewesi's door. She rapped lightly with her knuckles, resisting the urge to pound on the door. Fewesi came to the door dressed in a long white caftan, her head wrapped loosely in a colored shawl.

"Maya! So happy see you. I make *Bunna* now. Come in and share coffee wif me."

"That's not why I'm here, Fewesi."

Maya had given up trying to control her anger. Her voice was raw, accusatory.

She pushed past the young Ethiopian woman and walked into the kitchen area located at one end of the large central room. She stood there, arms planted on her hips, scanning the objects lining the wooden counter. Her nostrils filled with the tantalizing aroma of fresh roasted coffee beans and the heady fragrance of incense. She quickly shut them out of her consciousness. She replaced them with the image of poor Vered, lying prostrate on her narrow bed, in pain, her beautiful green eyes pressed shut.

"What, Maya? What wrong?"

"Did you give Vered cake to eat last night?"

Fewesi smiled.

"Not cake. Cookies. We bake together after you leave. Cookies in shape of new moon. Very sweet. I teach you."

"What did you put in them?"

Fewesi's smile broadened. She took Maya's hand and led her closer to the wooden counter. Lined up against the wall of white tiles were many colored bottles of spices and herbs, a few small clay pots with lids, and some paper bags. One by one, Fewesi selected a container, opened it, and brought the ingredients close to her visitor's nose. Maya easily identified vanilla, powdered sugar, and almond extract. Not the same spices that had flavored the cake Fewesi had served during the *bunna* ceremony the other day.

"Did you have any visitors last night while you were watching Vered?"

"Visitors?" Fewesi shook her head. "No one come."

Maya then told her about Vered's sudden illness, the sick cat, the cake crumbs on its paws, and Vered's comment that an Ethiopian woman had given her cake to eat.

Fewesi looked troubled. She began shaking her head and muttering under her breath.

"Tell more to me. 'Bout Vered. How she act."

"She says she has a terrible headache. And she can't open her eyes because the light hurts them. She's very weak. Her heart rhythm is unstable."

Maya wasn't sure that her neighbor understood all the Hebrew words. She was trying to keep it simple.

Fewesi closed her eyes, crouched down, and began to rock back and forth on her heels. She chanted some words in her native tongue, a tuneless song with a syncopated beat. Her hands began to carve the air like a blade, slicing up and down. Then abruptly, she stopped moving, straightened up, and grabbed Maya's arms.

"Zar!" Her eyes were wide open, the black pupils eclipsing the whites. "Zar! Zar!"

She kept repeating the word until Maya broke free of her iron grip. Fewesi's fingerprints lingered on Maya's fair skin like angry welts.

"What are you talking about?"

"Vered have Zar inside her. Someone use food to put spirit inside. Someone want to harm her. I heal her, make Zar her friend."

Maya had enough. She whipped around and stormed out of Fewesi's apartment. Fewesi ran after her and grabbed her by the shoulder, but Maya threw her off.

She walked over to her own door and checked to see that it was locked. She then headed down the stairs, not responding to her neighbor as the young Ethiopian woman called after her in a plaintive cry: "I heal her! Make Zar her friend!"

Maya didn't stop to catch her breath until she reached the ground level four stories down. But even as she yanked open the steel door and hurried outside, she could still hear Fewesi's voice echoing in her ears: "Zar! Zar! Vered have Zar inside."

46

EVEN FROM A DISTANCE, MAYA could tell that Café Menelik had seen better times. The blue lettering on the sign above the door was faded. The green, yellow, and red wooden flag painted as background was splintering at the edges. No customers sat at the small round tables set up outside, even though it was a warm, sunny day. In the bright light of late morning, the inside of the small Ethiopian coffee shop looked dark and uninviting.

Why had Rasta chosen to meet her here of all places? She was paying for his lunch. Why hadn't he insisted on meeting at some fancy restaurant like he usually did? Roni always blew up when he saw the bills from these lunches. Well, maybe the young man had suddenly come into some money. No longer needed handouts to survive.

Maya walked into the narrow café and headed toward the back of the room, choosing a square table for two. She seated herself with her back against the rear wall. As her eyes grew accustomed to the dim light, she saw that there were several people perched on high stools at the counter that ran the length of the narrow room. At a table near the front, seated at an open window, two young Ethiopian women lingered over their coffee, chattering away like magpies.

She checked her watch. The old Poljot informed her that it was a few minutes after eleven. She wasn't surprised. Rasta was never on time.

While she waited for her confidential informant to show, she decided to check her voicemail. Sarit had finally given up calling and left a message. Maya sighed and clicked "Play." Sarit's voice boomed out of the phone, high-pitched and breathless.

"You really need to pick up when I call, Maya!" A gasp of exasperation. "The killer's struck again! Elvis Aklilu was found dead this morning at a playground in Mexico Park. Stabbed by the same sort of knife used on his sister and stepmother. The guy left behind another of his cryptic signatures—some kind of amulet with a picture of a hyena. I've just wrapped up at the crime scene. Call me as soon as you can."

So, now Elvis had joined the pile of corpses. That made three murders in a week. Why had the killer waited so long between Hagar and Elvis? It didn't fit the typical pattern. Once their murder spree began, serial killers usually accelerated the pace of their killing, leaving less and less time between victims as their compulsion to kill hijacked their pre-frontal cortex. Maybe the killer had not planned to kill Elvis. Did something happen to trigger this third death? Or maybe the whole Aklilu family was on the killer's hit list. Only three of its members now remained alive—Moshe, his daughter-in-law Shulamit, and his grandson Bekeli. Who would next fall victim to the killer's double-edged blade?

She had to stop him before he killed again.

But to stop him, she needed to figure out his motive. Who benefited most from these deaths? That was always the crucial question. Her money was still on Moshe Aklilu. Based on what she'd already found out, the MK was involved in criminal enterprises up to his eyeballs. He stood to lose the most if all his dirty secrets came out. His real estate business had been under investigation by two government agencies for over two years. A recent exposé in the press had unearthed numerous legal and ethical improprieties in his recruitment of immigrant workers. And who knew what other shady enterprises the man had his hands in? Both his admirers and detractors agreed that Moshe Aklilu's meteoric rise from poor immigrant to wealthy MK could not have happened without a fair bit of unscrupulous conduct.

But would he resort to murder to maintain his privileged status? Kill his pretty, young wife, his own children? Perhaps they'd uncovered some of his dirty secrets and threatened to expose him. Yet despite his reputation for vindictiveness, she found it hard to believe that Moshe could be that cold-blooded.

But if he wasn't behind the killings, who was?

Moshe probably had dozens of enemies, all eager to take his place or get even. But nothing so far pointed to anyone in particular. The clues they had to work with—a ritual knife, hyenas, an amulet—were utterly baffling. The stuff of folklore and superstition. The killer had no doubt purposefully planted them at the crime scenes to throw them off his scent. She'd be wasting her time to follow that trail. No, she needed to go back to square one and probe for the usual motives for murder—greed, jealousy, or revenge.

47

HER THOUGHTS WERE SUDDENLY INTERRUPTED by someone calling out her name.

"Maya, baby!"

Her confidential informant had finally arrived.

Everyone looked up when Rasta entered the room.

Whenever he walked into a room, the lanky, large-boned Ethiopian always drew attention. With gleaming skin the color of hot tar, black dreadlocks rippling below his shoulders, and a braided salt-and-pepper beard so long that he wore it like a boa, the lengthy plait coiled around his neck, it was as if a movie star or famous athlete had descended from Olympus. Even more striking was the man's stride. Up, down, up down, like the painted horses on a carousel. He'd been born with a left foot so misshapen that his toes pointed straight up toward his torso, making his long body lopsided. But what Rasta lacked in grace, he made up for in charm. His handsome face bore a bright, toothy smile. Dark coals burned bright in the center of his eyes. His jubilant presence lit up any room he entered.

Maya waved him into the chair across from her.

"Sorry I be late, sweetheart, but you know, bizness wait for no mahn."

Maya nodded, used to the man's insouciant patter. Though he'd grown up in the Israeli port city of Ashdod, Rasta spoke Hebrew as though he'd been born in Jamaica. His accent was rendered even more exotic by sprinklings of Amharic and Caribbean patois.

"So, what do you have for me, Rasta?"

"Wait 'til I order somet'ing, darlin'. My belly cryin' somet'ing fierce!"

He eyed the items listed in yellow chalk on a blackboard behind the counter, smacking his broad pink lips and humming to himself. He then beckoned to the barista, a slender young Ethiopian man with a diamond stud in one ear, who approached their table with his pen poised.

"Shalom, mahn!" Rasta said. "What be happenin'?"

He winked at the barista and held up a fan of splayed fingers in a high five. The young man stood frozen like a statue, his pen immobile over his pad of paper.

Rasta shrugged and dropped his hand. Then he rolled his large pink tongue over his lips.

"I be havin' your best *bunna* and your sweetest sweet. I leave it to you to do da choosin'." He nodded to Maya, who had not yet ordered. "And for you, my sweet lady, what you be havin'?"

Maya spoke to the barista, eager to release him from Rasta's manic burlesque.

"Same for me."

The barista pivoted and made a swift beeline for the counter.

Maya turned to face the CI, half-smiling despite her resolve to keep her manner strictly professional. She was no match for Rasta's wiles. Despite the predictable blowback from Roni, she always looked forward to these lunches.

"OK, Rasta, shoot."

"So much to tell."

Rasta shook his head, his long dreadlocks whipping like whirligigs. Then he bent forward, his sharp, crooked nose almost touching Maya's forehead. She caught a heady whiff of marijuana emanating from the man's hair, beard, and skin like strong cologne. He smiled and leaned back against the wooden chair. Then he winked at her.

"Mister Moshe, he now have t'ree bodyguards keep him safe. T'ree big goons." He mimed a Popeye cartoon, flexing his own impressive biceps. "He scared, I tell ya, scared for him life!"

Maya wondered whether the bodyguards were a ruse, meant to show the authorities that Aklilu saw himself as victim, not perpetrator. But maybe his fear was genuine.

"More important, *yene fikire*, he plannin' to get rid a' *dat woman*."

The barista arrived, carrying a tray with two large ceramic coffee cups, filled with steaming black liquid, and two small plates with pieces of moist, golden cake. When he set the cups down in front of them, Maya was delighted to see a milky floral design swirling in the surface of the dark brew. Before she took a sip, she first inhaled the toasty fragrance of the roasted beans. Then she tilted the warm cup into her mouth, feeling the rich coffee enfold her tongue.

Rasta, hostage to his own frantic tale, ignored his coffee and cake. His large hands deftly carved and whittled the air.

"Dey hate each ot'er, Mister Moshe and dat Shulamit. Dey like jackal and viper. When she around, he fidget like a bad boy stuck fast wit' him finger in da jam jar. Now dat Elvis dead, he itchin' to t'row her out."

"Why do they hate each other so much?"

"Dunno. De old barya she tell me dat woman a witch. Has da Buda eye. But I don't t'ink dat da reason. I t'ink Elvis woman know too much 'bout Mister Moshe. He 'fraid a' her."

Maya lifted up the sticky dessert and took a bite. The cake tasted of cinnamon, sugar, and honey. It quickly melted on her tongue. She took another sip of the strong coffee to temper the sweetness. Her nerves tingled. Her mouth was in ecstasy.

"So, how does Moshe plan to get rid of his daughter-in-law?"

"I hear him talkin' on da phone." He paused. "To dat Filipino ladyboy. Joey Villanueva."

Villanueva! Why had the name of that Filipino gangster popped up again? Was he the killer? What did Moshe have on him?

"He plannin' to give dat woman to Joey. To sell off."

Rasta stopped talking, his nostrils quivering. He grabbed his cup of coffee with both hands and took a long sip, his eyes closed.

"Aah! Dat good *bunna*!"

He took a second sip and swished the cooling liquid around in his mouth. His eyes opened, sparkling with pleasure.

"Hey, man!" he shouted to the barista, who looked up from wiping off the counter, startled. "I tell all my friends 'bout your *bunna*! *Maksim*!"

Rasta thrust his giant thumb up toward the ceiling.

The slender barista nodded toward him, a wide grin relaxing his jaw. Rasta winked, then rubbed his thumb and forefinger together. He winked again. Angling for a commission, no doubt, a finder's fee. Rasta never missed an opportunity to earn a shekel.

"What do you mean 'sell her off'?"

"For sex slave, don' ya know. Joey, he big in da trade. He global now. Sell Beta Israel girls and also Filipinas and girls from Eastern Europe. Big money in dis."

Maya visualized Shulamit Aklilu. It was true that the woman was beautiful, tall and thin, with regal features, but she seemed too old to fetch much in the underground meat market. She must be pushing thirty. But there was no accounting for taste when it came to lustful men.

Rasta leaned forward and dialed down his deep voice to a whisper. Maya leaned in to catch his words.

"Mister Moshe he do somet'in' very bad to Joey years ago. Rumor say he double-cross him. Moshe owe him big time. Maybe he now payin' back dat debt."

Maya sat up, picked up her half-empty cup, and slumped back against the slatted back of her chair. How deeply was Moshe Aklilu in hock to Joey Villanueva? Deep enough for the latter to dun him by killing off his family? Deep enough for Moshe to offer his daughter-in-law as repayment? Would this transaction finally cancel his debt to the mobster? Or did he owe still more? Who else would have to die?

48

THIS TIME MAYA WALKED THROUGH the Aklilus' front door without knocking. She didn't know whether Ethiopian Jews observed this Ashkenazi custom, sparing mourners the awkwardness of playing gracious host in their grief. When she found the heavy front door unlocked, she simply pushed it open and stepped into the spacious foyer.

The house was packed. Maya craned her neck to see into the living room, but the crowd was too dense. It was a very mixed group—black men and women in long, white *shammas*; some of the men in suits, some of the women in dark dresses. Several white men in suits or more casual attire. White women in black pant suits or modest dresses. A few children threaded through the crowd, some grasping pieces of injera in their hands or glasses of juice.

She'd come to speak to Shulamit, but she needed privacy to say what she had to say to her. That wasn't going to be possible indoors. This crowd wouldn't thin out for hours.

Then she spotted the younger housemaid coming out of the kitchen. The small black woman carried a bamboo tray holding empty glasses and a pile of paper napkins. Maya beckoned to her with her forefinger. The maid looked alarmed, confused. She looked around, scouting for her mother. But the old barya was nowhere in sight. The girl set the tray down on a small wooden table and limped toward Maya. As she came closer, Maya noticed how disfigured her face was, cratered like the surface of the moon, the dark skin inflamed.

"I need to get a message to Shulamit Aklilu," Maya said.

The maid looked at her, not comprehending.

Maya reached into her large shoulder bag and extracted a small black notebook. She tore off a blank sheet and scribbled a few words on the top half. Then she folded it over and wrote "For Shulamit's eyes only" in Hebrew on the outside. She then thrust the folded paper at the maid, who immediately threw up her hands in surrender. Of course. The girl was illiterate.

"Shu-la-mit," Maya said. She pointed her finger toward the crowded living room. Then she pointed to the paper. "Give...this... to...Shulamit."

She knew it made no difference whether she spoke slowly or in a normal rhythm. The maid did not understand Hebrew. But she nodded to Maya and took the folded paper between two slender fingers. She pointed to the living room as Maya had done, then to the paper, and said, "Shulamit." She smiled tentatively, perhaps embarrassed by her slight lisp. Her smile quickly vanished. Her face lapsed back into dullness.

Maya watched her nimbly insinuate herself into the welter of guests and disappear. Maya waited nervously. Perhaps the maid would dutifully give the paper to Moshe, the head of the household. It was risky for her to do otherwise, to obey orders given to her by a white stranger. What had she been thinking, trusting this ignorant village girl to deliver a message she couldn't even read? Maybe she should leave before the maid came back.

But there wasn't time. The lame girl now stood before her, head bowed. She no longer held the note. Without saying a word, she took Maya gently by the hand and led her to the sliding glass doors that opened into the garden. She pushed one of the glass panels open and led Maya to a wooden bench set against the back wall. Still without speaking, she released Maya's hand and limped back into the house, sliding the double doors shut behind her.

Maya still wasn't sure whether her message had gotten through. In her note she had written: "Meet me in the backyard. I have something important to tell you. Please don't say a word about this to anyone. Just come. Quickly." She hadn't signed her name, assuming that the maid would tell Shulamit who had sent the note.

While she waited, she stared at the large white tent filling most of the grassy backyard. Through the clear vinyl walls, she watched a line of guests filling their plates with food from the long tables set up against the sides of the tent, pouring water and hot tea from carafes, talking and laughing as if they'd forgotten they were at a house of mourning. The thick plastic walls held the voices in, shielding the mourners inside the house from the consolers' levity.

Suddenly the sliding back doors whooshed open. Maya twisted around to watch Shulamit emerge from inside the house, dressed in a dark blue dress. Her feet were bare. So was her head. In the late afternoon sun, her russet hair blazed like burnished bronze. She was indeed a striking woman. Her amber eyes gleamed like cats' eyes. Maya noted that her eyes were dry. If she had shed any tears, they were long gone.

Riding on Shulamit's hip was her young son, Bekeli. The child's face and dark gray smock were crusted with crumbs. In his pudgy hands he still clutched a remnant of cake. When he saw Maya, his eyes widened, then he laughed, pointing at her with a stubby finger. He babbled a few words, then laughed again.

Maya caught a heady scent drifting toward her. It came from the little boy. A cloying sweetness. Where had she smelled that before? But she had no time to wrack her brain before Shulamit began speaking.

"Why have you come here? Can't you leave us alone in our grief!"

"You're in danger, Shulamit! I have reason to believe that you're next on the killer's list. You have to leave here now!"

Maya wasn't expecting the other woman's response. Shulamit opened her mouth wide and laughed. Her son joined her, although he obviously didn't know what was so funny. Neither did Maya. It was almost as if Shulamit knew the killer's mind.

"Where did you get this crazy idea?"

"I'm afraid I can't tell you. You'll just have to trust me."

Shulamit's face suddenly turned into a mask, devoid of emotion. But unlike the young housemaid's dull mien, hers was specular like polished jet. Maya thought she saw fear in her amber eyes. But when she looked again at Shulamit's face, it showed no expression. Her golden eyes gazed steadily at Maya, almost serene. Had she only imagined the fear?

"I've arranged for you to stay in a safe house," said Maya. "You and your son will be out of harm's way until we catch the killer. You'll be guarded 24/7."

"But I'm perfectly safe here!"

Bekeli began to squirm on his mother's hip. Shulamit bounced him up and down a few times, then switched him to the other hip. The baby giggled. She kissed his almost hairless head and gently smoothed the soft skin with her palm.

"I don't know where you've gotten your information, Agent Rimon, but I assure you that I'm in absolutely no danger."

"I have to insist! It's not—"

Shulamit interrupted her.

"I think it's best that you leave. Immediately." She turned her back to Maya and headed resolutely for the glass doors. She stopped before sliding them open.

"If you want you can walk around the side of the house, so you won't have to deal with the crowd inside. I'll tell my father you were here to offer your condolences."

And then she was gone.

49

WHEN DANI SOLOMON PUSHED THROUGH the door at the urgent care center, he felt as though his chest was about to split open. His heart hammered like a stamping press. His breath sawed in and out of his lungs in short, jagged heaves. His skin was cold and damp. His muscled calves and thighs quavered as though he'd just run a marathon.

"Help me!" he cried as he burst into the crowded waiting room. "I'm having a heart attack!"

The room was filled with Ethiopians patiently awaiting their turn. Some of the older ones looked up when Dani entered. The younger ones stared down at their smartphones. They noted his Western clothes—faded jeans, a white polo shirt with a tiger embroidered over the left breast, and American running shoes. His gnarly hair was neatly trimmed, his bespectacled face smooth-shaven and unmarred. What did he have to complain about? Hadn't they been waiting here for hours, some bleeding from accidents, others with high fevers or dying from cancer or riddled with parasites? It was always the young, spoiled ones who demanded all the attention. Many had been born here in Israel, never knowing the hardships their elders had suffered back home. They'd already been ruined by a native sense of entitlement, expecting the state to take care of their every need. One by one, the elders looked away from Dani, back to their books or their magazines or their weathered hands.

Behind a tall plexiglass pane facing the entrance sat the receptionist, a middle-aged white woman with airbag cheeks and a bouffant hairdo. After a few moments, she looked up from her phone. Dani rushed up to her, his hands flapping like loose sails.

"You've gotta help me! I need to see a doctor immediately! I'm having a heart attack."

With a loud sigh, the woman put down her phone and turned to her computer screen.

"Name?"

"Solomon, Dani. Will you please summon a doctor!"

"Address?"

Dani told her where he lived, his voice quivering like a withered reed.

"Government medical ID?"

"I can give all that to you later. Can't you see that this is an emergency!"

The woman typed rapidly on her keyboard, then paused.

"I can't admit you without a proper government ID."

Dani fumbled in his pants pocket and pulled out his wallet. He flipped it open and showed the woman his national healthcare card. She nodded and typed in the information.

"Nature of your complaint."

"Heart attack! I told you already!"

"I need you to calm down, *adoni*. Everyone thinks he's an emergency. Symptoms?"

He detected a Slavic accent. He smelled cabbage and sour cream on the woman's breath.

"Heart palpitations. Shortness of breath. A cold sweat. Weakness in my legs."

Dutifully, the woman keyboarded all the information. Her desk phone rang. She held up a fat index finger toward Dani and turned away to take the call.

Dani banged on the plexiglass window, though he knew it would only annoy her, probably make her drag out his registration even longer. The woman bent down over the phone and whispered conspiratorially into the receiver. Dani took in a deep breath, counted to ten, then scratched the scarred surface of his left palm with the clipped nail of his forefinger. Finally, she turned back to him.

"When did you first notice these symptoms?"

Dani patiently answered all her questions while his heart tapped out its fateful tattoo against his rib cage. He felt the breath draining from his lungs, emptying out of the alveoli until they gasped for oxygen like beached fish. His legs threatened to give out at any moment, tumbling him to the tiled floor.

"Okay, *adoni*, you're in the system. Kindly take a seat in the waiting room, and we'll call you when a doctor is ready to see you."

"Can't you move me to the head of the line? I might die before my name's called."

The woman clucked her tongue as though he were a naughty child. She nodded toward the plastic chairs set out in four rows in the white-walled room. Almost all of them were occupied. Single men and woman, old people bent over or snoring, pregnant girls not much over fifteen years old, three generation families. Mounted high on one wall, a large plasma screen played a popular Israeli cooking show. At this moment the chef was demonstrating how to make rugelach.

Dani staggered over to the nearest empty chair and fell into it. He dug into his pocket and fished out his mobile phone. Maya was already in his "favorites." He pressed her name and waited impatiently for her to answer.

"Maya Rimon."

"It's me, Dani!"

"What's the matter? You sound terrible."

"I think I'm having a heart attack. I'm at the Meyerhoffer Clinic on Bilu Street, near my apartment. Can you come?"

What am I doing, calling her now? Does she have protekzia here? Can she force them attend to me sooner?

The truth was that he didn't want to die alone. He had no family to call on. He wanted her here so she would hold his hand when he breathed his last.

"I can't come now, Dani. I'm on my way to my parents' house to check on my daughter. She's taken ill."

"It can't be as serious as a heart attack!"

It wasn't fair of him to pressure her like this, but what choice did he have? He might die any minute!

"Okay." Her breathy sigh was loud. "I'll call to check on Vered, then head out to you. This late in the day traffic shouldn't be too bad. Be there in about twenty minutes."

She was there in fifteen. She hurried into the waiting room and dropped down next to him, her face tense with concern. She offered him her hand. He took it gratefully, placing it on his lap, not caring that his coarse left palm raked her smooth skin. They sat like that for the next hour, their breathing gradually synchronizing into a fast but even rhythm.

And then, finally, he heard his name.

"Dani Solomon!"

The nurse led them through double steel doors with glass portholes at the top, then down a long corridor and into a tight rectangular space surrounded by a light-weight green and white curtain that hung from a U-shaped metal track fastened to the ceiling. With Maya's help, Dani changed out of his street clothes into a baggy green hospital gown, placing his clothes, watch, and glasses into a large plastic bag with a cinch tie. He handed his wallet and housekeys to Maya. Then he slid under the sheet and lay back against the pillow, staring up at the perforated white ceiling tiles.

The doctor appeared almost immediately. He was a short black man with black-framed glasses and a shaved head. Seen through the thick lenses, his eyes seemed about to pop out of their sockets.

"So," he said, perching with one hip and thigh on the thin mattress, "what seems to be the problem?"

"Heart attack!"

The doctor chuckled. His glasses slipped down his thin, angular nose. He pushed them back up with his middle finger.

"I doubt it, young man. I don't think you could have sat for over an hour in the waiting room and gotten yourself to this bed on your own feet if that were truly the case. Let me check your vitals."

With astonishing speed and dexterity, the doctor ran through the usual medical protocols, checking Dani's blood pressure, pulse rate, temperature, oxygen saturation level, muscle reflexes. All registered as normal.

The doctor winked at Maya, then smiled warmly at Dani.

"Just as I suspected. There's nothing wrong with you."

"But an hour ago my heart was pounding like it was going to explode! I couldn't catch my breath. My whole body was drenched in cold sweat."

"Tell me, Dani, do you believe in witchcraft?"

Suddenly, Dani's whole body began to shake. With both hands he clenched the front of his hospital gown. His eyes bounced from side to side like black steel balls ricocheting inside a pinball machine.

"And what about the Zar?"

Dani expelled a loud whoosh of breath. His eyes closed. One of his long arms fell limply over the side of the bed. Then he passed out.

"What's happened?" Maya's voice was shrill with alarm. "Is he dead?"

The doctor laughed out loud. He pushed his glasses back up to the bridge of his nose, then winked at her with a sly grin.

"Not to worry, young lady. Didn't you ever hear of a person being 'scared to death'?"

"That's just a figure of speech."

"But it can also refer to an actual medical condition. Vagal inhibition. If someone becomes sufficiently frightened, he can actually trigger in himself a series of physical symptoms that resemble a heart attack. Shortness of breath. Lightheadedness. Blurred vision. He can stop his own heart. He can even die."

Maya recalled reading about this disorder in her initial research into Ethiopian superstition.

As the doctor finished speaking, Dani groaned and opened his eyes.

"What's going on? Did I die and need to be resuscitated?"

The doctor leaned over and patted Dani affectionately on the shoulder.

"Nothing of the kind, *adoni.* As I was just explaining to your sweetheart here, you gave yourself a dangerous scare. But it was all in your head. I'm going to discharge you. And I'm going to put in my orders a recommendation that you see a psychiatrist at your earliest convenience. It would be best to consult one of our own people."

After the doctor left, Dani quickly changed back into his clothes, retrieved his personal items from the plastic bag and his wallet and keys from Maya, picked up the doctor's instructions from the receptionist, and hurried toward the front waiting room.

Maya had to run to catch up to him. She called out his name.

He halted but did not turn around.

"I can come back to your apartment if you'd like," she said. "Make sure you're all right."

He turned and extended his hand to her.

50

As soon as Maya stepped into Dani's apartment, she smelled it. The same maple syrupy aroma she'd detected on little Bekeli's clothes and Fewesi's cakes. She waited near the door while Dani settled himself on the yellow vinyl couch, placing a thin pillow behind his back, took off his running shoes, and stretched out his long legs on the low wooden table. Then she walked over to the couch and sat down at the opposite end, facing him.

"What's that sweet smell coming from your kitchen?"

Looking puzzled, Dani thrust his large, splayed nose into the air and sniffed. He glanced toward the kitchen area, then grinned.

"Tonight's dinner." He pointed to the cast iron pot sitting on the stove. "I was just about done cooking it when I felt the terrible pain in my chest." He chuckled. "It's lucky I remembered to turn off the burner before heading over to urgent care. Otherwise, it would've burned to a crisp."

Maya stood up and walked over to the kitchen area. She bent her head down, bringing her nose close to the uncovered pot that sat on the stove. The mixture of spices exuded a dizzying aroma. She could only identify a few of them: ginger, garlic, lemon, cloves, cinnamon. But she guessed there were at least half a dozen others that baffled her olfactory bulb.

"What is it?"

"*Doro wat.* A kind of spicy chicken stew. A big favorite in my family."

She noticed, lined up against the back of the kitchen counter, a low wall of small glass bottles, each identified by a white label. Beginning with "allspice," she unscrewed each plastic cap and brought the open bottle to her nostrils, inhaling deeply. It didn't take her long to find what she was looking for. Fenugreek. Uncannily reminiscent of maple syrup.

She held out the open bottle toward Dani.

"We call it *abish*," he said. "We use it in a lot of our dishes."

"I smelled this on our cat after she ate some cake that must have dropped on the floor. Damn near killed her. My daughter ate some of that same cake and is now deathly ill. And I smelled the same spice on Shulamit Aklilu's little boy. He reeked of it."

"What's your point?"

Maya slammed the spice bottle down on the wooden counter and yanked her mobile phone out of her pocket. She scrolled rapidly through her favorites, then jabbed a key with her index finger.

"I need to speak to Vered!" A brief pause. "I need to ask her where she got that cake." A longer pause. "Then wake her up!" Another long pause. "I'll call you later, Ima!"

With a loud whoosh of exasperation, Maya abruptly stabbed at the screen to disconnect the call. Then she laid the phone down on the counter and hammered the chafed wooden surface with her fist.

She looked up at Dani but didn't see him. Her eyes were unfocused, peering into the distance.

"I'm not sure how all this ties together, but I can feel in my bones that it does. I just have to figure out how."

She tilted her head back and looked up, noticing for the first time a maze of thin fissures that scored the white ceiling. Was there a pattern there? She couldn't find one. Slowly she lowered her gaze until she was staring at Dani. Her gaze was so intense he was forced to look away.

"I suspect that Shulamit is not as innocent in all this as she seems. The way she looked at me when I was at her house earlier today...I thought I saw something like despair in her eyes."

Dani tried to hide the shudder that shook his frame, but Maya noticed. And when he turned to face her, she saw that his features were disturbed as though strafed by a chill wind.

51

"WHAT IS IT, DANI?"

He shook his head.

"Nothing. Just a chill. It's too late in the fall to be wearing short sleeves."

She recalled the moment when the doctor questioned Dani about witchcraft and the Zar. How strongly he'd reacted.

"What are you hiding, Dani? Out with it!"

She walked back to the couch and sat close to him. She placed her hand on his jean-covered thigh, then pressed down gently.

"We all have embarrassing secrets. I'll tell you mine if you tell me yours."

She tried to keep her tone light, jocular, but she felt that familiar *frisson* on her skin that told her she was onto something.

Dani laid his hand over hers. His large hand completely swallowed up her hand and wrist.

"What do you know about Ethiopian superstitions, Maya?"

"I've read a few articles. About Buda. And the Zar. Some kind of spirit that takes over a person's will and personality, right?"

Dani stood up and began pacing back and forth across the large room, his hands tussling with each other until he clenched them into fists and thrust them into his pockets. Then he walked back to the couch and folded his long-limbed body into a seated crouch, his head nestled in his palms.

"I lied when I told you I didn't put much stock in such primitive notions. The truth is that my mother and grandmother raised me on all kinds of magic and superstitious beliefs. They totally swore by that stuff. Spirits and demons. My father used to make fun of them, so they stopped talking about it in front of him. But they certainly made it seem real enough to me. Whenever I misbehaved, my *ayati* would threaten to curse me with her dark powers. And she swore that some women in our family, her own mother, for instance, were haunted by spirits. She warned me not to choose a wife who was possessed by a Zar."

Dani laughed. Or attempted to laugh. His lower face twisted into a grimace that refused to surrender to his effort at humor.

"I guess getting involved in this case brought it all back. I've really managed to spook myself, haven't I?"

Maya reached out her hand and stroked his dark velvet cheek. She was pleased to see his mouth slacken into a soft grin.

"Nothing to be embarrassed about, Dani. You should hear my mother talk about the evil eye, which she feels has singled out our family for special attention. She's got more amulets and oddball rituals than anyone I've ever met. I have to confess that I've even adopted some of them myself."

She lifted up her large shoulder bag from the floor and rummaged around inside it. Out of its dark maw, she pulled a blue glass disk, about the size of her Poljot watch face, decorated on its surface with concentric circles of black, light blue, white, and dark blue. Threaded through a loop at the outer edge of the thick glass circle was a braided blue string, at whose other end dangled a smaller version of the ringed blue eye.

Maya shrugged her shoulders and grinned sheepishly.

"It can't hurt, right?"

Dani's shoulders eased down from their stiff perch next to his ears. His smile widened. Maya felt a rush of blood warming her cheeks.

Suddenly, he sprang up from the couch and dashed into his bedroom. Moments later, he returned, clutching a small white envelope in his hand.

"I meant to call you as soon as I received this. But then my heart started pounding, and I rushed off to urgent care."

He handed the envelope to Maya. She flicked the flap back and extracted a single folded sheet of white paper. The computer-printed message in Hebrew was brief:

"Stay away from Maya Rimon! She put your life in the danger. If you do not stay away, you will to be sorry."

The message was unsigned.

"It's obvious the author's not a native speaker," Dani said. "Whoever sent this is afraid you're getting too close. So, it's either the killer or someone who's protecting him."

Now it was Maya's turn to shudder.

"Oh, Dani, I'm so sorry! It's bad enough that I've put my daughter at risk. Now I've made you a target too. Maybe we should stop seeing each other for a while. At least until we catch the killer."

Dani walked back to the couch and sank down beside Maya. He took both her hands—how tiny they looked cradled in his large palms—and peered intently into her gold-flecked green eyes. She shuddered again, this time with pleasure.

"I can help, Maya." His voice was soft and pleading. "The killer most likely is someone from the Beta Israel community. He's using our superstitions to try to intimidate you, to scare you off. You need someone like me to get inside his head. Please let me help you."

Maya felt torn. Despite his protests to the contrary, Dani was clearly terrified of these superstitions. And he was a lawyer, not trained in gathering intelligence or using weapons. It wasn't fair of her to put him in harm's way. But he was right about her being an outsider. Even with her natural instincts, she'd probably miss or misinterpret crucial clues.

Seeing her ruddy eyebrows shift from decision to ambivalence and back again, Dani smiled.

"While you figure out how to respond to my offer, how about staying for dinner?" He paused, then chuckled. "If you can stand the smell of fenugreek."

52

DANI'S *DORO WAT* WAS DELICIOUS. Her nose and mouth tingled from the intoxicating blend of aromas. And when she sampled the simmering stew with a wooden spoon, her mouth practically sang in joy. Although Maya had dined in Ethiopian restaurants before, she'd never experienced such a broad kaleidoscope of tastes. Sweet and hot, salt and sour, onion and garlic, and *berbere*, a fiery salmagundi of a dozen spices unique to Ethiopian cuisine. The chicken was so tender it was falling off the bone. She couldn't wait to taste the savory hard-boiled eggs floating in the stew, stained dark brown after marinating in tomato sauce and spices.

While they were waiting for the doro wat to finish cooking, Dani offered Maya some of his home-made tej. She probably should have refused. But she found herself growing increasingly fond of the honeyed drink. And her fevered mouth craved something cool and sweet. The syrupy mead felt like soothing aloe on a burn.

After two glasses Maya's head began to spin. She had to grab on to the edge of the counter to keep from falling. She sat down on a nearby wooden stool and drained the glass of water Danny had poured earlier. The cool, clear liquid had no effect. Maybe once she had some food inside her. She couldn't remember when she'd last had something to eat.

Dani dipped the wooden ladle into the doro wat for one taste, then spooned it into a large, glazed clay pot, which he set down on the counter. Next to it he set a plate holding a tall stack of injera. He took two dinner plates down from one of the cabinets, filled them with heaping portions of the steaming wat, and set them down on the counter next to the stack of injera.

Then he walked over to the sink and reached up to a high kitchen cabinet. Reaching inside on tiptoe, he withdrew two glass beakers with rounded bottoms and long, narrow necks.

"*Bereles*," he said. He filled both glass vessels with more of the golden tej. "This is how we drink tej back home."

Balancing their bereles, the steaming plates of doro wat, and the plate of injera, they walked into the living room and sat down on the couch to eat their dinner. Dani seemed embarrassed not to have a proper table and chairs. But the couch and low table were well-suited for eating with their hands. They gobbled down the fiery stew and went back to the stove for seconds. Although there were only two of them, the stack of injera dwindled rapidly as they dipped the soft bread repeatedly in the pungent sauce. Maya couldn't recall the last time her mouth had been so happy.

She didn't notice how many times Dani refilled her berele. She had floated too far away. Drifting on a cloud made of honey mead and maple syrup. It wasn't only her mouth that tingled now, but her whole body. Her skin shivered as though submerged in a bucket of ice. But this chill was unlike any she'd ever experienced. Through every vein, her blood coursed like a flashflood through a wadi, simultaneously cold and searing hot. She fell back against the yielding vinyl of the couch, emptied of strength.

"How about some music?" Dani asked. His voice came from far away, like an echo in a winding canyon.

Was that nervousness Maya heard in his voice? She wasn't sure. Her hearing was playing tricks on her. The loud hum from Dani's refrigerator was giving her a headache. The rap music thundering down on their heads from the upstairs apartment assaulted her ears, thumping and pounding. She thought she heard a cat in heat caterwauling nearby.

"Whatever you play, play it loud," she said. "Drown out that godawful din."

He chose something African. Or maybe it was Caribbean. It pulsed hotly through her bones. Her head filled up with the jangle of steel drums, throaty wails of song, black hands pummeling stretched skin. Without consciously willing it, her body rose up and began to sway. She circled slowly around the coffee table. And then she was standing between Dani's knees, swaying, leaning into the seated man's chest. His hand stopped her from toppling over on him.

She reached out her hand, beckoning to him with her slender fingers.

"Dance with me."

Dani looked up at her, his face a cipher to her. *I've never been any good at reading men,* she thought to herself, *especially in situations like this. That's when all my investigative instincts quit on me. Make me act like a fool.* She lurched back, but her movement was too forceful. She fell backwards on to the floor, landing on her rump. The fall jarred her tailbone, making her cry out in pain.

Dani rose from the couch and lifted her up with his hand. Had she become weightless or was the man even stronger than he looked? The touch of his fingers immediately freed her of pain. And sent a jolt of energy through her body that electrified every nerve. Then she was in his arms, and they were drifting up toward the ceiling. Like a damp fog, his blackness completely enveloped her. Like a second skin. She was being drawn into him like sap into the dark tissues of a tree. She tasted honey on her tongue.

"I think we need to stop," said Dani.

He pulled away from her and stood for a few moments, not speaking. But he still held her with his eyes. Then he turned and walked over to the kitchen counter. He stared down at the dirty dinner dishes piled high in the sink, the empty bereles on the counter. The room still smelled of onions, garlic, and fragrant spice. His back stiffened as he faced the back wall.

Maya sat up, focusing her eyes on his broad back. The room spun, then stilled. Had she ever been this drunk? She didn't want to stop dancing. She wanted him to hold her for the rest of her life. But she knew she was a danger to him. He was inexorably being sucked into her murder investigation. It was selfish of her to let their bond grow deeper. But how much she wanted him! *Don't be a fool, Maya! Where is your professionalism? Dani Solomon is your informant.* Suddenly, her limbs felt like lead. Her eyes smarted.

Without a word, Dani returned to her. His face was a mask. His eyes too dark to fathom. He sat down at the opposite end of the couch and directed his gaze at some invisible point outside.

What should she say to him? *Let's just have a quick fuck. Then forget it ever happened. Blame it on the tej.* Her heart seized in her chest. Then her blood ran cold. She shivered. She looked over at him, her gold-green eyes caressing the taut muscles of his arms, the planes of his broad nose, the generous sweep of his brow, the strafed palm of his left hand. What now? Was it her move or his? Would she ever master the bewildering puzzle of human intimacy?

Dani reached for her hand and gently cradled it in his. She stared down at his palm, pocked and cratered like a scabrous moonscape. She shook her head.

"I don't know what we should do."

Dani grinned.

"That makes two of us. Pretty pathetic for a pair of college-educated professionals, huh?"

They both laughed.

Maya reached down and cupped her fingers around Dani's hand. Tenderly she stroked the rough gnarl of his palm, then brought it to her lips and kissed it. She felt his skin tremble against her mouth.

"Look, Maya, I haven't known many women. Never even had a serious girlfriend."

He paused, then quickly averted his eyes. His breathing was shallow and rapid.

"You don't owe me a confession, Dani, or an apology. I think you're right that we should stop...this," she paused, then grinned, "whatever 'this' is. Let's just stick to working together on this investigation. Then, when it's over, maybe we can pick up where we left off."

Later, when she thought back to that pivotal moment, she couldn't remember who made the next move. She wanted to believe it was Dani, scooting over to her side of the couch and taking her in his arms, kissing her with an urgent tenderness. But she knew this was a lie. What did the psychologists call it? A false memory. The credit—or blame—for what happened next was entirely hers.

It all happened so fast. Before she realized it, she'd broken free of gravity. It was as if some unseen force, a Zar, had invaded her body and taken over her will. This alien force pushed her toward Dani, pressed her against his muscled chest. And once skin met skin, she was powerless to stop herself. And so was he.

Unlike their earlier dalliance, they now moved hurriedly, like ravenous feral beasts. They flew at each other, clawing at clothing, clutching at skin, hair, bone, and muscle, bent on exorcising whatever inimical spirits were holding them back.

Afterwards, they lay on top of each other, Maya resting on Dani's bare chest, their skin damp, their breath sawing in and out, their eyes shut against the intrusive lamplight. They didn't talk much before they drifted off to sleep.

Maya woke first. She thought about washing the dinner dishes before driving home, but she was too tired. Quietly, she fixed herself some strong coffee. She didn't wake Dani to say goodbye. Just before midnight she closed the door softly behind her and walked to her car.

When she finally reached home, she could barely keep her eyes open. The alcohol had worn off, leaving behind a leaden fatigue. She stumbled up the four flights of stairs to her apartment and tumbled through the door, collapsing on the orange loveseat and falling asleep immediately.

She failed to notice that her neighbor, Fewesi, was watching her through a crack in her door.

53

Shulamit's Diary

November 9

I fear that I've offended my Zar. My headaches have gotten so bad I sometimes go blind with pain. I don't know what's riled them so much.

Ayati told me that the best way to calm an offended Zar is to prepare bunna. The aroma of roasted beans seems to soothe their spirits. So, that's what I'm going to do as soon as the rest of the house is asleep.

Then, tonight and every night until Sigd, I'll perform the conjuration ceremony just as Ayati Ga'wa taught me. Adorn my hands and neck with henna. Light the incense and the seven black candles. Hang around my neck the special kitab amulet Ayati Ga'wa made for me. It, too, will soothe a nettled Zar.

Soon you will be able to rest in peace, Emayay. In a week's time I will finally fulfill the promise I made to you so long ago. But at what a high price!

So it is fated. What must be done will be done.

As you used to be so fond of saying: Awaqin matalel, qimru tirf no. *If you cheat someone, the only profit you get is their hankering for payback.*

DAY 9

Tuesday

54

When Maya walked into JEJI's front reception room slightly after 10 a.m. the next morning, she was surprised to see two plastic card tables set up in the middle of the room. A couple of white men in pale shirts and sports jackets sat at each table, facing each other, typing on laptops. In the middle of each table perched a pile of dark green bookkeeping ledgers. Next to each laptop were a large magnifying glass, a colored plastic ruler, and a water bottle.

Several Ethiopian clients sat in the plastic chairs lined up against two of the light green cinderblock walls, some looking down at their mobiles, others staring up at the disembodied legs visible through the basement room's high windows, cut off at the knees, walking by on the sidewalk. Dani's assistant, Esther Azazew, sat in her usual place by his office door, clacking away at her keys, glancing up frequently to watch the visitors clacking away at theirs.

Maya walked over to Esther. The young woman stopped typing and leaned toward Maya. Her eyes bulged out of their sockets like frightened fish.

"An audit," she whispered loudly. "The Jewish Agency is investigating our finances. But it's really just politics. There's nothing wrong with our books. Rumor has it that the Agency took some funds meant for our immigrants and 're-allocated' them"—Esther paused to sculpt quotation marks in the air with her fingers—"to build a French Cultural Center for newly arrived Frenchies. Now they're trying to 'reframe the narrative'"—up went the crooked fingers again—"to distract the media's attention."

A fifth figure in a white shirt and jacket came hurtling down the corridor, carefully balancing a wobbling stack of loose spreadsheets as if he were holding a baby at a *bris*. He hurried over to one of the card tables, deposited his paper stack on top of the ledgers, then whipped around and disappeared back down the corridor. *Like the White Rabbit,* thought Maya. *At the beck and call of some bureaucratic Queen of Hearts.*

"I have an appointment with the director," Maya said. "Can you let him know I'm here?"

Esther stood up and turned to face the closed wooden door beside her desk. She rapped twice with her knuckles. Moments later, Dani poked his head out, saw Maya, whispered something to Esther, then closed the door. Esther gestured for Maya to take one of the seats in the reception room. Maya sat down between two elderly Ethiopian women. They smiled at her, then went back to chatting over Maya as if she weren't there. Maya noticed that the two old crones didn't share a complete set of teeth between them.

Ten minutes later, Dani emerged from his office and beckoned to Maya with a long forefinger. She entered his office and sat down in the slat-backed wooden chair positioned across from his desk. Avoiding his gaze, she directed her eyes to the curved billawa hanging high on the wall to her left, its sharp point aimed at the bare plaster ceiling.

Dani's dark eyes followed the direction of her eyes.

"Still have no idea about who used one of these to murder his victims?"

Maya turned to face him, her face expressionless. She'd dreaded coming here today. Of course, Dani would want to talk about what happened last night. What it meant. Where they would go from here. She didn't want to deal with any of that right now. She was mad at herself for having lost focus because of her foolish involvement with this man. She needed to get a grip—and fast.

"I wanted to look at that file again," she said, turning her eyes away from the curved knife hanging on the wall. She looked at Dani, but his eyes quickly dropped to the floor. She swallowed a thick lump of saliva. "Kidist Adanech. Wasn't that her name, the woman from Gultosh who wrote the diary? Now that we know Aklilu and Kidist came from the same village, I want to see if I can find any connection between the two. Maybe there's something you missed."

"About last night, Maya—"

"I don't want to talk about it! I'm here strictly on business."

Dani was fidgeting with his left palm, brushing his right forefinger over the rutted skin. He brought the palm to his face and rubbed it against the smooth dark skin of his brow. He glanced over at Maya, saw her staring at the hand. As if suddenly cut loose from a rope, his left hand plummeted behind the desk.

"The file?"

"I told you I can't give it to you, Maya. Client confidentiality. I've already told you more than I should have."

"Then I guess we're done here."

She was about to stand up when a loud knock rattled the wooden door.

It was one of the auditors, looking very agitated. Beads of sweat pearled on his forehead, although it was a chilly day. A pair of murky brown eyes peered out through coke-bottle lenses. His bulbous lips were chapped and raw.

"I need to show you something, Director," the man said. "It's highly irregular!"

Dani rose and followed the man out of the office. Moments later he returned, his face taut like a wound spring.

"I have to step out for a bit. Shouldn't take long. Ask Esther if you need anything. We have cold water and some sodas."

He closed the door, leaving Maya alone in the small room.

As soon as she heard the click of the latch bolt, Maya sprang up from her chair. She began rooting through Dani's desk drawers, beginning with the top right drawer. She kept at it until she found what she was looking for in the bottom left drawer. The Adanech file.

The manila folder wasn't very thick. A few pages covering the woman's brief stay in the UN refugee camp in Sudan, a few more pages about her surviving family, a daughter named Sisayu. A photocopy of the girl's transfer documents from Ethiopia to Israel at age ten. Some notes about her placement in an Ethiopian foster family in Kiryat Malakhi. After the girl left the foster family at age sixteen, the Jewish Agency had lost track of her.

Maya went back over the documents in the file. She skimmed through the girl's initial interview at the Jewish Agency. She slowed down when she came across the name, "Negasi," mentioned in the girl's account of her family's journey to the refugee camp in Sudan. Sisayu told the case worker that the man had a scar on his neck. Maya tucked the detail away in her mental file.

And then she found a small certificate she'd missed in her first pass. The paper was stuck to the back of one of the pages. It was a government identity document, stamped and notarized, dated March 12, 2001. It explained that Sisayu Adanech's name had been officially changed soon after arriving in Israel. Her legal name had been changed to "Shulamit." The certificate was signed: "Batya Bodenheim, Caseworker, The Jewish Agency."

A coin dropped into the slot. *Shulamit was Kidist's daughter.*

Dani returned, looking upset. He found Maya calmly seated in her chair, the manila folder on her lap. He was carrying a bottle of water, which he drained in a few gulps.

He nodded his head toward the file, his tense expression snapping into impassiveness.

"I had to see what was in the file, Dani. Call it a hunch or just my training. I was pretty sure I'd find something relevant to my investigation."

"And did you?"

She nodded, her green-gold eyes flashing with excitement.

"Kidist's surviving daughter was named Sisayu. But when she got to Israel, her name was changed. To Shulamit."

Dani snorted and shook his head.

"It happened to most of us, especially in the early airlifts in the '80s and '90s. The government authorities couldn't wait to turn us into 'real' Israelis. They decided we were better off becoming Yael or Shira or Noam or Daniel instead of remaining Abaynesh or Mulualem. They thought it was better for us to forget where we came from and focus on the future. I'm not surprised Sisayu was forced to take a new name."

Maya swallowed, then took a deep breath and let it out slowly. What she was about to say would no doubt sound crazy to Dani, a wild shot in the dark. But she knew from the goosebumps prickling her skin that she had uncovered something vital to her case.

"If Sisayu came to Israel in 2001," she said, "that would make her twenty-eight now. That's the same age as Shulamit Aklilu. And Sisayu's mother, Kidist, came from the same village as Moshe Aklilu. They may well have known each other back home. It's got to be more than a coincidence that Sisayu ended up in Moshe's home. In his family."

Dani shrugged. He looked down at his watch. His left hand traveled up to his forehead, lingered there for a moment, then landed on his desk, next to a pile of papers and files.

"Whatever," he said.

His voice sounded hollow, as though all the air had been sucked out of it.

"Look, Maya, I've got a lot of work to do. I have to spend a substantial amount of time with the auditors on top of my regular responsibilities. I'm not happy that you looked in the file without my permission, but there's nothing I can do about that now. Give me a call if you have any more questions I can help you with."

He didn't wait until she was out of the room before turning to his paperwork. When she turned back from the doorway, he was bent over an open file. Neither of them said goodbye.

55

THAT NIGHT MAYA COULDN'T SLEEP. She tossed and turned, unable to settle down. She got up to pee, played a few games on her phone, then closed her eyes, hoping that sleep would finally come.

When it did, she had one of her "lucky dreams." That's what she called them. These occasional oracular dreams often provided keys to unlock puzzling cases. Like the clairvoyant rabbis in Morocco that her mother used to tell her about. People would come to these rabbis with their problems and the holy men would write amulets posing questions to be answered in dreams. She sometimes wondered if her unconscious worked the same way.

She awoke with her dream still fresh in her mind:

She was standing before an open iron gate, its bars tipped with sharp, spear-like points. Inside was a lush garden. Date palms, tamarisks, fruit trees of all kinds. Shrubs heavy with bright red berries and white blossoms. Flowers of all colors and shapes. Butterflies, bees, and shimmering hummingbirds, drunk on nectar, flitting among the flowers.

She was alone. There were no people in the garden.

As much as she wanted to enter the garden, something held her back. Not fear but a premonition. A feeling that she might not be able to leave once she stepped inside.

A ghostly form appeared before her, two silvery wings fluttering at its sides. The figure was androgynous, like a child. Long silky hair fell over its shoulders in golden waves. Though the figure appeared benign, Maya felt chilled when she looked into its eyes. They were transparent like glass, without irises. She tried to flee, but her feet were riveted to the ground.

The figure raised both hands. Above its head appeared a giant curved sword, its blade flashing red-hot like metal beaten at a forge. The sword began to whirl as if wielded by an unseen hand. Slicing the air, contrails of white smoke curling in its wake. Mesmerized, she watched the sword swivel and spin. And then the sword suddenly vanished, followed by the ghostly form.

Her feet were set free, and she fled.

What was this strange dream telling her?

The flaming sword was easy enough. It was the murder weapon. A billawa. But who did the winged figure represent? The killer? His victims? Her? And what about the garden and the gates? And why weren't there other people in the garden?

Some faint recollection prodded her memory.

She was in fifth grade Bible class. They were reading a story about this sword. Something to do with the Garden of Eden.

Maya rose from the sagging orange loveseat and padded into Vered's room. Because there was a half-moon in the cloudless night sky, she found her way without turning on any lights. Not that she would have disturbed Vered. Her daughter's small bed was empty. Vered was still at her parents' house, recuperating from her bout with poisoned cake.

She found her daughter's Tanakh in the small white bookcase and carried it over to the window. In the glow of bright moonlight, she leafed through the first few pages of Genesis until she came to the end of chapter 3. And there it was: "He drove the man out and stationed east of the garden of Eden the cherubim and the fiery ever-turning sword, to guard the way to the tree of life."

What did this sword symbolize in the Bible story? Adam and Eve had just sinned by eating from the forbidden tree. Not the Tree of Life, but the Tree of Knowledge. Their punishment was exile. And without access to the Tree of Life, they were destined to die. Their lives were being cut short because of...of what? Disobeying God? Eating the forbidden fruit? Rebelling against heaven?

And then the answer snapped into place. This was a story about human willfulness and its consequences. What mattered more than the sin committed by the first two humans was the sentence that this sin levied upon them. Never-ending guilt. For the rest of their lives, Adam and Eve would feel the sharp blade of remorse.

That's what this serial killer was after. He was punishing his victims because they'd committed some sin against him. The billawa was his sword of vengeance!

She finally had her motive. This was a blood vendetta. The killer had sentenced the whole Aklilu family to death. *Dum butlab dum*, as the Arabs would say. "Blood begets blood." Which meant that the three surviving members of the family still had a target on their backs.

Maya's mind sifted and resifted through all the evidence she'd gathered so far. Did any clues point to an egregious wrong committed by someone in this family? How long ago had that injury been inflicted? What was the connection between Sisayu and the Aklilu family? And where did Negasi fit in?

Then she remembered Moshe's scar. When Sisayu had first arrived in Israel, she told the people at the Jewish Agency that Negasi, the man who had betrayed her family and left them to die, had a scar on his neck. What were the chances...?

She was almost there. And she had a hunch about who held the next piece of the puzzle.

56

THIS TIME WHEN MAYA SHOWED up at Shulamit Aklilu's front door, the tall Ethiopian woman made no effort to hide her resentment toward the intelligence agent. As soon as Shulamit opened the door, her eyes raked over Maya's body like twin blades. She did not invite Maya and her two agency colleagues into the spacious vestibule. Instead, the young black woman stood facing the three agents, her arms planted firmly on her broad hips, her topaz eyes ablaze.

Maya smiled. Shulamit narrowed her eyes into slits. Stiffening her shoulders, Maya forced her smile to stay where it was, tacked steadfastly to the corners of her lips. She nodded, then tilted her head toward the living room, which was empty of visitors at this early hour.

"We have a warrant to search the house."

"Have you no shame?" Shulamit yelled at Maya. "We're in mourning!"

"This is an ongoing investigation. Time is of the essence."

Without realizing it, Maya had raised her voice to match Shulamit's.

Hearing loud voices, Moshe made his way from the kitchen to the front vestibule. He was dressed in blue silk pajamas, a white terry-cloth robe, and slippers. Maya noted that the skin under Moshe's eyes was bruised with dark smudges. Thin red veins filigreed the whites of his eyes. Taking a deep breath, Maya informed him of her intention to search the house.

"This is outrageous! Obvious police harassment!"

He spun on his heels and marched down an unlit corridor. Maya, Masha, and Ziggy followed. Shulamit shuffled a few paces behind.

Pushing open the wooden door to his office, Moshe walked to his large mahogany desk and dropped down into the leather chair. He dug into the pocket of his robe and pulled out his smartphone. As he scrolled in his Contacts for the Security Minister's phone number, his large fingers fumbled with the screen. Twice he jabbed at the keys only to discover he'd called the wrong number. As his frustration mounted, he cursed under his breath in Amharic.

Finally, he succeeded in reaching the Security Ministry's office. He barked rudely at the Minister's secretary, then waited impatiently for Arik Ophir to come to the phone. While he remained on hold, his fingers hammered on the shiny wood of his desk like a ticking bomb. Suddenly, he snorted, then slammed down the phone.

"The nerve of that man! Treating me like some mid-level civil servant. I'm a member of the Knesset, for God's sake!"

Calmly, Maya twisted to one side and reached into her shoulder bag. She dug out her small black notebook and flipped to a blank page. Then she pointed her pen at Moshe. He gazed up at her, scowling.

"I'm sorry to have to question you during this…awkward time, sir, but it's important to gather information while memories are still fresh."

Moshe turned his face away, struggling to regain control of himself. Then he turned back toward the three agents, his dark eyes inscrutable. Maya forced herself to focus on his face.

"Can you tell me about your life before you came to Israel, MK Aklilu? Our records of those early years are quite spotty."

"I don't see what any of this has to do with the murder of my wife and children!"

Moshe's shoulders had inched up, almost touching the bottoms of his pendulous ear lobes. His nostrils flared like those of a riled horse.

"Let me be the judge of that," answered Maya. She ran her fingers through her moussed tangle of auburn hair.

"It's all on my official website. I was born in Gultosh. Gondar Province. Orphaned twice in Ethiopia. Airlifted to Israel in 1995.

There, you know all my secrets. Now go and do your job. Find my family's killer!"

For a few moments Maya said nothing. She had reviewed Moshe Aklilu's history that morning before coming to the house. The story he'd just told her matched the official version. Except for one important detail. In his official biography on the website, his home village was listed as Sagade. But Moshe had just named a different village as his birthplace. Gultosh. Why lie about that? And what else had he fabricated about his past?

This was precisely the kind of slip Maya had been hoping for.

Maya then noticed that Shulamit Aklilu was no longer in the room.

Leaving her colleagues to search Moshe's office, she quietly snuck out and returned to the vestibule, then headed upstairs to the second floor.

She found Moshe's daughter-in-law in what she assumed was the couple's bedroom. No photographs of Elvis hung on the walls, either solo portraits or pictures with his wife and son. The king-sized bed was unmade. Women's clothes and shoes lay scattered on the carpeted floor. In one corner of the large room was a small table, upon which sat seven black candles with burnt wicks, arranged in a circle. The air was filled with the pungent smell of incense. And something else. Burnt paper.

Shulamit sat on the floor, leaning her back against the foot of the bed. On her lap she cradled a cloth doll with silky yellow hair. When Maya entered the room, she glanced up dully, then went back to murmuring inaudibly to the doll.

Maya now noticed wisps of gray smoke curling up from a small metal wastebasket. She dashed over to it. A few embers flickered among the feathery ashes. She recognized the tight wire coil of a loose-leaf binder. Quickly, she ran into the hallway, filled a cup with water from the bathroom sink, and ran back into the room. She flung the water into the metal can. The embers hissed briefly, then went out. But whatever it was that Shulamit had burned was beyond recovery. At the bottom of the wastebasket lay a soggy, black mess.

"I assume you know it's a crime to destroy evidence."

No response from the seated woman. She was now gently stroking the doll's yellow hair.

"Shulamit!"

Maya's loud shout startled the seated woman. She looked up at Maya, her golden eyes quickly regaining their customary watchfulness.

"I need to ask you a question."

"I'm tired of your questions, Agent Rimon. Why can't you just leave us alone!"

The tall black woman rose and took a step forward, as if to push the intruder out. Maya stood her ground. Their angular noses, one white, one black, hovered only inches apart.

"Does the name 'Kidist' mean anything to you?"

Although Shulamit tried to conceal it, Maya caught the fleeting look of shock on Shulamit's face before her mask snapped back into place. She caught the surprised eyes, the sleek brows knit into an inverted "v", the high cheek muscles pinching her long nose. Shulamit was unable to suppress the gasp choking off her breath.

"I know no one by that name," she said. She didn't even try to make her denial sound sincere.

Maya quickly recounted the parts of Kidist's story she had learned so far: the Adanech family's brutal trek from their village to Sudan. Their arrival at the refugee camp. Kidist's quick surrender to cholera. Ten-year-old Sisayu's transport to Israel, where her name was summarily changed to Shulamit.

As Maya related these events, she studied the other woman's reactions. Shulamit had become as impassive as stone. A skill perfected over a lifetime practicing deception. Her amber eyes revealed nothing. Her chest barely moved when she breathed.

"I know you're keeping secrets, Shulamit. And I can assure you that I'll ferret them out."

Shulamit suddenly erupted into laughter. So violent was her outburst that she doubled over, clutching her belly with both arms.

Maya wasn't fooled. This woman was on the verge of nervous collapse. Her dark eyelids fluttered. Her eyes rolled back, the black irises almost disappearing under the lids, leaving only the whites like eviscerated eggs. Her slender limbs trembled as if stung with cold.

Shulamit sank down to the floor and resumed stroking her doll's silken hair.

When she next spoke, her voice was eerily calm. Like ice.

"Search to your heart's content, Agent Rimon. You won't find anything. I have nothing to do with these awful murders. I'm just a grieving widow."

Maya sucked in a long breath and pressed on.

"One last question. What do you know about Buda and Zar?"

Shulamit stared at Maya as though the other woman had just asked her if she believed in three-headed dragons. Then she smiled wryly.

"Ah, I see. You think we're all primitive savages, don't you? Conjuring up the evil eye to curse people. Keeping company with invisible spirits. Using dark magic to afflict our enemies." She chuckled. Then her face reverted to stone. She began singing softly to the doll in Amharic.

57

RONI QATTAWI SIGHED. HE SHOOK a cigarette out of the new pack and lit up, drawing the bitter smoke deep into his lungs, then exhaling it with a forceful blast. He took a second drag, then stared at the silver-framed photograph of his father perched at one corner of his wooden desk.

Poor Baba! He'd given up a successful import-export business in Alexandria to bring his family to Israel after the Sinai war, only to find himself packed off to a remote customs house operated by the Israeli Tax Authority. What tedium he must have endured, monitoring imports and exports, levying taxes, and prosecuting customs violations. His health had deteriorated rapidly after he'd turned forty, worsened by his fondness for Arak. Roni didn't want to end up like him. Forced out of his job at fifty because of repeated absences and erratic performance. Dead at fifty-one. The older Roni got, the more he realized what a miserable life his father had lived. No, he definitely would not follow in his Baba's footsteps.

Like his Baba, Roni had come to loathe his job. No matter how hard he tried, he remained pitifully maladroit at interdepartmental politics, which was why he still hadn't gotten a promotion. His time at the office was increasingly taken up with paperwork. It had been ages since he'd been out in the field. He was working such long hours now that his social life was a shambles. And damn that pigheaded Maya Rimon! If he wasn't careful, she'd report him for drinking on the job. And that would be the end of his career.

He looked up and checked to make sure the mini-blinds were all the way down over his office door. Then he bent down and unlocked the lower right-hand drawer of his desk. He reached in and brought out the half-empty bottle of Lagavulin 16. Carefully, he placed the bottle of Scotch in the center of the desk. Then he reached back down and took out a glass, which he placed next to the bottle. Lined them up precisely like cadets at parade. He poured himself a finger of the golden liquid, then added a second finger.

He lifted the glass and held it up to the fluorescent light. Then he swirled it, watching the whirlpool of viscous liquid sparkle in the harsh light. He brought the glass to his thin lips.

The phone rang.

Peeved, he set down the glass, careful not to spill any of the precious single malt, and reached for the black handset.

"Qattawi."

"Sarit Levine."

What did she want now? That woman was so damn eager to move up her own food chain that she was forever prodding him for intelligence she could leverage to her advantage. One day he was going to tell her to go fuck herself, find someone else to use.

"What is it, Sarit? I'm busy at the moment."

"Just got a call from the Prime Minister's office. Moshe Aklilu's invited him to speak at next week's Sigd celebration. It'll certainly boost Aklilu's stock among his constituents to have the big man there. And the PM is clearly angling to win over the Ethiopian bloc in the next election. One hand washing the other."

"Why're you telling me this, Levine? I know all about this already."

Silence at her end. What was she cooking up in that devious mind of hers?

"Don't you think it's a bad idea for the PM to go? I mean, the crowd will be huge. Every year's festival is bigger than the one before. Add the presence of the PM..."

What was she getting at?

"If I was planning a murder," Sarit finished up, "this would be the perfect setting, don't you think? Especially if the killer and his target are both Ethiopian."

The Aklilu case.

Sarit thought their serial killer was targeting another victim at the Sigd celebration.

"So, what do you want me to do?"

"I assume Intelligence is sending over a team to protect the PM and monitor the crowd."

"So?"

"I'd like to offer to send in my best team as backup. Let's hope we can catch this guy before he kills again."

Roni snorted. *Everyone wants a share of the glory.* The Security Services didn't need Sarit's cops horning in at the *kushis'* party. Even if Sarit's hunch about the murderer proved correct. What a headache this Aklilu case was! Roni couldn't wait until they caught the killer and shut down the investigation. *The sooner we catch him, the sooner I get Arik Ophir off my back.*

Sarit cut into his thoughts.

"Call me when you've worked out the details so we can coordinate comms."

She hung up.

Roni grabbed the glass of Scotch, downing it in two gulps. Its strong, oaky bite made him cough. What a waste of fine single malt, chugging it like cheap beer, but he needed something to relax him.

Then he poured himself another two fingers of the Scotch. He sipped it slowly. The liquor slithered down his throat like raw oysters. He tilted the last drops of Lagavulin into his mouth, snaked his tongue around the golden liquid, and swallowed. Yes, he could definitely feel a weight lift from his shoulders.

He bent down and opened the bottom desk drawer. He slipped in the bottle of Scotch together with the glass. Then he closed the drawer and locked it.

When he sat back up in his desk chair, the room swirled around him like a whirling eddy. It was not an altogether unpleasant sensation.

58

THE DAY WAS UNUSUALLY WARM for mid-November, especially for Jerusalem. The temperature was supposed to hit twenty-four degrees by three o'clock.

Shulamit took advantage of the mild weather to take Bekeli out to the backyard to play. She wore a short-sleeved coral blouse that showed to advantage her amber eyes and russet hair. Although her father-in-law didn't like her to wear jeans, even around the house, she wore her tightest fitting pair, drawing attention to her sleek runner's body. She was barefoot. She loved to feel the tickle of soft grass on her toes. Before coming to live at the Aklilus' grand house in their exclusive neighborhood on Cremieux Street, she'd never walked on freshly mown grass.

A late season honeybee buzzed near her left ear. She shook her head, then swatted the bee away. As she swung her head, she felt the weight of the silver clasp that bound her shoulder-length hair at her nape. She shivered despite the heat. Why had she decided to wear the clip on a day when Moshe was home? What if he noticed? Wouldn't the clasp's singular design betray her theft?

The truth was she no longer cared if he found out she was a snoop. They were nearing the endgame.

Bekeli's shrill squeal snagged her attention. Her two-year old son had spotted a small animal nosing about in one of the flowerbeds. He was chasing it as fast as his stubby legs could carry him. In his excitement his arms pummeled the air.

Giving up on catching his elusive prey, Bekeli ran to a corner of the lawn where a mud-covered soccer ball lay. He bent down and lifted it up with both hands, running toward his mother with an enormous grin creasing his plump, round face. But his balance was thrown off by the slight heft of the ball, and he tripped over his own feet. He went down, his nose smashing into the hard ball. He began to cry.

Shulamit ran over to him and scooped him up in her long arms, pressing him to her chest. His sobs pierced her like a sharp blade.

"Don't cry, *yene woo'ehd*, my treasure! You're okay."

Bekeli wailed louder. She looked down and noticed that the top of his right foot was red and swollen. A tiny barb poked out from his tender flesh. A bee sting. He must have crushed one when he fell. With two fingernails, she plucked it out. Then she brought his pink foot to her lips and kissed the inflamed area.

"Oh, my poor Bekeli, already the world is wounding you. Don't cry, my love. *Emayay* will soon make all your pain go away."

Swinging her son onto her hip, she started walking toward the double glass doors leading into the house. But she stopped short when she saw the dark figure of her father-in-law staring at her from the other side of the glass. Like her, he was dressed casually in dark trousers and a short-sleeved shirt, but on his feet were what he called his "political shoes," shined to a high black polish. The expression on his face was jubilant, despite the fact that they had only gotten up from *Sevat Ken* the day before. No sign of mourning remained in that photogenic smile.

He slid open one of the glass doors and stepped into the backyard.

"Why the tears, grandson?" he asked when he noticed Bekeli's wet cheeks. "Was your *Emayay* mean to you?"

Shulamit glared at him. Her father-in-law never missed an opportunity to mock her. If only his admirers could see how truly sadistic he really was. Only in public or in front of the camera was he the benevolent MK. At home, he was a tyrant.

"A bee stung him. I'm going inside to put some ice on it."

"Before you go, I wanted to tell you that I'll be taking Bekeli with me to the Promenade tomorrow for the Sigd celebration. It's not too early for him to learn about his people's heritage."

Shulamit took a step back, stunned.

Moshe was bringing her son to the Sigd Festival? Why hadn't he told her sooner? She hadn't planned on this.

She shuddered, her bony shoulders shaking even more visibly than they had when she'd become worried about wearing her mother's hair clasp at home. Then, suddenly, she became calm. Maybe this was meant to be. Fated. Deep inside she felt her Zar gripping her bowels.

"If Bekeli goes, so do I. You'll be too busy shaking hands and signing autographs to watch him."

"No, he will remain with me the whole time. Everyone loves to see political leaders with little children."

He walked forward and chucked Bekeli under his double chin.

"Especially when they're as handsome as this one."

Moshe laughed. His protruding belly jiggled. Shulamit clenched her teeth. Even when he wasn't performing for the public, Moshe's laughter sounded insincere.

"He's my son!"

"And my grandson. We will have no more argument about this." Moshe breathed in deeply, then took a few steps back. "I will have bodyguards. They will watch out for him." He paused, then grinned. "The boy stays with me."

"For the photo ops, eh? 'Popular MK poses with handsome grandson.' You don't fool me, Moshe!"

Bekeli began squirming in Shulamit's arms. She set him down on the grass and stood up, her back like an iron rod. Under Moshe's intense stare, she felt herself shrinking like melting wax. She reached back to touch the hair clasp. It had pulled loose and now dangled near one ear. She reached back with both arms and re-fastened the clasp.

Moshe's dark eyes followed her arms. He tilted his head. Then he stepped to the side and gazed at the back of her head.

Suddenly he spun around and marched back toward the double doors. He slid one side open, then twisted around. His smile, cunning and full of spite, made her blood run cold.

"No need to worry, my dear. The boy will be completely safe with me."

He stepped inside the dark house, then slammed the glass door shut. The panes shivered, then stilled.

Shulamit walked back into the middle of yard, oblivious to the velvety grass, the honeybees softly purring around her head, the warm breeze on her cheek. She bent down and seized the soccer ball. With a mighty heave, she threw it toward the chain-link fence bordering the yard. She smiled as the mud-spattered ball cleared the top of the fence and sailed out of view.

59

"I CAN'T BELIEVE YOU'VE NEVER come to one of these celebrations before!"

Dani's voice was teasing but Maya picked up a faint note of censure. Though she'd heard about the Sigd Festival for years, she'd never felt drawn to attend. What did she know or care about the Beta Israel? When she'd tried to imagine the scene—a large, boisterous crowd of black Jews, speaking and praying in Amharic—she couldn't see herself enjoying the experience. What sense could she make of any of it?

But when Dani had asked her to come to the annual festival on her day off and to bring Vered along, her curiosity had been piqued. More to the point, she relished the idea of spending a whole day with him, away from her exasperating investigation, away from Roni's constant needling. And she was eager to see how Dani and Vered would get along. Not that she expected their relationship to go anywhere.

As she always did when she was anxious, especially when she was about to face an unfamiliar social setting, Maya had thrown herself headlong into research mode. She'd learned that *Sigd* meant "a day to bend the knee" in the ancient Ge'ez language. For two thousand years the festival had been observed only by the Jews of Ethiopia. But in 2008 the government had declared it a national holiday.

Falling fifty days after Yom Kippur in a month otherwise bereft of Jewish holidays, Sigd commemorated the day that God gave the Israelites the Torah on Mount Sinai. Each year on this day, their Ethiopian descendants renewed that covenant. It was also the day the Beta Israel recalled the return of the Jewish exiles from Babylonian captivity. In their colorful celebration, the community re-enacted the dramatic moment when Ezra the Scribe, appearing before the repatriated exiles and the surviving remnant in Jerusalem, read the Torah for the first time in public. Reminding them that they were finally home.

Back in Ethiopia, the far-flung communities of the Beta Israel used to travel for days to gather together in villages near the Semien Mountains. While they waited for the holy day, they would reconnect with distant relatives and friends, arrange marriages, and share stories and meals. When the day of Sigd dawned, they would ascend the mountain in a grand procession, led by their priests, the qesoch, who carried with them colorful umbrellas and the precious Orit, the Ethiopian Torah. On the mountaintop they sacrificed animals, tore their clothes, and faced Jerusalem to pray.

Nowadays the annual celebration in Jerusalem drew tens of thousands of Ethiopian Jews to the Armon Hanatziv Ridge, one of the highest points in Jerusalem. The women donned their finest jewelry and scarves; the men, their purest white shammas and turbans. Carrying brightly colored umbrellas and the timeworn Orit, the qesoch led them in a grand parade, though the climb was no longer as arduous as ascending Jan Amora nor the autumnal Jerusalem sun as scorching. At a long table covered with a white cloth, the turbaned priests would then chant from the Orit in Ge'ez in an ancient oriental melody.

Most of the day was spent in prayer. Fasting all day, the Ethiopian Jews confessed their sins before God and begged for forgiveness. The women prostrated themselves on the ground, weeping copiously and ululating. The priests exhorted the people to remain faithful to God and their traditions, and the people thundered back, "Amen!"

At sundown, fifteen thousand Ethiopian Jews, joined by a host of outsiders—photographers, journalists, government officials, tourists, and gawkers—would then join together for a state-sponsored meal. And when their hunger was sated, they would erupt in joy, singing and dancing to the sounds of horn blasts and drums.

What a *balagan*, as Israelis would say.

A scene tailor-made for murder.

As the Egged bus pulled into the Haas Promenade parking lot, Maya looked at the crowd and felt her stomach heave. She hated crowds. All around her, the passengers began to leave their seats. As she placed her feet on the baking macadam of the parking lot, Vered dashed back into the bus to retrieve the small cloth shoulder bag she'd left on her seat. It was Dani's "getting acquainted gift" to her. The bag was embroidered with a brightly colored scene of Ethiopian children at play. Maya thought it a sweet gesture. During the ride, Vered had clutched the bag to her chest, peeking inside every once in a while to marvel at the small wooden baboon Dani had carved for her out of mpingo wood and hidden inside the bag.

The three of them walked along the tree-lined paths of the Haas Promenade, threading their way through the jostling crowd. It was still early. This high up on the Armon Hanatziv Ridge, the air was pleasantly cool, fanned by a light breeze. Glaring at Maya, Vered yanked off her yellow sweater and flung it at her mother. They'd fought about the sweater before leaving the house. A preview of her headstrong daughter as a teenager. She'd been no different when she was Vered's age. As her mother was forever reminding her.

Most of the Ethiopian Jews at the Promenade were dressed in white from head to toe. The women's heads were covered by long netelas; the men wore turbans, fedoras, or *kippot*. The crisp air was filled with exotic smells. Maya recognized a few familiar cooking spices, but most of the aromas confused her nose. Strains of music wafted overhead. Nasal melodies that reminded Maya of Arab *maqam*. Singsong chants in indecipherable tongues. A number of women, mostly middle-aged and elderly, lay prostrate on the ground, their foreheads pressed to the grass or concrete. Some sobbed. Others screeched like strangled cats, carrying on like women at a Moroccan Jewish wedding.

Maya's head whirled. She felt dizzy, even a little afraid.

"Let's get closer," said Dani.

He grabbed Maya's hand and pulled her further into the crowd. Maya reached back for Vered's hand. But her daughter was no longer there.

"Vered!"

Maya's voice was calm, but she could feel the adrenalin already blazing through her like a burning current through a wire.

"Vered!"

She jerked her hand out of Dani's grasp. Dani whirled around and stared at her, his eyes wide.

"She's gone! I don't see her!"

Together they ran through the milling throng, pushing people aside, stepping on sandaled feet. There were few white children in the crowd. Each time Maya came upon a white girl, she grabbed her by the shoulder and spun her around, gawping into an unfamiliar face. Her heart thumped wildly. She couldn't breathe. Her eyes fogged with tears.

And then, suddenly, there was she was, standing in a small open space amid the crowd. Beside her, holding her hand, stood Sarit Levine.

"Lose something, Maya?"

Sarit's grin toggled fitfully between sympathy and amusement.

"It's lucky I was here to snag her."

Sarit released Vered's hand. The young girl ran toward Maya and threw her arms around her waist, burying her face in her mother's blouse. Maya nodded to the petite police inspector, then mouthed her thanks.

"I'm surprised to see you here, Sarit," Maya said. "Expecting trouble today?"

"The Prime Minister's speaking here a bit later. Trying to score a pre-election photo op. We're just being extra careful."

Maya glanced around and spotted the uniformed cops near the festival entrance. She'd missed them on her way in, too overwhelmed by the dense sea of black skin that had so quickly swallowed her up. A sudden fear, unloosed from some pit deep inside her, had slipped its icy fingers around her throat and squeezed. Never before had she been around so many dark-skinned people. Vered, in contrast, seemed oblivious, which both confounded and pleased her mother. *Oy, Camille, did you do a job on me! Here I am in love with a black man, and I'm still bedeviled by your racist whispers.*

Maya spotted a knot of police surrounding several black limousines parked at the edge of the crowd. The Prime Minister's motorcade. It took her a few more minutes to spot the undercovers. Most were Ethiopians, dressed like everyone else, but their black closed-toed shoes gave them away. As did the coiled wires spiraling from their ears.

"Looks like you've got it covered," Maya said.

The two women parted with perfunctory waves.

Dani led them to a shaded spot, near the long, cloth-covered table where the qesoch sat, looking regal in their high turbans, white *shammas*, and gold-embroidered capes. The treasured *Orit* lay before the priests, its weathered boards and parchment leaves as fragile as old bone.

"They haven't begun chanting from the Torah yet," said Dani. "Let's walk around and take in more of the scene."

Vered groaned. Her freckled face scrunched into a grimace. From her shoulder bag Maya dug out a slim container of dried fruit, nuts, and sesame sticks and handed it to her daughter. Vered immediately began stuffing the snack mix into her mouth. Maya resisted the urge to chide her awful manners. This outing wasn't much fun for a six-year-old.

Maya glanced nervously at Dani, whose eyes were fixed on the ancient qes sitting in the center of the other priests. The old man's face was so wrinkled that his eyes looked like black beans pressed into dried clay.

"If we stay until sunset," Maya bent down and whispered to her daughter, "there's a huge party with lots of singing and dancing. I think you'll like that."

Vered shrugged her shoulders. She tipped her head back and drank some water from Maya's thermos. Then she pulled open her new shoulder bag and winked at the wooden baboon huddled at the bottom of the bag. When she looked up, her grimace had eased itself into a grin.

Maya sighed and relaxed her shoulders. Then she looked around for a way out of the packed crowd.

That's when her eyes fell upon Roni Qattawi.

60

LIKE ALMOST EVERYONE ELSE AT the festival, Roni was dressed in white—loose pants and a short-sleeved button-down shirt—but his sharp Egyptian features and saddle-leather skin would never let anyone mistake him for an Ethiopian. Before Maya could turn away and lose herself in the crowd, Roni saw her and began making his way in her direction.

He halted abruptly when he noticed Dani. He eyed the tall, slender black man from head to toe as he might appraise a horse he was considering putting money on. Then he looked at Maya and chuckled.

"*Melkam Sigd!* Fancy meeting you here, Agent Rimon. Who's your...friend?"

Reluctantly, Maya introduced the men to each other. Dani was almost a head taller than Roni and more muscular. Several of Dani's features—the high forehead, straight black eyebrows, and long fingers—suggested a delicacy that Roni's rough-hewn features lacked. Dani smiled at Maya's boss, who nodded his head but did not return the Ethiopian's broad smile.

"I see you've brought your cute little daughter as well. Nurit, isn't it?"

Roni bent down and stroked Vered's auburn hair with his hand. Vered recoiled and shrank back against Dani's legs.

"Wrong flower, Roni. She's named for a rose, not a buttercup. Her name's Vered."

Roni shrugged, then aped Dani's generous grin.

"Well, enjoy your anthropological outing!"

He turned to leave, but Maya grabbed him by the forearm and yanked him back.

"Why are *you* here today? Sarit seems to have brought enough firepower to protect the whole Knesset."

"You're right. I came for a different purpose. To catch your 'hyena-killer.'"

Maya disliked the name the papers had given the murderer. Hyena-killer. It made him out to be some magical creature with superpowers. She wished the media would stop making murder sound so fascinating and glamorous. But it's what boosted ratings and ad revenue.

Roni guffawed, exposing small, stained teeth in crooked rows.

"It's not a joke, Roni! This festival is just the kind of setting this killer would choose, using the pandemonium of Sigd as cover."

"And who will he kill this time? The Prime Minister?"

Should she share her suspicions with Roni, that Shulamit and Moshe Aklilu were somehow linked together in this crime? That something in their shared past was behind the murders? She didn't want to say anything until she'd put the whole puzzle together. She wasn't yet ready. But she was close.

"*Nu*, Maya, so who's next on his hit list?"

She sucked in a deep breath, then slowly blew it out between pressed lips.

"I think it's likely that Moshe Aklilu will kill his daughter-in-law or vice versa. I'm not sure which. But I'm pretty sure that this is the last act of the play."

Roni started to laugh but choked on his own saliva. What came out was a loud snort. His flinty black eyes speared hers.

"Is this another of your cockamamie conspiracy theories, Rimon? Do you have any evidence to back it up? Or even a motive? Why would Moshe Aklilu want to kill the members of his own family? His only son? His daughter? His pretty, young wife? His daughter-in-law, for heaven's sake! Why? And what possible motive could *she* have for killing them? This time you've gone completely off the rails!"

Maya said nothing. Roni was right. It all sounded crazy. She had no way of proving that either of her suspects was the killer. She shouldn't have said anything, even at the risk of pissing off her boss. It was better that than appearing ridiculous.

Standing nearby, Dani nervously shuffled his feet. His eyes explored the ground under his sandals.

Suddenly, he called out, with far too much cheerfulness: "Hey, Vered! How about if we look for a bathroom? I don't know about you, but I could sure use one."

Vered giggled. She reached up and took Dani's left hand—Maya was surprised that her daughter seemed unfazed by the roughness of his scarred palm—and off they went, quickly disappearing into the crowd.

"This is precisely why I didn't assign you to the team I brought here today," Roni said. He flicked the tail end of his cigarette at the ground and lit another one. He inhaled a lungful of smoke and let it out slowly. "I knew you'd go off half-cocked like this. Go home, Maya. It's your day off. And take your *kushi* boyfriend with you. And your flower child."

Roni shook himself loose from Maya's grip and marched toward the bevy of black limousines at the perimeter of the crowd.

Maya stared at his back until his slim form was lost amid the PM's entourage.

61

As soon as Roni was gone, Maya felt restless. She felt the need to do something, anything, to stop feeling so...what? Mortified? Inept?

She looked around. No sign of Dani and Vered. Must be a long line at the port-o-potties.

The crowd had swollen to fill the plaza. It surged toward the table where a young acolyte was chanting from the Orit, swaying over the ancient codex, his voice tremulous with fervor. Behind him sat the qesoch, their turbaned heads shielded from the bright sun by colorful umbrellas. Behind them stood other white-robed men, leaning over the elderly priests to hear the holy words in ancient Ge'ez. A few women tried to stretch themselves out on the ground, but there was no longer room for that. Maya felt herself squeezed in a human vise. She smelled sweat and sour body odors. Most of the Ethiopian men standing around her towered over her. Clouds suddenly scudded in front of the sun, throwing everything into shadow.

Looking beyond the turbaned heads of the qesoch, she saw that the area behind them was almost empty. Mumbling *yikirita*, "excuse me," one of the few words she knew in Amharic, she shouldered her way through the crowd. It took her almost five minutes to make her way to the edge of the throng, and a few more to reach the relatively clear area behind the qesoch. The site was a haphazard jumble of electrical cords, sound and video equipment, pallets of water bottles, stacked plastic folding chairs, and boxes of colored flyers. Techs scrambled over the equipment, shouting to each other in Amharic and Hebrew. An elderly woman bent over a small iron stove, baking *dabo*. The oily smoke brought tears to Maya's eyes.

At one end of the grassy area stood a cluster of dignitaries, several wearing Western-style suits. They talked quietly among themselves. The group included Moshe Aklilu, who was ostentatiously dressed in a flowing white *shamma* and black cape, trimmed with gold embroidery and fastened with a band of gold cloth. On his head he wore a large white kippah, likewise trimmed with gold. Sitting at his feet was little Bekeli, wearing a miniature version of his grandfather's outfit. The toddler played with a stick in a patch of dirt, drawing circles, then rubbing them out with his pudgy fingers.

Suddenly, a tall figure leapt into the middle of the grass. The figure was dressed as an animal, covered from head to foot with heavy ochre cloth. Sharp metal talons protruded from its hands and feet. On its head was a terrifying wooden mask. The unnaturally large eyes of the creature were shiny black, amplified by two concentric white circles surrounding the dark iris. Its ears and snout were also enlarged, thrusting out from the face like sharp projectiles. But the beast's most frightening feature was its yawning mouth, serrated with sharp spiky white teeth.

Before anyone had time to react, the costumed figure ran over to Moshe Aklilu, bent down, and snatched up Bekeli, who cried out in fright. Thrusting the screaming child under one arm, the beast fled, disappearing over the guard rail bordering the stone promenade. The child's cries grew progressively fainter until they faded away altogether.

Even after the figure and its captive prey had disappeared from sight, no one at the scene moved or spoke. A hundred feet away, the swollen crowd continued to listen raptly to the qes's chanting, unaware of what had just occurred. The techs, their hearing muffled by headphones, continued to scramble over tangled cables, shouting instructions to each other. Only Moshe Aklilu and the other dignitaries stood stock-still and open-mouthed, staring at the low stone fence and metal rail, over which a frightening apparition had just bolted with a kidnapped child under its arm.

Maya was the first to react. She raced to the low stone fence and stared down the rocky slope, spotting the costumed figure scrambling over rocks and low brush, struggling to hang on to its wriggling prey. For such a tall person, the figure displayed surprising agility, never stumbling over the uneven terrain. Maya was too far away to hear Bekeli's cries, but she knew the toddler must be frantic with fear. Where was his mother, Shulamit? Had she let Moshe take the boy off by himself?

Not hesitating, Maya grabbed the metal rail with one hand and catapulted over it, landing several feet below on a patch of caked soil. Her sandaled feet were unable to find a purchase on the slurry of pebbles and dirt. Her feet shot forward, and she fell backwards, breaking her fall with her right hand. When she looked down at the hand, she saw that it was badly scraped. She wiped the bloody hand on the front of her slacks, then started running, keeping the receding figure in her sights. A few times she stumbled over rocks and rutted soil, but she did not slacken her pace. She began closing in on the other runner, who must be tiring by now. Bekeli had to weigh a good thirty pounds.

Maya was also getting winded. It took a tremendous effort to run in sandals over rough ground. But the race would have to end soon. A hundred meters ahead, the slope of the Armon Hanatziv Ridge flattened out and ended abruptly at a paved road. At the moment, traffic on this road was heavy. There was no way the kidnapper could get across without getting hit. And there was nowhere else to go. On either side of them the field was bordered by dense bushes. The beast was trapped.

Maya was only a few meters away from her target. She slowed, then stopped. She was wretchedly aware that she carried no weapon. She didn't even have the Swiss army knife she always carried in her purse. She'd shed the shoulder bag before hurtling over the guard rail. And her adversary had a good six inches on her.

The two of them now stood opposite, staring at each other, gasping for breath, their chests and shoulders heaving from their exertions. Bekeli was strangely quiet, clinging to his abductor as though somehow deriving comfort from the contact.

From this close distance, Maya finally got a good look at the kidnapper's costume. And all at once—*click*! Her brain put the clues together. The tawny hide with dark spots, the low slope of the beast's forehead, the sharp, jagged teeth. Of course, the figure was dressed as a hyena! Her mind flashed to the image of the hyena carved into Hagar's bloody brow. The caricature of the hyena spray-painted on the Aklilus' garage. The hyena drawn on the amulet stuffed into Elvis's mouth.

She took a step forward, her hands raised, palms facing out.

"Please don't harm the boy. He's only—"

Harsh laughter erupted from behind the beast's mask.

Maya took another step forward.

Reaching inside an open seam of the costume, the kidnapper pulled out a long, curved knife. Maya immediately recognized it. A billawa. The sharp blade glittered in the late afternoon sunlight.

"One more step and I'll slit the child's throat!"

62

Maya froze. The angry voice sounded familiar, but she couldn't quite place it.

The hyena-figure now yanked off its mask and flung it away. Maya gasped.

It was Shulamit Aklilu!

The young black woman threw the mask to the ground and spit in the dirt.

"But he's your own child! Why are you doing this?"

Gently, Shulamit set Bekeli down on the ground beside her. The little boy found a stick and began poking at the dirt. Shulamit lowered the billawa but did not release it. She glowered at Maya.

"You white Jews think you understand all about us, but you know nothing!"

Shulamit wiped her mouth with the back of her free hand. Maya saw that her lips were cracked and dry. Maya's mouth, too, was parched. Her thermos of cold water lay at the bottom of her shoulder bag up on the ridge along with her pocketknife. She licked her chapped lips and tasted salt.

"You want to know why I'm doing this?" said Shulamit. Her amber eyes blazed in the dying light of day. "Why I'm killing the people in this family? In the name of justice! Though some might call it revenge."

Maya desperately needed water. Even though it was early November, the air at the bottom of the ridge was stifling. They needed to head back up to the Promenade while it was still light. She needed to convince Shulamit to end the stand-off, to give herself up.

Bekeli suddenly started to cry. He looked up at his mother and reached up with his stubby arms. Undoubtedly, he was thirsty too. And hungry. Shulamit let the knife drop to the ground. She reached down and picked up her son. Her face softened.

Maya nodded to her, keeping her own face expressionless.

Shulamit's shoulders sagged. A loud sigh escaped her desiccated lips.

"Twenty-five years ago, my family escaped from our village in Gondar. Conditions had gotten very bad for Jews there. I was only four years old. My grandmother was very frail, but she wanted to die in the Holy Land. There were eight of us—my old *ayati*, my parents, my three sisters, my brother, and myself. The youngest, Tenanye, was only a baby. We left with two other families. None of us knew how to get to the refugee camp in Sudan. My sister Hawi's boyfriend, Negasi, said he could lead us there. He claimed to know the way."

Bekeli suddenly let out a sharp cry. Shulamit looked down and eyed the big toe he was pointing at with a stubby finger. The toe was covered in red ants. She brushed the ants off, then kissed the swollen toe. Then she spit into her palm and rubbed the saliva over the bites. Bekeli grinned up at her. She swung him onto her other hip and re-adjusted her footing. Her son began poking at the dark spots on her costume with the stick he still grasped in his hand.

"*Ay-ay*, Negasi knew the way all right. He waited until we became weak with hunger and thirst. Then he robbed us! He took everything we'd brought with us—all the money we'd saved to start our new lives in Israel. The silver hair clasp my father made for my mother. Even my precious doll, Gudit, just to be spiteful." She paused, then kissed her son tenderly on his head. "And then he left us there to die."

"Only *Emayay* and I made it to the camp. But soon after we arrived, she got sick with cholera. Before she died, she made me swear to stay alive for all of them. And she made me promise to bring Negasi to justice."

Maya wanted to ask Shulamit a question, but she dared not interrupt her. The woman was speaking as if in a trance, her amber eyes opaque and glittering.

"I spent six years in that horrible camp, waiting. Eating sickening food, dodging the indecent eyes and hands of men, fighting with other children over our pitiful rations, watching many die. Finally, they put me on a plane to Israel. They placed me with an Ethiopian foster family in Kiryat Malakhi. Those people did not treat me well. The only good one was Ayati Ga'wa. She taught me all she knew about magic and spells and potions."

So, it was Shulamit who had poisoned Vered and the cat. And tried to frame Fewesi. And no doubt planted drugs on Titi to try to frame her husband.

The storyteller seemed lost in her own tale, replaying tapes she'd listened to in her head for a quarter of a century. Maya lost patience.

"And where does Moshe Aklilu fit in?"

Still lost in her reverie, Shulamit bent down and picked up the billawa from the baked ground. She raised it above her head and began slicing the air, startling Bekeli. He reached for the glimmering blade, but his mother roughly shoved his hand away.

"I lost track of Negasi after he left us in the mountains to die. I came to Israel and began trying to create a new life here. Then one day I saw him on television. He had just been elected to the Knesset. I recognized the sickle-shaped scar on the side of his neck."

So, Maya had been right to finger Moshe as Negasi.

"Of course, he had changed his name," continued Shulamit. "Did you know that in Amharic Negasi means 'he will wear a crown'? Well, there he was on TV: King Negasi! Seeing him on the screen with that high and mighty grin, his chest puffed out for everyone to see, telling everyone all the wonderful things he was going to do for 'his people'—it made me want to vomit! From that moment on, I devoted every waking hour to tracking him down. I found out where he lived. I learned that he had a son five years younger than me. I decided I was going to marry that son and get close enough to Negasi to make him pay for what he did to us."

"So, you killed his wife and two children to get revenge."

Shulamit nodded. Her eyes blazed with triumph. And with something else. Profound sorrow. Maya was heartened to see even that fleeting trace of remorse, but she quickly reminded herself that this woman had taken three lives, at least one of them wholly innocent.

"And Bekeli? What does he have to do with what Moshe Aklilu did? How could you even think of killing your own child!"

Was it the angle of the setting sun that changed the expression in Shulamit's dark eyes? Or was it something from inside her? Her amber eyes became hard like burnished stone. Her voice, too, now had a brittle edge to it.

"I decided that the best way to avenge my family was to let Negasi live, aware that I'd taken from him everyone he loves, including his beloved grandson. I'm willing even to make the ultimate sacrifice if it means increasing that man's suffering. Why shouldn't he be condemned to live his whole life grieving? It's what he has forced me to do!"

Maya couldn't help sympathizing with this woman's pain. She had heard similar testimonies of inconsolable misery from Holocaust survivors and from parents who had lost children to terrorist bombs. But she also knew that revenge would never take away the pain.

"Why not let the Israeli criminal system bring Moshe to justice? My investigation into his various enterprises here in Israel has uncovered more than enough crimes to lock him away for a long, long time."

Shulamit had a strange look in her eyes. She gazed off to the side, her pupils unfocused and glazed. She began muttering under her breath. The tendons in her neck became rigid. Her breathing stuttered. The hand holding the billawa began to weave back and forth in front of her, the blade swimming like a circling shark. Fascinated, Bekeli watched the knife's movement. Back and forth. Back and forth.

"Hand the boy over to me, Shulamit. Your arms must be tired from holding him. Let's go back up to the Promenade and get some water. Something to eat."

Shulamit appeared not to hear her. She abruptly stopped swinging the knife. She brought the sharp blade close to her son's neck. She looked up into the cloudless sky.

"Here I am! Here is the knife! And here is the sacrifice!"

She closed her eyes.

"*Emayay*, forgive me!"

63

"No!"

Maya screamed and lunged forward, her open hands grasping for the painted hilt of the billawa.

Shulamit swiveled her wrist and tilted the curved blade down, then thrust it out toward Maya like a spear. Maya sucked in her abdomen and jumped backward. She looked down and spotted a sharp rock several feet away.

But before she could bend down to grab it, Shulamit began to babble incoherently in a loud, gruff voice, the sound rumbling from deep within her throat.

And then, suddenly, she began to laugh. Bekeli joined in, but his eyes were wary.

Still laughing, Shulamit swung the child off her hip and set him down carefully on the ground. He reached up to her with both arms, but she shook her head.

"My precious son, you, too, must forgive me."

Whispering these last words, Shulamit swept the knife up toward her own throat and lightly nicked the dark skin with the blade. A few drops of blood pearled on the polished steel.

And then her hand froze, the glinting blade poised motionless at her neck. A single bead of dark blood snaked slowly down toward her delicate breastbone.

What stayed Shulamit's hand at that moment? Was it some invisible angel? Or perhaps her Zar releasing her from its merciless grip? Or had the deadly caress of the razor-edged blade finally brought her to her senses? Whatever it was, those few seconds of hesitation gave

Maya just enough time to fly at the other woman and snatch the billawa from her hand.

Her strength suddenly gone, Shulamit sank to the ground and buried her face in her hands. Bekeli scooted over on his bottom and clutched her trembling head between his pudgy hands. Then he began kissing her russet hair with loud smacks.

Maya lowered herself to the ground, resting on her knees. She took a few deep breaths. Although adrenalin had temporarily staved off her hunger and thirst, she suddenly felt extraordinarily tired. She laid the billawa down on a tussock of dried grass. Shulamit's smeared blood had dried on the blade, making the metal look tarnished.

"You can't let him win," said Maya. "You've come too far for that."

Shulamit began to sob. Bekeli stroked her hair so tenderly that it seemed as if he were the parent comforting his child.

"You made two promises to your mother," said Maya. "The first was to bring Negasi to justice, which I assure you will be done. The other promise was to live. For all of them. You're still a young woman, Shulamit. I'm sure the judge will be compassionate."

Shulamit's sobs were subsiding. But now Bekeli began to cry. His hunger and thirst kicking in.

Maya rose to her feet, then reached her hand out to Shulamit.

"Come on. Let's go back up to the Promenade." Maya sniffed the air, then smiled. "Even from here I can smell the *doro wat* and *bunna*. I don't know about you, but I'm starving."

Shulamit slowly stood up. Then she bent down and scooped up Bekeli, settling him securely on her hip. He thrust a pudgy thumb into his mouth and began to suck. As the two women headed toward the sloping field, he fell asleep.

Shulamit shuffled a few steps behind Maya, her head drooping as though she, too, were falling asleep. She extended her splayed hand out toward Maya, who cradled the long black fingers tenderly in her palm.

Then the three of them began their ascent up the Armon Hanatziv Ridge.

Epilogue

Three months later

THE WINTER HAD BEEN PARTICULARLY brutal. So much for global warming. Although it had snowed only once in the Jerusalem hills, bitter rain had pelted the city frequently. The icy pellets scalded one's skin like a raw burn. No matter how warmly Maya bundled up, she was always chilled. Trekking back and forth to her office every day left her feeling miserable and short-tempered. It was already early February. The almond blossoms should be out by now. But the stubby trees were bare.

Today Maya woke early even though it was Shabbat. She had lost the ability to sleep in on her day off. Her body was always wound like a clock, springing into wakefulness soon after the sun rose. But regardless of how early she woke up, it still took her forever to get ready for the day. Feeling the habitual grogginess, she reproached herself for staying up late last night reading a detective novel. She'd be a zombie by evening.

She peered out of the living room window at the thermometer hanging in a stone recess. Only nine degrees! She shivered. She dressed quickly in jeans, heavy socks, and a sweatshirt.

As she laced up her hiking boots, her thoughts segued to the phone call she'd received yesterday from her ex's lawyer, Rafi's brother, Avi. Rafi was scheduled for a parole hearing in two weeks. He had told his brother that he had every intention of suing for sole custody of Vered once he was out of prison. Maya had enjoyed the eighteen-month respite from their endless squabbles over their daughter. But it looked like the war was about to resume.

At least justice was being served in the case of Moshe Aklilu. Over the past few weeks, Moshe and his partner in crime, Joey Villanueva, had been on trial for sex-trafficking and money laundering. The case had garnered sensational publicity because of Aklilu's position as an MK. His opponents, especially his perennial rival, Benny Tzagai, were gloating over Aklilu's spectacular fall from grace. The government had frozen all of his assets and seized his mansion in the German Colony together with his three luxury cars. And the Knesset had ignominiously expelled him from its ranks. Three days ago, the judge had handed the case over to the jury. They were still deliberating.

Maya wondered what would happen to Shulamit. After she'd surrendered to the authorities, she'd undergone an extensive psychiatric evaluation. The doctors recommended that she be remanded to a special unit at Hadassah Medical Center that specialized in treating PTSD. After a year of treatment, she would be re-evaluated as to her fitness to stand trial. One of the examining psychiatrists described her mental state as a "cultural manifestation of trauma"; another, as a delayed grief reaction to losing her family as a young child. Maya recalled Shulamit's muscle twitches, her *basso profundo* vocalization, and her incoherent mutterings during their final confrontation near the Promenade. And she remembered what she had read about Zar possession. Which diagnosis was closest to the truth?

She took a deep breath and smelled coffee brewing across the hall. She sighed. The aroma was not the piquant fragrance of Fewesi's spiced *bunna* but ordinary Turkish "mud." Her new next-door neighbors were a family from Venezuela, fleeing that country's collapse. In early December Fewesi had moved out without saying goodbye or leaving a forwarding address. Nigist Fredo-Wasa, Maya's prying neighbor on the second floor, had confided to Maya that Fewesi had returned to Ethiopia to resume her work as an herbal healer. Fewesi had told Nigist that she just hadn't been able to adjust to life in Israel.

A key turned in the front door. Dani and Vered had returned from their outing.

"Ima!"

Vered bounded into the living room. Maya leapt to her feet. Vered ran up to her mother and hugged her fiercely around the waist.

Maya peered down at her six-year-old daughter. Her ruddy curls swirled over her head like storm-swept seaweed. Her fingers were covered in chocolate. And when Vered looked up, Maya saw that her pale cheeks were daubed with brown smears like slapdash rouge. A broad smile crinkled every feature of the young girl's face.

"Dani bought me two scoops of chocolate ice cream!" Vered held up two slender fingers. "Can you believe it? Ice cream in February! It made my teeth shiver."

Dani stepped into the room. He wore dark slacks, a dark gray turtleneck, and a light brown cable-knit sweater. He also wore wool gloves and a black watch cap. Maya laughed.

"It's nine degrees out, Dani, not fifty below!"

"What can I do? I was born in the tropics. I'll never get used to this cold."

He smiled. Maya felt warmth suffusing her skin. Even though they'd been together for three months already, she still thrilled at the sight of his luminous smile. She had come to love every part of him—the pearl-white teeth, so bright against his obsidian skin; the strong nose that widened into a river delta at the nostrils; and most of all, the deep pools of his eyes. When he held her in his firm, sinewy arms, she felt invulnerable.

Now that the Aklilu case was closed, she and Dani had no more excuses to see each other professionally. But she wasn't yet ready to talk about him at the office. Except to Masha, of course, who had been sworn to secrecy. She certainly wasn't ready to bring him home to meet her parents. Of course, Camille kept sniffing around with that big Moroccan nose of hers, but Maya refused to open up to her about Dani.

Maya fished her mobile out of her pants pocket and speed-dialed Camille.

"Is it still okay if Vered sleeps over at your place tonight?" she asked her mother when she picked up. "I know that Saturday night's your regular night out with Abba. You sure you don't mind?"

"You have a date, Maya?"

Her mother paused, waiting for a response that didn't come. But she was not someone who surrendered without a fight.

"Well, do you? Who with? I hope it's not with that *kushi*. You know what they say: 'The minute an Ethiopian man marries a white woman, she becomes black.'"

"Can Vered sleep over, yes or no?"

"Of course she can."

Maya discerned the pout in her mother's voice. She visualized Camille's glossy lower lip clamped over her upper one, that great scythe of a nose slicing the air, her plump, bejeweled hands wringing like flags in a stiff breeze.

"Okay, then," said Maya. "I'll pick her up early tomorrow and take her to *gan*."

She hung up before her mother could come back with a tart retort.

Vered was sitting cross-legged on the floor, playing with Bezoona, bopping the black cat on the head with one finger until the cat took a sharp swipe at her, drawing blood. Vered bopped him once more on the head, much harder than before, sending the cat skittering under the loveseat. Vered licked the scratch with her tongue, then ran into her bedroom. Maya soon heard her talking animatedly to Kofi, the small wooden baboon Dani had carved for her.

She felt Dani's warm hand on her cheek. She spun around and found him staring at her, gazing at her face as though preparing to paint her portrait. She blushed. Dani winked at her.

His grin was teasing, but his dark eyes brimmed with feeling.

She smiled at him, reaching up to stroke his cheek.

Dani reached out his scarred palm and brushed her auburn hair. He leaned down. His kiss was gentle, but his full lips soon pressed against hers with mounting passion. Maya responded eagerly, parting her lips as his tongue probed deeper. Then she abruptly broke away.

"What is it, Maya?"

She tossed her head in the direction of Vered's bedroom.

Dani shrugged and sank into the loveseat.

Maya plopped down next to him.

"Sorry. I just don't want Vered to get her hopes up too high. About us. She's really become fond of you."

She cupped Dani's chin with one hand and planted a quick kiss on his lips.

"Can I sleep over tonight?" he asked.

From Vered's bedroom came the high, throaty bark of a baboon.

THE END

Glossary

Abba: Father, Daddy (Hebrew).

Abish: Fenugreek (Amharic).

Adoni: Sir (Hebrew).

Araqe: Ethiopian alcoholic drink made with gesho and fermented grain. Similar to *ouzo*. (Amharic).

Ars: Pimp, low-class person (Arabic).

Ashkenazi: Jew of European descent (Hebrew).

Awakiy balazar: Shamanic healer (Amharic).

Ayati: Grandmother (Amharic).

Baba: Father (Arabic).

Baksheesh: a bribe (Persian).

Balagan: tumult (Hebrew, derived from Russian).

Barya: slave. Lowest caste in Ethiopian society (Amharic).

Berbere: mixture of a dozen spices unique to Ethiopian cuisine (Amharic).

Berele: glass beaker with round bottom and long, narrow neck. Used for drinking *tej* (Amharic).

Bezoona: cat (Judeo-Arabic; Iraqi Arabic).

Billawa: ceremonial double-edged blade from Ethiopia (Amharic).

Bris: circumcision (Hebrew).

Buda: evil eye (Amharic). A person possessing Buda is believed capable of cursing others by casting a malevolent gaze.

Bunna: Ethiopian coffee ceremony (Amharic).

Chik-chak: slang for "ASAP" (Hebrew).

Dabo: honey bread, eaten by the Beta Israel on Shabbat and holidays (Amharic).

Dikkalla: Bastard (Amharic).

Doro wat: Spicy chicken stew (Amharic).

Dula: traditional Ethiopian walking stick made of hardwood or bamboo (Amharic).

Igziabeher: Lord of the World or Creation; name of God (Ge'ez).

Emayay: Mommy (Amharic).

Falasha: "landless"; derogatory name for Ethiopian Jews (Amharic).

Freier: Sucker, loser (Yiddish).

Ge'ez: ancient Ethiopian language, used in the sacred scriptures of the Ethiopian Church and the Beta Israel.

Giveret: Madam, ma'am, Mrs. (Hebrew).

Hamor: Donkey (Hebrew).

Haredi: ultra-Orthodox Jew. Literally, "one who trembles" (Hebrew).

Harira: thick, spicy Moroccan soup made with tomatoes, beans, lentils, and chickpeas (Amharic).

Havivati: Dear, darling, fem.

Habibi: Sweetie, darling, masc. (Hebrew).

Ima: Mother, Mommy (Hebrew).

Injera: Ethiopian flatbread, made out of teff flour (Amharic).

Jebena: tall vessel with delicately curved neck and spout, used in making coffee (Amharic).

Jeddah: Grandmother, Grandma (Arabic).

Jib: hyena (pl, *jiboch*) (Amharic).

Jnoun: dwarf (used by North African Jews as an insult; Arabic).

Kippah: skullcap or yarmulke (Hebrew).

Kitab: amulet made of leather or metal to ward off the evil eye (Arabic).

K'ria: a Jewish mourning ritual in which mourners tear their garment or wear a torn ribbon. Literally, "a ripping" (Hebrew).

Maksim: literally, enchanting. Derived from (Hebrew) word for magic. Can also mean fantastic, derived from maximum.

Mamzer: Bastard (Hebrew).

Maqam: Arabic melody type (Arabic).

Melkam Sigd: Happy Sigd! (Amharic).

Mizrachi: Jew of North African and Middle Eastern descent (Hebrew).

Motek: Sweetie (Hebrew).

Mud: Israeli slang for Turkish coffee.

Netela: handmade scarf-like two-layered cloth made of cotton worn by Ethiopian women (Amharic).

Nu: interjection meaning "so" or "well" (Yiddish and Russian).

Orit: The Ethiopian Torah, consisting of the Pentateuch as well as the Books of Joshua, Kings, and Ruth (Ge'ez and Amharic).

Protekzia: influence, personal connections, (Hebrew) slang, from English "protection" (Hebrew).

Qes (pl. *qesoch*): Ethiopian Jewish priest, the Beta Israel equivalent of a rabbi (Amharic).

Rooskis: slang for Russians (Hebrew).

Rugelach: Eastern European Jewish pastries, usually stuffed with fruit (Yiddish).

Sevat Ken: "Seven days," the seven days of mourning observed by Ethiopian Jews. Similar to *shiva* in Ashkenazi tradition (Amharic).

Shamma: white robe worn by Ethiopian men and women as their daily outer garment (Amharic).

Shvartz(es): Black people. Derogatory (Yiddish).

Tanakh: the Hebrew Bible (Hebrew acronym).

Tej: honey wine, made with leaves of an Ethiopian bush (Amharic).

Um Raquba: United Nations refugee camp on Sudanese border.

Wat: Ethiopian stew made with meat, vegetables, and spices (Amharic).

Way-ya: Exclamation of distress (Amharic).

Yene Fikire: My love (Amharic).

Yikirita: Excuse me (Amharic).

Zar (pl. *zayran*): Spirits believed to inhabit people as controlling presences, based on Ethiopian creation legend (Amharic).

Postscript

THE EVENTS AND CHARACTERS IN *The Hyena Murders* are for the most part imagined. But many of the particulars are based upon real events and people. In this brief Postscript, I will attempt to separate fact from fiction in my novel. But the reader should know that such a boundary is always permeable.

The story of Ethiopian Jewry is long and complex, its ancient origins shrouded in myth and scholarly controversy. In their own narrative, Ethiopian Jews trace their ancestry back to King Solomon, Israel's third king, and the Queen of Sheba, who visited Jerusalem to test Solomon's legendary wisdom. Impressed by his ability to unravel her riddles, she converted to Judaism. The queen returned home and bore a son fathered by Israel's king. Ethiopian Jews consider this son, King Menelik I, their ancestor.

Other accounts date the arrival of Jews to the destruction of the First Temple in Jerusalem in 586 B.C.E. Still others claim they probably arrived in trading caravans between the first and sixth centuries of the Common Era.

Over the many centuries, the Jews of Ethiopia endured many periods of persecution and destitution, punctuated occasionally by moments of triumph.

According to Ethiopian, Coptic, and Arabic sources, in the 10th century C.E., a Jewish queen, known variously as Gudit (or Yodit or Judith) or Aster (Esther), conquered the northern Kingdom of Axum, which had ruled Ethiopia since 400 B.C.E., burned many churches, and deposed the king. In most accounts, she was a convert to Judaism. She sat upon her throne for forty years. Despite recent scholarly challenges, Ethiopian Jews proudly claim her as one of their own. In my novel, Sisayu names her beloved doll after this warrior queen.

Beginning in the 15th century, Christian kings forced many Jews to be baptized and denied them the right to own land. From then on Ethiopian Jews were known by the pejorative term, *falashas*, an Amharic word meaning "exiles," "wanderers," or "landless." This derogatory label has now been officially replaced by "Beta Israel," Amharic for the House of Israel, a name Ethiopia Jewry has claimed since ancient times.

Isolated from the mainstream of Jewish life for millennia, the Beta Israel settled primarily in the northwest section of the country, notably Gondar Province, occupying about 500 small villages. They developed a form of Judaism that diverges in many ways from rabbinic tradition which the community predates. Until its mass relocation to Israel in the second half of the 20th century, the community's practice mainly consisted in following the legal sections in the Hebrew Bible, observing the Sabbath, and observing the purity laws concerning menstruation, birth, and death. Their Torah, called the *Orit* (from the Aramaic *Oraita*) consists of eight books: the Torah and the Books of Joshua, Judges, and Ruth. They did not begin observing the post-biblical holidays of Purim or Hanukkah until they came to Israel. The uniquely Ethiopian holiday known as Sigd became an official holiday in Israel in 2008.

Landless, poor, and victimized for centuries, Ethiopian Jews yearned to immigrate to Israel. Their dreams finally became a reality in the late 20th century when the international Jewish community mustered sufficient resources and political clout to fly them to freedom.

Through a series of dramatic airlifts—aptly entitled Operations Moses, Joshua, and Solomon—57,000 Ethiopian Jews were flown to Israel over twenty years. The most extraordinary airlift, Operation Solomon, took place on May 24-25, 1991, when thirty-five non-stop flights transported 14,000 Ethiopian Jews to Israel in thirty-six hours. An El Al 747, stripped of its seats, broke the world record for the most people carried on one plane, 1088, including two babies born in flight.

Unfortunately, when the Ethiopian Jews arrived in Israel, they discovered that their romantic fantasies of the Promised Land did not match the reality they found there. In a few hours, they'd traveled centuries, from pre-industrial times into the 20th century. They had to learn the basics of hygiene, modern housing and transportation, a new language, and a very different version of Judaism than the one they'd practiced back in Gondar.

They also faced a new kind of discrimination, different from the anti-Semitism and exclusionary social policies of their birthplace. Israeli authorities forced the new immigrants to discard their Amharic names and take new Hebrew ones. (In the novel, Sisayu became Shulamit; Negasi became Moshe.) Later immigrants did not face such demands. More recently many Ethiopian Jews in Israel have reclaimed their original names or taken new Ethiopian ones.

They also face racial discrimination in their new homeland. Placed initially in down-at-the-heel development towns from which most don't escape, they occupy the lowest rungs of Israel's socio-economic ladder. But in response to public pressure from Ethiopian activists and advocacy organizations (such as JEJI, a non-profit I invented), the government is gradually making more resources available to this community.

Even though Israeli rabbinical authorities have recognized the official Jewish status of the Beta Israel, they still regard Ethiopian Jews as not "fully" Jewish. So, for instance, Ethiopian funerals must include an Orthodox rabbi in addition to a *qes* (as happens at the Aklilu family burials). Beta Israel are encouraged to replace their prayers and melodies with Ashkenazi and other mainstream Jewish liturgies. Community customs are also changing. In Ethiopia, only Christians tore their clothing as a sign of mourning, so Jews refrained from doing so. But once in Israel, new immigrants began observing the traditional custom of *k'ria* (as does Moshe Aklilu). Younger Ethiopian Jews, however, have not followed the older generation's adaptation.

The one exception to the acculturation of Ethiopian Judaism and Jews into the Israeli default is Sigd.

Sigd is an Amharic word meaning "prostration" or "worship." (It has the same root as *masjid*, the Arabic word for mosque.) For centuries, only the Jews of Ethiopia observed this holiday. It is celebrated on the 29th day of the Hebrew month of Heshvan, fifty days after Yom Kippur. According to Ethiopian Jewish tradition, this is the day Israel accepted the Torah at Mount Sinai. Sigd also celebrates the Jewish people's return from Babylonian exile to Jerusalem, modeled on events described in the Book of Nehemiah. The major themes of the day are repentance, the renewal of the Israelite covenant with God, and a longing for Jerusalem and the Temple.

Back in Ethiopia, the whole community, dressed in their finest clothing, walked on this day to the highest point on a mountain. The *qesoch* (rabbis) carried the *Orit* as well as colorful parasols. Some old people carried heavy rocks on their shoulders, casting them off on top of the mountain, symbolically casting off their sins. During the day all the adults fasted and confessed their sins. The *qes* read the Ten Commandments and other passages from the *Orit*. Blessings and psalms were recited in Ge'ez. The *qes* delivered a sermon about remaining faithful to Judaism and the Torah.

At the end of day, a small horn was blown to mark the return of the *qesoch* and *Orit* from the mountaintop. Then among much singing and dancing to drum, gong, cymbals, and violin, the community shared a pot-luck meal (*se'udah*) together.

Since 2008, Sigd has become a national holiday in Israel, though it continues to be celebrated mainly by the Beta Israel.

The largest celebration is on the Promenade in East Talpiot, overlooking the Old City (which is where the last part of the novel takes place). The flamboyant pageantry, featuring colorful umbrellas and gold-and-purple cloaked *qesoch* wearing white turbans, draws photographers from around the country. Many worshippers prostrate themselves on the ground. Many of the women ululate. At the conclusion of services, worshippers accompany the *qesoch* with ululation, applause, and trumpet blasts to a tent and break their fast with a communal meal. Sigd festivals, featuring contemporary and traditional Ethiopian music, dance, crafts, clothing, and food, also take place in other parts of the country.

Perhaps the most exotic aspects of Ethiopian culture presented in this novel are the superstitions known as Buda and Zar. Remnants of pagan and pre-monotheistic beliefs, these ideas hold sway to this day. Although a full discussion of these beliefs is beyond the scope of this Postscript, you can explore further using the many resources available online.

For centuries Christians and Muslims in Ethiopia have embraced the belief that Jews possess Buda, the power of the evil eye, activated by their envy of others' good fortunes. Those who are *bouda* (possessing this power) can curse others with an evil eye, visiting harm upon others. Jews were believed to derive their extraordinary powers by making pacts with the Devil, acquiring the ability to turn into were-hyenas at night and rob graves, consuming the corpses. It was also believed that their Faustian covenant empowered them to create things of beauty. And because Jews shunned raw or bloody meat, a delicacy in Ethiopia, they were regarded suspiciously. Non-Jews believed that eating charred meat (required by Jewish dietary laws) was a sign of Buda practice.

Divested of land, Jews had no choice but to specialize in handicrafts, especially metalworking, weaving, and pottery. Because they were able to master fire and shape metal, they were regarded as magicians. Their dual nature as outcasts and sorcerers made them paradoxical in the eyes of their detractors.

Those cursed by Buda suffered a variety of ills: wasting sickness, domestic accidents, infertility, bad luck, sick livestock, and blighted crops. Victims could even be "scared to death" by a physiological reaction known as vagal inhibition, characterized by the sudden stopping of the heart, often leading to death. (That's what happens to Dani Solomon.)

To protect themselves from the evil eye, non-Jews resorted to familiar anti-demonic measures: invocations, exorcism, charms, and amulets. Some carried an amulet or talisman, known as a *kitab* to ward off the ill effects of Buda. Although many Ethiopian Jews, especially the older generation, continue to affirm the reality of Buda, they refrain from using it against fellow Jews. In the novel, Sisayu comes close to resorting to Buda against her enemies, but ultimately resorts to a more conventional murder weapon, the double-edged blade.

The phenomenon known as Zar arose from a well-known Ethiopian Jewish folktale, shared by all three Abrahamic religions: Adam and Eve had thirty children, half of whom were very beautiful. Eager to protect them from divine envy, Eve tried to hide them in the Garden of Eden. God was angered by Eve's actions and declared that these children would remain invisible for eternity. The fifteen unhidden children became the ancestors of humanity, while the invisible children became the forebears of a class of envious and unpredictable spirits called Zar. Zar spirits possess individuals, mostly women, and cause discomfort or illness (typically headaches, infertility, bad luck, or madness). What would be termed mental illness in modern psychiatry is attributed by Zar believers to spirit possession.

Zar spirits are not considered gods, nor even supernatural, but rather humans transfigured by God. As a rule, *qesoch* do not consider these beliefs antithetical to Judaism but rather as an effective way of mediating social conflict, managing mental illness, helping couples cope with infertility, resolving marriage difficulties, and helping the community adjust to intense social and cultural change.

A person possessed by a Zar spirit can be restored to health through a ceremony performed by a shaman as well as through participating in *bunna*, the daily coffee ritual that Maya's neighbor Fewesi introduces her to. A sufferer can also attend a Zar healing ceremony, during which she enters a trance. As a result of such an experience, the Zar spirit is not exorcised but befriended, promising to withhold further affliction if the sufferer agrees to undertake certain commitments, such as performing certain rituals, attending regular Zar ceremonies, wearing special clothing or jewelry, or ingesting specific foods or other substances such as tobacco to appease the spirit. I leave it to the reader to decide whether Sisayu makes peace with her Zar by the end of the novel.

All of the characters in the novel are my own invention. Any resemblance to real people, living or dead, is purely coincidental.

A Note about Language and Terminology

I have chosen to include a number of untranslated foreign words from Hebrew, Yiddish, Arabic, Russian, Amharic, and Ge'ez. Israel has long been a multi-lingual society. In Israel today, although Hebrew is the dominant language, significant minorities speak Jewish dialects, notably Yiddish, as well as Ladino and Judeo-Arabic, English, Arabic, and Russian. Many Ethiopian Jews speak Amharic in addition to Hebrew. My decision to include a few foreign words in my book honors this multilingual reality. I've included a Glossary of foreign words and expressions as well.

The Jewish community uses a different calendar than the Gregorian, dating back almost six thousand years. I have substituted the abbreviations B.C.E. ("Before the Common Era") and C.E. ("Common Era") for the more familiar B.C. ("Before Christ") and A.D. (Anno Domini, "the Year of our Lord").

Selected Bibliography

I consulted many books, articles, people, and online resources while writing this book. I'd like to single out a few that were particularly helpful.

I learned a great deal about the Ethiopian Jewish community from the writings of several scholars:

BenEzer, Gadi. *The Ethiopian Exodus: Narratives of the Migration Journey to Israel, 1977-1985*. Routledge, 2002.

Edelstein, Monik D. "Lost Tribes and Coffee Ceremonies: Zar Spirit Possession and the Ethno-Religious Identity of Ethiopian Jews in Israel," *Journal of Refugee Studies* Vol. 15, No. 2, 2002.

Feldman, Micha. *On Wings of Eagles: The Secret Operation of the Ethiopian Exodus*. Gefen Publishing, 2012.

Kaplan, S. and H. Rosen, "Ethiopian Immigrants in Israel: Between Preservation of Culture and Invention of Tradition," in *Jewish Journal of Sociology*, 35 (I): 35-48, 1988.

Quirin, James. *The Evolution of the Ethiopian Jews: A History of the Beta Israel to 1920*. 2010. Tsehai Publishers, Hollywood, CA.

Rosen, C. (1989). *Getting to know the Ethiopian Jews in Israel by means of their proverbs. Information (International Social Science Council)*, 28 (1), 145–159.

Salamon, Hagar. *The Hyena People: Ethiopian Jews in Christian Ethiopia*. University of California, 1999.

Seeman, Don. *One People, One Blood: Ethiopian Israelis and the Return to Judaism*. Rutgers U Press, 2010 (ISBN: 0813549361).

Wagaw, Teshome G., *For Our Soul: Ethiopian Jews in Israel*. Wayne State University Press, 1993.

I am especially indebted to the scholarship of and my conversations with Professor Hagar Salamon for insights about the Ethiopian community. In addition to her book, *The Hyena People*, I found the following articles particularly useful:

"Holy Meat, Black Slaughter: Power, Religion, Kosher Meat, and the Ethiopian-Israeli Community" in *Political Meals*, Regina F. Bendix and Michaela Fenske, eds., *Wissenchaftsforum Kulinaristik*, LIT, 2014.

"Blackness in Transition: Decoding Racial Constructs through Stories of Ethiopian Jews," *Journal of Folklore Research*, Volume 40, Number 1, January-April 2003, pp. 3-32, published by Indiana University Press.

Several novels focused on the Ethiopian Jewish community—Omri Teg'amlak Avera's autobiographical novel, *Asterai* (French translation, Actes Sud, 2009); Jane Kurtz's *The Storyteller's Beads*; and Sonia Levitin's *The Return* (Fawcett, 1988)—inspired me to try my own fictional version.

Acknowledgments

IT WAS OVER THIRTY YEARS ago that I first met an Ethiopian Jew. It happened at a Sigd celebration arranged by Dr. Jeffrey Schein, a Jewish educator who belonged to our Philadelphia synagogue. As he was planning the program, he invited me to share a few Ethiopian Jewish folktales that I knew: how Moses became king of Ethiopia; how Moses met his death; and of course, how the Queen of Sheba traveled to Jerusalem to test King Solomon with riddles and then had a son with him, Menelik I, who became the ancestor of the Beta Israel. As part of this festive celebration, which included injera and other Ethiopian foods, a young Ethiopian Jew spoke about his life in Ethiopia and in Israel. I bought a hand-made scarf narrating the history of Ethiopian Jewry in colorful comic-book-like panels.

Ever since that first encounter with Ethiopian Jewish culture, I've been fascinated by this ancient Jewish community that managed to keep Judaism alive through millennia of isolation from the rest of the Jewish world. I'm grateful to Jeff Schein for starting me on this exploration.

In addition to the books, articles, and videos I consulted during my research, I'm also indebted to several individuals who shared their expertise and experience with me. Professor Hagar Salamon, Senior Lecturer at the Jewish and Comparative Folklore Program, Institute of Jewish Studies, at Hebrew University, provided me with invaluable information about the Beta Israel community in Ethiopia and Israel. Her contributions came both from her book, *The Hyena People: Ethiopian Jews in Christian Ethiopia* (which gave me the title of my own book) and numerous scholarly articles, and also in private correspondence. I'm also grateful to Professor Salamon's doctoral student, Bar Kribus, who reviewed the finished manuscript for errors.

Watching the documentary, *Bal-Ej: The Hidden Jews of Ethiopia* (2016), made by film-maker Irene Orleansky, apprised me of the problems still plaguing the Jews who remain in that country today. And I'm glad that my friend, Mindy Shapiro, put me in touch with Yuvi Tashome, an Ethiopian Jewish immigrant who now runs an Israeli non-profit, Friends by Nature. Yuvi generously shared with me personal experiences from her life in Israel, which informed several incidents in my book.

I'd also like to thank our AirB&B landlords, Monique and Marcel Girard, whose charming casita in San Vito in southern Costa Rica provided the birds, flowers, serenity, and warm hospitality to nurture the writing of this book.

The folks at Wicked Son Press and its parent company, Post Hill Press, provided tremendous support, especially Wicked Son founders, Adam Bellow and David Bernstein, whose enthusiasm, trust, and collaborative style made working on this novel such a joy. I'd like to thank managing editor Aleigha Kely for her professionalism and responsiveness. And kudos to my copyeditor, Mal Windsor, who not only knows her stuff when it comes to usage, grammar, and diction, but also suggested adding a chapter to the final draft that improved the book. Thanks also to Glen Pawelski, Project Manager at Mapping Specialists, Ltd., for providing the detailed maps to help orient readers to the exotic settings in the story.

Most of all, I want to acknowledge the steadfast encouragement and perceptive counsel I received from my life partner and writing buddy, Herb Levine. His sharp ear and unerring eye helped me avoid some of my writerly pitfalls. And his suggestions about marketing and outreach to readers have been spot-on.

All errors in the book are my own.

Guide For Book Groups Reading
The Hyena Murders

IN PREPARING FOR YOUR BOOK group on The Hyena Murders, we strongly suggest that all participants read the author's postscript.

1. This book exposed you to a great deal about Ethiopian Jewish culture—both in Ethiopia and in Israel. What are some of your take-aways?

2. This novel explores racism in contemporary Israel. Were you surprised to discover so many instances of racism in so many characters?

3. Racism is said to be systemic when it infects the institutions of a society and not just the personal views of individuals. Do you see instances of systemic racism portrayed in this novel?

4. What do you make of a character like Roni? How does someone like Roni get so far in his chosen profession?

5. This novel has two detectives separately researching the case. Do you see a contrast between the method of Sarit Levine, of the Jerusalem Police, and Maya Rimon, of the Service?

6. This novel has made revenge the motive for the murders. Probably the most famous revenge story in English is Shakespeare's *Hamlet*. What do you think of revenge as a driving force for a murderer?

7. Discuss the character of Shulamit, the murderer. Do you have any sympathy for her? What do you think of the diagnosis of PTSD?

8. This novel has two journals or diaries embedded within it. The reader has access to both of them, but Maya had access to only one, and Sarit to none at all. How does this determine the way the solution to the murder unfolds?

9. Have you read the first Jerusalem Mystery by Ellen Frankel, *The Deadly Scrolls*? If so, how would you say your sense of Maya's character has evolved?

10. Are you rooting for the romance between Maya and Dani to succeed? Do you expect it to last into a third novel or to fizzle out?